I0665235

THE
WISHING
ROCK
Theory
of Life

a novel with recipes

Book 2 in the Wishing Rock series

THE
WISHING
ROCK

Theory of Life

a novel with recipes

PAM
STUCKY

Wishing Rock Press

This book is a work of fiction. Names, characters, places, and incidents either are products of the author's imagination, or are used fictitiously. Any resemblance to actual events or locales or persons, living or dead, is entirely coincidental.

Copyright © 2012 Pam Stucky

All rights reserved. No part of this publication may be reproduced, distributed, or transmitted in any form or by any means, including photocopying, recording, or other electronic or mechanical methods, without the prior written permission of the publisher, except in the case of brief quotations embodied in critical reviews and certain other noncommercial uses permitted by copyright law. For information and permission requests, contact pamstucky.com.

Published in the United States by Wishing Rock Press.

ISBN (print): 978-0985125202
ISBN (ebook): 978-0985125219

wishingrockpress.com

AUGUST

From: Alexandra
To: Ruby, Erin, Millie, Claire, Carolyn
Sent: August 5, 2010
Subject: I see naked people

Hello ladies!

I've just been informed by a client that the Moon Bay community center will be holding figure drawing classes starting on the 10th. Weekly classes, seven dollars per person per class, drop-ins allowed. I've wanted to take a figure drawing class forever. Who's going with me? You don't have to have talent. All you need is the willingness to try!

From: Erin
To: Alexandra, Ruby, Millie, Claire, Carolyn
Sent: August 5, 2010
Subject: RE: I see naked people

Figure drawing? That's naked people, right? Just one naked person per week, or many? Sure, I can't draw at all but heck with it, I'm in. What time is the class? Should we do dinner in town before?

From: Millie
To: Alexandra, Ruby, Erin, Claire, Carolyn
Sent: August 5, 2010
Subject: RE: I see naked people

I'm in! Wonderful idea, Alexandra! Thank goodness one of the three towns on this little island has a community center. Their new director is bringing in some great instructors. I say yes!

From: Alexandra
To: Ruby, Erin, Millie, Claire, Carolyn
Sent: August 5, 2010
Subject: RE: RE: I see naked people

Erin: Yes, naked people. One naked person at a time I think. I believe there's supposed to be one long pose, that is, a pose held for a longer time whilst we capture it with our vast drawing expertise, and then several shorter poses. The class lasts about an hour or so.

Millie: I knew I could count on you!

All: Class starts at 7:00. I think dinner beforehand sounds lovely, if everyone would be able to meet by 5 or 5:30?

From: Ruby
To: Alexandra, Erin, Millie, Claire, Carolyn
Sent: August 5, 2010
Subject: RE: RE: RE: I see naked people

That's the day after Ed's birthday. We were thinking of going in to Seattle on the 9th overnight but should be back the afternoon of the 10th. That works for me. Is it naked men or naked women?

From: Erin
To: Ruby, Alexandra, Millie, Claire, Carolyn
Sent: August 5, 2010
Subject: RE: RE: RE: RE: I see naked people

Ruby: Did you and Ed already tell me you'll be out of the office? I don't remember that. Is this paid time off? Hmmm? Nice to be sleeping with the boss. No, no, don't worry about me, I'll be fine without you.

From: Ruby
To: Erin, Alexandra, Millie, Claire, Carolyn
Sent: August 5, 2010
Subject: RE: RE: RE: RE: RE: I see naked people

Erin: Am I wrong or didn't you sleep with the boss first? Don't answer that. I don't want to think about it.

So who all is in? Carolyn and Claire, we haven't heard from you?

Alexandra, do we need to supply our own paper and pencils and such? What are we supposed to bring?

From: Millie
To: Ruby, Erin, Alexandra, Claire, Carolyn
Sent: August 5, 2010
Subject: RE: RE: RE: RE: RE: RE: I see naked people

I may have to skip dinner or at least be late. I'll see if Ben can close the store for me that night; it's one of the nights in the week when I'm open later. I think I have some art supplies in storage, too. I'll check.

From: Alexandra
To: Ruby, Erin, Millie, Claire, Carolyn
Sent: August 5, 2010
Subject: RE: RE: RE: RE: RE: RE: I see naked people

Claire usually checks e-mail only about once a day and probably won't get on until the evening. I just remembered Carolyn was heading in to Seattle today to pick up supplies for Ed's party tomorrow. I'll call them later.

Ruby, they sell paper and drawing implements at the studio or you're welcome to bring your own. Millie, let us know if you find any in storage.

I don't know if it's naked men or naked women. I suspect both will make their appearances from week to week. If it matters to you I'd be happy to call and find out which we'll have on Tuesday.

Figure drawing it is, then! I am very much looking forward to this. Wonderful, ladies!

From: Ruby
To: Pip
Sent: August 6, 2010
Subject: Hey mama-to-be!

So, apparently Jake isn't taking too well to my being in a relationship with Ed. He's ignoring my calls and e-mails, and he's ignoring Ed's messages too. I understand why he's not talking to me; I hurt him something fierce. But I feel bad for Ed. They were such good buddies. And it's not like Ed went in with some nefarious plan to woo me while dressed up as an olive on a martini float. It just happened. Then again, they're guys, eventually they'll do a belly slam or slap each other's asses or something and call it good.

Regardless, Jake will be back at medical school soon with tons of smart young ladies vying for his attention. He doesn't need me holding him back. I know I'm not old old, but he and I are at totally different phases in our lives. He's wise and mature for his age but sometimes he's just so twenty-four.

Ed, however, is another story. He's turning forty on Monday, he's settled into himself, he knows who he is and he's fine with it. He's mature and solid. I like Ed so much, Pip. He makes me laugh. We're having a big birthday party for him on Saturday. Thank goodness Claire and Carolyn have done most of the planning!

Okay, I'm heading over to Ed's for dinner, so I'd better get myself prettied up. Give Captain Gavin a kiss for me. I miss you. I miss Gavin too, even though I hardly know him. Maybe we all should visit Gavin's sister in Ireland and do a wee road trip there? I've probably done enough traveling for a while, but one day I'll come over and we'll do just that!

Let me know when I can tell Erin and/or Ed about the baby!!! You've known Erin forever, can't we tell her? And Ed?

Talk to you soon,
Love,
Rubes

From: Ed
To: Alexandra
Sent: August 7, 2010
Subject: Naked people?

Lex,

I can't believe you've invited a group to go draw the beautiful, sumptuous human form and you didn't include me! Where is the love, Lex? You know that naked people are—I mean art is—my passion! I'm picturing you all getting naked to draw the naked people, just to make them feel at home, right? Will someone be taking pictures? I do have a birthday coming up, you know.

Speaking of which, I need to get downstairs and out to supervise the pre-party happenings on the lawn. Carolyn has the ice cream custard mix all cooked up; now it's up to us burly Brooks men to crank that dairy into submission. Take no prisoners. I hope she didn't try to get fancy again with the flavors this year. Home made ice cream is supposed to be vanilla only, that's the Brooks tradition and that's all there is to it. I can't believe Michael married such a rogue scoundrel. Chocolate cookie bits have no place in home made ice cream. Hopefully she learned her lesson. And don't you go putting strawberries on yours again this year. Don't think I didn't notice, traitor.

Ed

From: Alexandra
To: Ed
Sent: August 7, 2010
Subject: RE: Naked people?

Ed,

You are right, as usual. Yes, we will all be au natural whilst we draw. In fact whenever we women get together, we always choose to forego clothing, as women do. Your fantasies are, of course, correct.

This is a girls' night out, my apologies, darling. We'll do something else for you. Speaking of which, the last few days you've been rather fully occupied, have you not? All going well? I'm delighted that you and Ruby finally saw the light, looked into each others' eyes and discovered one another within. About time. I know it was her hesitation not yours so I won't harass you about it. Plan on my ripping you away from your beloved some night soon, though, darling, so we can catch up. I want to hear how you're doing. And turning forty! Such an old man. Trust me, you will love your forties. Far better than one's thirties which of course are legions better than one's twenties. Let me know when you have time to come over for a drink.

I will undoubtedly see you before you even get this message. Downstairs I go now to join in the birthday festivities. I will take this opportunity to tell you how much I cherish you, and that I wish you love, laughter, joy, good health and good cheer in the coming year, and always. Be that as it may, I am putting strawberries on my ice cream, and Carolyn has told me that not a single one of the flavors she's made is plain vanilla. The woman rebels so rarely, I have to support her when she does, you know.

I love you, my sweet.

Alexandra

Text from Ruby to Erin
Sent: August 7, 2010

Hey just FYI, after the party outside is done, a smaller group of
us will be gathering at my place for a more cozy birthday celebration. You are invited, of course, and David too—would you let
him know? Time TBD; it's pretty informal.

Text from Erin to Ruby
Sent: August 7, 2010

Sounds good. I'll tell David. Are you down at the lawn already?
Do you need anything? I'm about to head down.

Text from Ruby to Erin
Sent: August 7, 2010

I think we're good. Carolyn and Claire are amazing and have it all
under control. Thank goodness for Carolyn and Claire!

Text from Erin to Ruby
Sent: August 7, 2010

Great, I'm on my way. See you soon.

From: Ed
To: Alexandra
Sent: August 8, 2010
Subject: RE: RE: Naked people?

Sorry for the delay; I'm just now checking e-mails after the birthday shenanigans. It's almost one in the afternoon and we're only now waking up. What a party that was! Worthy of a king. Was it part of my dream or did Tom try to balance a chair on his forehead?

Lex, you know I love you too, even if you do insist on besmirching generations—nay, eons—of Brooks family ice cream traditions. Ol' Grandpa Meriwether Brooks must be rolling over in his grave after the wanton disregard of ice cream rules we witnessed yesterday. Next time I'm making that custard myself so no more chocolate or mint or berries or any other such blasphemy slips in. Sacrilege.

I'll let you know when I am free for you to pry into my love life. We're doing great so far but it's only been about a week. Plenty of time yet for either of us to mess it up. What about you? Don't you want love again? I have to say that even if it isn't macho of me to admit this, I find having a woman to be a mighty pleasing thing. No woman is an island. Don't you want someone to be there to kill the spiders, change the lightbulbs, keep the bed warm at night?

From: Alexandra
To: Ed
Sent: August 8, 2010
Subject: RE: RE: RE: Naked people?

Ed,

Don't worry about me. You know my history. I don't need a

love life. I am surrounded every day by more than my fair share of love with all my amazing friends. I am blessed. Furthermore, I catch and release spiders with a little blessing, I have somehow managed to learn to change lightbulbs on my own, and I have a lovely electric mattress pad to cozy up with at night.

If I don't talk to you before you and Ruby head into Seattle tomorrow, have a wonderful birthday, my dear friend. You managed to stretch this one out a good bit, didn't you? Well, I suppose you're worth celebrating for a few days in a row.

Love,
Alexandra

From: Ed
To: Alexandra
Sent: August 8, 2010
Subject: RE: RE: RE: RE: Naked people?

Lex, I do know your past but you can't close your heart forever. Yes, all your friends love you desperately, but the love of friends isn't the same. I know you want more, you can't fool me. Maybe you can fool the others, maybe you can even fool yourself, but not me.

Thank you, Ruby and I will have a wonderful time, I'm sure. You can't go wrong with a hotel with a whirlpool tub in the bedroom! That's life as it was meant to be lived!

So it's decided, we're due for a date, you and me, to talk about life. I don't know if Ruby can survive without me for an afternoon—or why she would want to—but she'll just have to manage. Let me know what night works for you.

See you soon,
Ed

From: Ruby
To: Pip
Sent: August 11, 2010
Subject: Figure drawing

Hey Pip and baby Pip! Have you disappeared? How are you, stranger? All is well here. Last night the poker ladies went to a figure drawing class out at Moon Bay, and we had a blast. Figure drawing is, of course, drawing the naked form. I was worried that I would be nervous and giggly but as it turns out I have apparently become a totally mature adult. What a surprise!

Last night the model was a woman. We got there before she had disrobed, and we were all just chatting with her like it was the most natural thing in the world that she would soon be stripping down in front of us. Turns out she's a nanny by day. Strange mix; I can't quite get my head around whether that would bother me if I were a parent of the children for whom she nannies, but she says they know and don't mind. Anyway, after everyone arrived she got up on the couch, peeled off her robe, and struck a pose, and we all just started drawing like we were drawing a flower or vase. It's just shapes, right? Not at all titillating like I thought it would be. Our group made up a little more than half the class; there were three men and two other women attending.

Claire enjoyed the class well enough but probably won't go back; she just wasn't confident in her ability. Erin actually showed a lovely propensity for the task; she was slow but her details were accurate. She spent a good amount of time focusing on the woman's feet. Feet don't look like you think they do, as it turns out. Neither do ears. I gave up on the feet and sort of drew them into shadows. One guy who was there was totally doing abstract art. I have no clue how what he was painting (you could use whatever medium you wanted) was related to what he was seeing, but

I guess that's what art is about!

Anyway, kudos to me for being fully mature. Other than Claire, the rest of us plan to go back again next week.

You still haven't written. How is life? How is Gavin? How is the wee Isle of Mull? It's so weird to think you're over there for good, never to return. That my niece or nephew will grow up with a Scottish accent. The strange twists of fate.

Speaking of the strange twists of fate, Ed and I are doing great. We went in to Seattle on his birthday and stayed at a posh hotel downtown, chocolates and champagne on arrival, complimentary thick gorgeous socks, the works. I know, socks are socks, but these were cushiony and luscious, like hugs for my feet. I love me a good pair of socks.

It feels like we're just getting to know each other now. (Ed and me, not me and my socks.) Even if we've known each other a while, our relationship is still so new. Intertwined and cuddled up, we talked until three in the morning. I haven't done that with someone in so long. It's like comfort food for the soul. I'm so happy, Pip.

Jake is still not talking to me nor to Ed. He's been going off spelunking with David a lot, or on hikes on his own, Ben tells me. I didn't realize I'd break his heart. I didn't think he cared so much. I thought he was just in it for fun, not that he really loved me. Claire is worried about him but Tom, his dad, says he'll be fine. And I'm sure he will be. It's fine if he's mad at me but I feel awful that he's not talking to Ed. They've been such good buddies for so long. I hope they get that back. It just doesn't seem to be worth it, to be mad at good people.

Pass on a hug and a kiss to Gavin and his family for me, and write back! Where are you?

Love

Ruby

August 12, 2010
Wishing Rock News
Millie Adler, editor
Letter from the Editor

Dear Rockers,

Gather up, friends, there is work to be done! I've just had a visit from the Dogwinkle Fire Marshall. This year we couldn't distract him from going into the basement on his annual inspection and he tells me he can't turn a blind eye to that mess we have down there. With so many of Wishing Rock's bachelorettes dating so many of our own bachelors, there's no need for us to lure Moon Bay's volunteer firefighter force out here with a fire, so it looks like it's time to clean up the basement of our beloved Box!

The Fire Marshall would like it done by the end of the month. The Powers that Be have met and set aside August 21 for a work party to get ourselves organized. If you can't join us down below in the belly of the building on that date, please try to clean out your personal storage area by August 31, and chip in by doing a little organizing in the community areas too.

If you can join us, the work party will start at 10 a.m. I haven't spoken to anyone else but I'm sure we'll have a potluck either at lunch for a break or afterward for a celebration of our cleanliness, or perhaps both! Watch this space or listen to the grapevine for more information.

I will coordinate gathering supplies we'll all need for the day, boxes, packing tape, and so on. Carolyn (whose storage area, as I am sure it will come as no surprise to hear, needs no cleaning or organizing), will be in charge of the community areas. If you have any questions let us know.

I suppose since we haven't cleaned out the basement in forty years, it's about time! We hope to see you there!

Millie

From: Ruby
To: Gran
Sent: August 14, 2010
Subject: Wishing rock theory of life

Hello, Miss Adele!

Gran, how I miss you! Wasn't your plan to be in Scotland through July? Check your calendar, missy, it's August 14! Don't tell me another MacAlpine has stolen away another of my family members. Pip and Gavin are living over there so if you and Liam are going to make something serious out of what's going on, it's only fair that you bring him over here. Tell him I said so. What are you two up to anyway?

All is well here. The whole town came out for Ed's fortieth birthday party. Those Brooks men, you gotta love them. I was initiated into their strange world of homemade ice cream rules. I'm not even sure what they all are; all I know is that Carolyn thinks they're ridiculous and so she purposely breaks them. One rule is that the ice cream must be vanilla, but since she's the cook she won't abide. She tosses in peaches or cookie bits or chocolate and mint or whatever suits her fancy, and what are they to do? It was delicious.

As a tribute to Ed's rabbit-on-antenna episode earlier this summer, Michael made rabbit shish-kebab for everyone. Can't say's I ever had rabbit before. It was okay, a bit gamey I thought, but with enough barbecue sauce almost anything is edible. He skewered it with parboiled carrots (for the bunny) and baby red potatoes. The vegetables were delish!

Gran, I'm very much enjoying Ed's company. We've been going on long walks on the beach each night (how cliché), and I've started gathering up my own collection of wishing rocks. So many people here have a bowl full of them on a counter or coffee table or book shelf. You'd think the beach would run out, but there are always more. Just like wishes, I suppose. I'm developing a Wishing Rock Theory of Life, even. Wishing rocks and wishes are like life in so many ways:

1. Wishing rocks sometimes have one really strong band of white, offering up one big wish. Just as in life sometimes you want one thing and you want it bad.

2. Or, sometimes there are multiple interwoven rings of white around a rock, just as in life sometimes your wishes are many and complex and interrelated.

3. Sometimes, the white band is a strong and complete ring, whereas other times it starts strong on one side but fades into nothing as it curves around the rock. In life, sometimes you start off with one goal but as life changes, so do your dreams. What once seemed so important fades away to make room for something else.

I'm sure there are tons more ways wishes and wishing rocks are like life. I'll keep you updated.

Anyway, Gran, I'm a little afraid to say it but I'm feeling truly happy. Each night that Ed and I collect rocks, there are so many wishing rocks that I could fill a bowl every time. But rather than getting greedy and collecting them all at once, I've been gathering them up and then when we're ready to go in I pick out my three favorites, and then throw the rest back into the ocean along with my wishes. Every time, I say at least two wishes for Ed and me to be happy together forever. He makes me happy.

I know I'm not supposed to tell anyone my wishes but you're like a part of me so it must be okay, right?

Love you! Write and promise me you and Liam will visit soon.

❖

From: Gran
To: Ruby
Sent: August 15, 2010
Subject: RE: Wishing Rock theory of life

Ruby, sweetheart! It's wonderful to hear from you. Life is full speed ahead right now. Yes, yes, I know I said my original plan was to head back around the end of July, but as you know, plans change. Liam and I are having a wonderful time together, and have decided to do some traveling. Millie's tales of Meriwether and Maddie inspired in me a desire to see Switzerland. With all that's been going on—Pip's wedding and now pregnancy, your troubles with Jake and subsequent hooking up with Ed—we felt it would be best to keep a low profile on our trip. But, our departure date grows near. We'll be leaving for Bern on the 24th. For now the plan is to travel around for a few weeks to a month. Who knows where the spirit will take us!

I appreciate your analogies of wishing rocks and life, especially the third. Life changes and so do dreams. As we get older and grow to know ourselves better, our priorities change. Along with that, what we want out of life changes as well.

I'm off to the library to read up on yodeling and fondue. Take care of yourself and I will write again when I have time. Liam says to tell you hello.

Love, Gran

From: Pip
To: Ruby
Sent: August 16, 2010
Subject: RE: Figure drawing

Hey Rubes—

Ugh. Sorry, I haven't been ignoring you. I am not feeling so good. No morning sickness; more like twenty-four/seven sickness. I've been throwing up for days. This baby had better treat me well when I'm old and senile, after all I'm going through to bring him/her into the world. Gavin is trying his best but honestly the smell of him after he's spent a day out on his boat is enough to make me hurl—literally. You'd think the fresh air smell would be good but I swear I can smell the fish molecules on him, the barnacles, the decaying whales, every foul-smelling thing in the sea, despite the fact that he's hardly near the water; all he does is captain a damn tourist boat. He's being so sweet but I just want to smack him.

I'm having trouble at work, too. The smell of sugar is so overwhelming. I don't know how I didn't notice that in all my years of baking but it's absolutely cloying.

Hopefully this all goes away soon.

Yes, you can tell a few people I'm pregnant, Erin and Ed, but not a lot yet please. We want to wait until the first trimester is over just to be safe, in case something happens. I don't want to tell everyone I'm pregnant and then have to tell everyone I'm not pregnant.

Of course, everyone on this damn island knows anyway. How do you live in such a small community? This is driving me insane. It's not quaint, it's intrusive. I don't need everyone to know everything about me. I feel like they probably know what color underwear I'm wearing on any given day. "Oh, Pip normally wears red panties on Tuesdays but this week she wore green! What do you think that means? Yammer yammer yammer."

So the doctor says I may have mood swings but I haven't seen it yet. I'm sure someone will let me know.

Gavin and I are thinking of hopping over to Ireland soon to visit his sister and her husband. We'll probably go soon, but maybe we'll wait until I can fly a couple hours without a barf bag. I've never been, so I'm very excited. Really I am.

Much love,

Pip

From: Ruby
To: Pip
Sent: August 16, 2010
Subject: RE: RE: Figure drawing

Aw Pip! Maybe you could find a nice neutral cologne for Gavin? No, the mood swings don't show at all, don't worry, you still seem your sweet old self.

Feel better soon!! Ireland sounds fabulous, keep me informed!

Love

Ruby

Text from Ruby to Ed
Sent: August 16, 2010

Want to go away this weekend? Everyone is going somewhere. Gran is going to Switzerland. Pip's going to Ireland. Let's go somewhere!

Text from Ed to Ruby
Sent: August 16, 2010

You want to go to Europe?? Weren't you just there?

Text from Ruby to Ed
Sent: August 16, 2010

Yes!!! No, somewhere local is fine. Also I was just talking with Claire and Jake is going to be home this weekend. I sort of want to avoid him.

Text from Ed to Ruby
Sent: August 16, 2010

Ahh now the picture is getting clearer, young grasshopper. You don't want to see if you can patch things up? I might like to.

Text from Ruby to Ed
Sent: August 16, 2010

Not so much just yet.

Text from Ed to Ruby
Sent: August 16, 2010

Sure then, where to?

Text from Ruby to Ed
Sent: August 16, 2010

Leavenworth? Victoria? Winthrop?

Text from Ed to Ruby
Sent: August 16, 2010

Leave it to me, I'll make plans. Being your knight in shining armor is more work than I expected. Thank goodness I'm so amazing.

Text from Ruby to Ed
Sent: August 16, 2010

Thank goodness indeed. ;) Love ya, dude. xx Thanks.

From: Millie
To: Jake
Sent: August 17, 2010
Subject: Ruby

Jake, darling. I hope you're having fun on your vacation with your friends. I had dinner with your family last night and they told me you're still angry at Ed. First of all, Ed is your friend, he's been one of your best friends for years. You and Ruby had already broken up when they started dating. I don't understand why you'd turn your back on that? I know it hurts now honey but you'll find someone else. Your mom tells me the female medical students are practically banging down your door. You don't have to move on but please talk to Ed. I know you've been ignoring his messages. Sweetheart, friendship is more important than jilted love. Life is too short for grudges. I'm old; I should know. Talk to Ed. Please do.

Come see me when you're back from your trip.

Love, Millie

From: Jake
To: Millie
Sent: August 17, 2010
Subject: RE: Ruby

Millie, all due respect, but it's no one's business. Wishing Rock is just going to have to deal with it. I have nothing to say to that guy. He broke the bro code. Every dude knows you don't break the bro code.

I'll be home soon, will see you then.

J

From: Ben
To: Millie
Sent: August 17, 2010
Subject: RE: Bro code?

The bro code is the code that says you don't date a friend's ex. Yeah, I'd say Ed should know it, it's not a generational thing. Every guy knows it. Jake just isn't over Ruby, that's all. He still thinks he can get her back.

Ben

From: Ruby
To: Pip
Sent: August 18, 2010
Subject: naked men

Are you feeling any better yet? I'm sure it will take a while. I was talking with some friends and they said candied ginger is the way to go. Can you get candied ginger over there? Do you want me to mail you some?

Here, hopefully this will cheer you up: My report of our second figure drawing class last night!

Remember how I had thought I was so mature last week, after having been completely nonplussed by drawing a naked woman? Apparently I was mistaken. Last night the model was a man, and that changed everything.

First, we got ourselves all situated. You don't know what pose the models will pick until they actually sit down (or stand or lie or lean or whatever), so there's no way of knowing what kind of angle you're going to get. When we walked in, the instructor introduced the male model to us (gold chain necklace, shirt unbuttoned), so we knew right then we'd be drawing a guy. (We're smart like that.) I picked a chair a bit off to the side so I could get a good angle but not sitting right in front of him—thinking that would be awkward. Got myself situated, set up my easel, etc.

The woman last week had changed into a robe before coming into the art room, so when the time came she just disrobed. Well, this guy did it differently. He was just in his street clothes until the time came for him to get naked, and then he just basically did a strip tease! You know I'm no prude but I felt a bit like a voyeur watching him. Something about the expression on my face must have caught his eye because he kept staring at me with a funny little smile. Then when he'd finally shimmied out of his skin-tight jeans and was all undressed, what did he do but pick a pose with himself in all his glory pointing right at me! And what's worse, he was looking me in the eye!

The thing is, once they pick a pose they're not supposed to move at all, so the whole class he was just staring at me, watching me study him. I could feel the red rise up my neck into my face, the beads of sweat accumulating on my forehead. It was so awkward, Pip. I started giggling and had to swallow the laugh and duck my head for a few minutes to try to contain myself. So much for being a mature adult! But I just couldn't bring myself to stare at his junk long enough to figure out the angles and curves of it, not with him watching me like that. I spent the greater part of an hour in intense study of his foot. As you may recall from last week, feet are very difficult. I do believe I am much better at feet now, having spent a good amount of time this week keenly surveying his and drawing them six times. Hairy toes, second toe longer than the big toe. Does that mean he's royalty?

Alexandra, of course, drew a lovely and lifelike representation of the whole man, which is nice, because I really didn't get a good look at him above his ankles.

Next time I'm totally going to stare him right in the balls. And draw them.

I'm jealous about Ireland, everyone is traveling somewhere! I've told Ed he needs to take me away somewhere this weekend, and he's obliging. Will let you know where we go.

Feel better soon, sweet Pip! All my love to you and Gavin.
Ruby

From: Millie
To: Adele
Sent: August 22, 2010
Subject: Switzerland

Dear Adele,

Hello, my friend. Are you off to Switzerland yet? Your grand-daughter keeps me up to date on all your comings and goings but I've forgotten to ask her about you as of late. I can't wait to hear your tales.

All is well here in Wishing Rock. We cleaned out the basement yesterday, for the first time in forty years. Seems we uncovered some old treasures! Ben was in a back corner and found a whole box labeled MBB—turned out it was letters Meriwether wrote to Madeline after she died. We're all eager to know what's in the letters but Ed and Michael agreed that Ben, who found them, would be allowed to read them first. I don't know if they took into consideration the fact that Ben is busy on his own adventures and might take a while to get through the letters! But, he'll alert us all to any important findings, I'm sure.

In other news, Ruby was helping Ed clean out his storage area and uncovered a bit of Ed's past, as well. Who knew our basement would be full of such intrigue and surprises! I haven't heard the whole story but Ed had a box full of an ex-girlfriend's belongings. It's not someone he dated while living here, so I don't know much and can't wait to find out the scoop. Ruby looked a bit peeved that Ed still had the woman's things. I'll fill you in on the story when I know it.

In my own tame world, I'm savoring the chance to slowly get to know my gentleman friend, Walter. You remember Walter? I may not have mentioned him by name before. He's the widower who started catching my eye a couple of months ago. We like going on slow walks and long talks around the island. I'm enjoying the opportunity to show him my little island. I find myself thinking about time, about the fact that his whole life and my whole life we were living our lives completely unaware of each other's existence, nearly seventy years on separate paths, only to find our paths converging in this moment in time. He was married before; his wife died a few years ago, complications of a stroke. Had we met ten years ago we might never have connected. Or would we have? If something is meant to be, will it find a way?

It doesn't really matter. All I know is I am having a lovely time with this gentle man. Life has given me another chance, another adventure, and I'm grateful.

All my best to you and Liam,
Millie

Text from Erin to Alexandra
Sent: August 24, 2010

Well, that was interesting. FYI Ruby just came by to let me know she's home. She didn't want to talk just yet. Said she was going to write to Pip.

Text from Alexandra to Erin
Sent: August 24, 2010

Thanks for letting me know. I'll check on her later. Wish we could have stayed in class. That looked like it was worth drawing.

Text from Erin to Alexandra
Sent: August 24, 2010

Haha! Worth drawing and so much more! ;) Don't tell David I said that. Love you, see you tomorrow. xx

From: Ruby
To: Pip
Sent: August 24, 2010
Subject: Jake

I'm just back from tonight's figure drawing class. Trauma. Drama. Ridiculous.

This is how it happened.

I walk in, we all walk in, tonight it's me, Alexandra, Erin. The others couldn't make it. About five other people in class, finding seats, getting settled.

The instructor is there but no model yet.

We set ourselves up. I'm off to the left, the opposite side from last week, hoping the model, whoever it is, won't stare at me again. It's getting close to time for class to start but the model isn't there yet.

I casually ask where the model is. The instructor says, "This one told me he's a little shy, didn't want to be here when people were getting ready. He just wants to come in and get started."

I'm busy sharpening my pencils when the model walks quickly past me so fast he creates a swish of wind. He swoops up on stage, disrobes, poses.

I look up.

Jake.

I'm frozen in space, my right arm raised with pencil in hand, my jaw open in disbelief. I look over at Alexandra. She's looking at Jake. I can't read her face.

I look at Erin. She has this tight grin, about to burst into a nervous laugh, looking at me. Seriously.

I stare at Erin, afraid to look at Jake. What am I going to see on his face? Anger? Defiance?

Slowly I peel my gaze away from Erin and look at him.

He's looking right at me.

The pain on his face, as naked as he is.

I feel it in that instant: I did that to him.

My heart just leaped into my throat, and tears into my eyes. I must have made a sound because suddenly everyone was looking at me.

I threw my things into my bag and raced from the room. Stopped outside in the doorway, calculating the distance to walk home. Alexandra drove us to the community center tonight.

While I was thinking, Alexandra and Erin came out.

"Are you okay?" said Alexandra, though I'm sure it was clear, even for a person without her psychic skills, I was not.

I didn't say anything. Just stared at them.

"We'll go home," said Alexandra.

"I'll get our stuff," said Erin.

She went in, while Alexandra and I stood there.

"What was he thinking, Alexandra? Why did he come here? Did he do that to hurt me?" I asked.

"I doubt he wanted to hurt you. I suspect he was trying to make a bold move to win you back." She paused. "Do you want to talk with him?"

Did I want to talk to him? I had no idea. Yes, but no. What would I even say? "I think he's … busy right now," I said.

"We can wait."

I don't know if she meant for me to wait inside, but there was no way that was going to happen. "I can't go back in there. I can't sit there and draw him."

Alexandra, ever calm, ever wise. "If you want to talk to him, we can wait in town and let him know we're here. What do you want?"

God, Pip, it was so awful. I can't say what it was but the look on his face, it just stabbed through me. He didn't look that hurt when I broke up with him. I didn't think he'd even cared that much. I thought I was the smitten one, that he was just humoring me but didn't actually love me. I never really trusted his love, Pip. Tonight I wanted to talk to him and I didn't want to. But that look on his face, I mean, I loved him once, I did. I still do. Differently but I still do. I couldn't just leave.

"I want to talk to him. If he wants to talk to me, that is. I owe him that."

"I'll tell the instructor to tell Jake to meet you at the cafe when class is over."

She went back in, she and Erin came out, we all went to the cafe. Eventually, Jake showed up and Erin and Alexandra left. They took my art supplies and drove home; I figured Jake would either drive me home or the walk would do me good; it was a nice enough night.

We just stared at each other for a while. Finally I spoke.

"Jake, what was that about? What were you thinking?"

He looked at me. "I don't know, Ruby. I had to do something. I want you back. You didn't give me a chance. When I was home this weekend, Mom told me you all were taking this class and I got this idea to surprise you. Stupid idea, in retrospect."

"You didn't have to surprise me naked. I would have talked to you."

"You're always with Ed. Ben tells me you guys are always together. I wanted to see you alone."

"First, that's not true. I'm not always with Ed. Second, you only had to ask and I would have met with you, without him.

And besides, you should talk with him too. He misses you, Jake."

"Nothing to say."

I sighed, looked at the cafe counter, noticed my mouth felt very dry. "I'm going to get a water. Do you want anything?"

He stood up. "I'll get it." Got in line, came back a few minutes later with a tray with two glasses of water, one slice of mixed berry pie, two forks.

I looked at him, then at the two forks, the one slice.

"I just ... if you're hungry. It's yours if you want it," he said.

"I'm not hungry."

He looked so defeated. I couldn't share a pie with him though, my favorite pie, right? That would be mixed signals. I couldn't do that to him.

"Jake," I started, then stopped. I didn't know what to say.

He pushed the pie aside. "Ruby, you didn't give me a chance. We could have talked about kids. Was that it? That was the whole reason you left, because I don't want kids? I'm young, Ruby, I just haven't thought about it much. I'm too young for kids right now, for sure. I'm twenty-four. I'm in medical school. It just doesn't work." He picked up a fork, surgically peeled the pie crust off the pie without eating any.

"I know you're young, and I know you're not ready," I said. "That's the thing. I'm not young enough to play around. If I want to have kids I have to do it soon."

"So you're just going to get with anyone who's ready to have kids? It doesn't matter if you love him?"

"I do love Ed," I said, and the second I said it, I knew it was the wrong thing to say. He flinched away from me as though I'd hit him.

I took the fork from his fingers, held his hand in both of mine. "I'm sorry, Jake. You know I still love you. I always will. But we're just not right. It's not just the kids thing. There's more to it."

"What, am I not smart enough? Not funny enough? Do I smell bad or something? What is it? I can fix it, Ruby."

What could I say? I had loved Jake, and but I'm not in love with him anymore, and I love Ed now. How to explain the heart? How to explain the heart, I suddenly realized, to someone who has never had his heart broken before? He'd always been the one to leave, in the previous relationships he'd had.

I suddenly felt thick and heavy with the realization that I was Jake's first real heartbreak, that I was the one he would look back on when he thought of the first woman who devastated him.

"Jake, it's not any of those things. You're a fabulous guy. I don't know. Something just snapped in me and I guess I realized we weren't meant to be."

He sat there, blinking forcefully, like he could blink my words away. He added his other hand to our hand-holding, and started caressing my palms, like he used to, when we'd be cuddled together on the rooftop under a cozy blanket, watching the stars, or in the morning, waking up on lazy Saturdays, or in the evenings, while we sat watching TV.

I pulled my hands away.

"I'm sorry, Jake."

He picked up the fork and played with the pie crust again. "Maybe you'll change your mind. You could change your mind, you know. It happens."

I watched as he dissected the pie crust from the back of the pie filling, and then the bottom. "I suppose anything is possible," I said.

He shot me a glance, a glimmer of hope in his eyes.

"I mean, no," I said. Why am I always saying the wrong things? "I was trying to be honest, I mean, anything is possible, that's true, but I just, I don't think so. No."

"Anything is possible," he said. Damn it. Why, Pip, why can't I have someone vet my words before they slip out of my mouth?

"That's all I need to hear." He wasn't smiling, but his aura (Alexandra might say) was happier.

I decided not to make it worse. Instead, "Will you talk to Ed?"

His shoulders stiffened.

"Okay, not yet," I said. "But sometime, Jake. He's one of your best friends. Don't let this ruin that. Friendship is far too important. Don't lose him over me."

He half nodded but I'm not sure it was a promise.

"Do you want me to drive you home?" he asked, looking hopeful.

I looked at the clock on the wall over the counter. Eight thirty, on a clear summer night. Just a few miles from Wishing Rock. "I think a walk will do me good," I said.

With a mix of disappointment and optimism, he gave me a quick kiss before I could turn away, and he left.

I walked home, thinking the whole time, how do I manage to mess these things up? What would I tell Ed? How do I discourage Jake, let him know it's over for real? I need to talk with him again but I'm scared I'll say all the wrong things and convince him I want to marry him or something. All I want is for him and Ed to talk again, but I think I've made that worse.

Oh Pip. I envy you and your morning sickness and husband who smells of the decaying ocean and your stable life. Give Gavin a kiss for me.

Love,
Ruby

Hey again—it's a couple hours later, I'm home again, and I just found this still in my draft e-mails. Never hit "send," I guess. After I wrote that I was still feeling unsettled so I hopped in my car and drove. As you might have guessed, there are not a lot of places to drive to on this island. I found myself up at the park out at Balky

Point. You'd think I'd have the place to myself but there were three other cars out there. One car clearly had a couple in it—probably teenagers—making out in the back seat. The others seemed to be empty; I thought I saw a shadow down at the beach but I'm not sure. I got out and walked to the edge of the park, looked out over the water for an hour, staring at the waves and the stars, thinking. Time seems nonexistent when I'm watching the waves. That vast expanse of ocean and world making me feel so small; the universe so huge. My problems seemed both tiny and insurmountable at the same time.

Ultimately, we're all alone, aren't we? Each of us, no matter how many people we have in our lives who love us, no matter whether we're married or single, ultimately we're alone. Tiny specks on this vast spinning chunk of earth. Amazing how caught up we can get in our dramas when ultimately each of us is so in-significant. But we're all we have. This is it.

Fear less, live more. Be kind.

R.

From: Pip
To: Ruby
Sent: August 25, 2010
Subject: RE: Jake

Ruby, you have got to stop thinking so late at night. Next time you get all philosophical and start staring at waves in the dark, do me a favor: go to bed. Sleep. This tiny blue dot of an earth will still be here in the morning, spinning away, but your brain will be spinning less and we'll all be grateful.

Worry less. Live more. Everything's going to be okay.

From: Adele
To: Millie
Sent: August 26, 2010
Subject: RE: Switzerland

Dear Millie,

Wonderful to hear from you. Yes, we're off to Switzerland in days. We will arrive in Geneva on Monday, then take the train to a small town on the north end of the lake, called Vevey. At present moment our plan is to toodle around that area for a while, and then head north. We'll see where the winds and cowbells take us. I have been researching and have found one man, the last man in Switzerland who still makes alpenhorns by hand, and we are scheduling a day to go to his workshop and see how it's done. Liam is especially excited about this as he enjoys woodworking, even if he doesn't do much of it. Neither he nor I speak any German and the alpenhorn maker does not seem to speak much English, but I am hoping we can work out hiring a translator.

Meriwether's letters to Maddie! What a find. I wish there were a way I could read them all myself. Does that make me a voyeur? I would never want anyone to read the letters Gerald and I wrote each other. Then again, Meriwether and Maddie have both passed so that changes things, does it not? I suspect once I'm gone I won't much care if people read our letters. At any rate, if you learn anything interesting from the letters, do let me know. How nice that Ben can read over them. It seems to me that the young people might sometimes get bored with island life. Nice to have something new to distract him.

Pip tells me that Jake is stirring up trouble over there, trying to patch things up with Ruby and causing Ruby to go into whirlwinds of overthinking. Do you know, one thing I've noticed over the years is that when a woman ends a relationship, there's usually not much that can be done to resurrect it. Women ruminate for so long about whether to end it that by the time they do, there's not much love left. Men, on the other hand, jump out of relationships without really giving it much thought sometimes, and then they realize what they've lost and try to jump back in. What I'm saying is that I understand Jake's efforts but I suspect Ruby was thinking about ending the relationship far earlier than any of us knew; perhaps far earlier than she knew. I doubt there's much hope for the young lad. Keep me updated on this front as well, Millie!

I'd best be going. Gavin's daughter's birthday was two days ago but she had her school friends over that night for a party, so tomorrow the family are gathering at Gavin and Pip's for a celebration. Gavin is bringing the boat out to pick up Liam and myself this afternoon, so I need to find a suitcase that isn't already packed for Switzerland and throw in a few things for tomorrow. We'll be back here on Saturday, one day then to finish packing and closing up our houses for the time being, and then we're off on a new adventure! Tschüss, darling! I believe that is Swiss German for "goodbye"! We are carrying along a laptop with us on our travels (how modern are we?!) and plan to stay at places with "wifi" on occasion, so I will be in touch!

Much love, Adele

From: Ed
To: Alexandra
Sent: August 27, 2010
Subject: Ghosts in the basement

Lexie, you gotta help me out here. Since Ruby hasn't been here long enough to have accumulated a mess in her storage area in the basement, she helped me clean out mine. She found a box of things from my ex in Alaska, from before I even moved here. Ruby wants to know why I'm keeping them. I couldn't seem to get it through to her that this woman means nothing to me anymore. She said if the woman meant nothing to me I'd have gotten rid of her stuff long ago. Says I wouldn't have moved the stuff with me in the first place.

What is with women? Would you do me a favor, Lex, and write a manual for me? I guess that would be a womanual? Haha! Damn I'm clever. How can Ruby be angry at such a clever guy? The female mind, it's a mystery.

Talk to her, will ya, Lex? You can fix anything, I am sure. You're a doll.

Love ya!

Ed

From: Alexandra
To: Ed
Sent: August 27, 2010
Subject: RE: Ghosts in the basement

Ed,

I would be more than happy to help you out but I must know first: Why indeed do you have a box of your ex-girlfriend's things in the basement? Why in the world did you move them with you? And further, my darling, don't you think it would be good for you to practice communicating with your beloved rather than passing the task off to someone else? Just a suggestion, love.

Alexandra

From: Ed
To: Alexandra
Sent: August 27, 2010
Subject: RE: RE: Ghosts in the basement

You mean you don't know that story? How is that possible? We all have skeletons in our storage closets, don't we? Never mind then, I'll deal with it myself like the modern sensitive man that I am.

In other news, I would like to state for the record that I need a robot that can read my mind. Earlier today I was hard boiling some eggs (being the amazing and sensitive new age man I am, I was making egg salad sandwiches for myself and Ruby). One time when I was up at the Inn, Claire told me that to avoid getting that unsightly green ring around the yolk you have to put the eggs right from the hot water into an "ice bath." Clearly I am far too manly to give anything an "ice bath," so as the eggs were boiling I was thinking up alternatives. When the eggs were done I ran them under cold water, but was that enough to prevent the Green Ring of Cookery Ineptitude? This is where the robot comes in. I thought, I could put the pan full of water and eggs straight into the freezer to complete this all-important cooling process, but then I could end up with a pan full of frozen water and eggs if, for example, I went off to wrestle a grizzly bear and forgot that I'd put the eggs in the freezer. If I had a mind-reading robot, though, the robot would know to get the eggs out of the freezer and dried off and into the refrigerator, and I'd be free to wrestle all the bears I wanted, without any worries.

Why no one has invented this for me yet, I don't know. However, you know lots of people around the world, right? And if anyone knows mind-reading it's you, right? Could you get someone on this? Thanks, doll!
E.

From: Alexandra
To: Ed
Sent: August 27, 2010
Subject: RE: RE: RE: Ghosts in the basement

Oh, Ed. There are so very many reasons I love you. Your need for a mind-reading robot is now added to the list.

Very well, then, don't tell me about your mysterious ex-girlfriend or the box of her belongings. I'll find out one way or another, you realize that of course? I am now intrigued and will not rest until I know. The secret loves of Edward Brooks! My next puzzle to solve. I am on the case!

From: Ed
To: Alexandra
Sent: August 27, 2010
Subject: RE: RE: RE: RE: Ghosts in the basement

Speaking of love, I'm serious, Lex. When are you going to get yourself out there again? Don't you crave it? It's human nature. Don't deny it. You must want to find someone again, one day.

From: Alexandra
To: Ed
Sent: August 27, 2010
Subject: RE: RE: RE: RE: RE: Ghosts in the basement

What are you now, my matchmaker? When the time is right, my love, when the time is right.

From: Ed
To: Alexandra
Sent: August 27, 2010
Subject: RE: RE: RE: RE: RE: RE: Ghosts in the basement

Allow me to be the Wise One for a moment: If we always waited for the time to be right, nothing would ever get done. I'm just saying. Don't put the walls up so high that no man can ever get around them. At some point, you have to move on. I love you, Lex, I just want the best for you. You know that.

From: Alexandra
To: Ed
Sent: August 27, 2010
Subject: RE: RE: RE: RE: RE: RE: RE: Ghosts in the basement

I know that, Ed. I love you, too.

From: Ed
To: Alexandra
Sent: August 28, 2010
Subject: RE: RE: RE: RE: RE: RE: RE: RE: Ghosts in the basement

Yeah, Ruby got mad at me about that too. She's not so sure men and women can just be friends, at least not as good of friends as you and I are.

From: Alexandra
To: Ed
Sent: August 28, 2010
Subject: RE: RE: RE: RE: RE: RE: RE: RE: RE: Ghosts in the basement

She'll come around, Ed. Have faith. Sometimes I think we all need to practice living from love, not fear. What the world would be.

I'm off on a conference call to Banff; work calls once again. I'll talk with you later.

From: Millie
To: Ben
Sent: August 29, 2010
Subject: M&M

Hello Benjamin,

You know I must be busy if I almost forgot to ask whether you've found anything interesting in Meriwether's letters yet. Have you?

I need to go down to the store for a bit this afternoon but will stop by after. Tell your mama that if she wants company for dinner, I'm happy to invite myself over. Been too long since I've spent the evening with you fine folks!

Love
Millie

From: Ben
To: Millie
Sent: August 29, 2010
Subject: RE: M&M

Hey Millie,

Not all the letters are finished. Sometimes Meriwether just started writing and stopped in the middle of a sentence or didn't finish his thoughts. I'm trying to put them in order. They were all mixed up in the box. I haven't seen much interesting yet. Mostly it's sappy romantic stuff. If I find anything good I'll let you know. :)

Mom says come on by for dinner, we're eating at six.

Ben

SEPTEMBER

September 1, 2010
Wishing Rock News
Millie Adler, editor
Letter from the Editor

Dear Rockers,

It's that time of year, my favorite time of year, do you feel it? Changing of the seasons, the waning days of summer, time for pumpkin bread and spiced cider and of course the annual cider press party. The time of year when the quality of the light in the sky is crisp and introspective, when the flannel sheets start to call out from the cupboard (only to be told "not yet, sheets, not yet!"), when there's just time for a few last bonfires on the beach, a few final s'mores. It's almost fall! I love it!

And, my dear friends, you are so lucky, so very lucky, to have me around. I don't mean to be immodest but it's true, be glad I am here to do the investigative research where our dear Ed is concerned. I got wind from someone over in Moon Bay that the new corn field planted out on the road to Balky Point had been planted by none other than one Edward R. Brooks, so I went in with my journalist cap and lots of questions, and Mr. Brooks, seeing that he was defenseless against me, obliged.

The corn field, Ed told me, is to fill a void. Not a void in the land but a void in our calendar. Regardless of whether you or I agree, Mr. Brooks feels that heretofore, our small island has had a shameful dearth of harvest season activities. No more, my people! Ed has a vision, and that vision includes a corn maze. Ed won't reveal just what shape the maze will take, but he promises it will be memorable. Harvest season and the corn maze will culminate in a Halloween Haunted House. Stay tuned for more details. If you're looking to pick up a little extra cash, Ed will be hiring a few positions to staff both maze and house. Give him a call if you want to find out more. He also has a top-secret crew working on design and construction of both, so if you're able to keep a secret (and I know you aren't, but give it a try), and want to help out with this, call Ed.

Speaking of corn, I am in search of a delicious corn bread recipe. I started thinking about corn and now cannot get corn bread off my mind. If you have such a recipe, let me know. Perhaps bring it to the next bonfire, which I will now announce:

Beach Bonfire, September 12, at the beach bonfire pit, in case that was not obvious. Festivities will also be held on the lawn. Croquet and other lawn games starting at 5; picnic potluck on the beach at 6. Michael found lawn darts in the basement when we were cleaning. He has threatened to bring the lawn darts to the party. Be alert! Despite the protests of the more sage members of the community, his mind is made up. If we have lawn darts they'll be far away from other activities but keep your heads up!

Millie

From: Ruby
To: Pip
Sent: September 2, 2010
Subject: Leavenworth!

Hey Pip! How are you? Feeling any better yet?

My not-so-subtle hints that Ed should take me someplace ("Ed! Take me somewhere!"—I'm subtle like that) paid off. Ed has come through and we're going to Leavenworth for the long weekend this weekend.

It scares me a bit how much I like him, Pip. Makes me want to pull back a bit to protect my heart. The last guy I loved like this left me at the altar. I feel like I need to prepare myself for the inevitable rejection.

Anyway, we're heading to Leavenworth tomorrow around noon; should get there by evening.

When are you and Gavin heading over to visit his family in Ireland? Where are they again?

❖

From: Pip
To: Ruby
Sent: September 3, 2010
Subject: RE: Leavenworth!

Hey Rubes,

Not feeling a whole lot better yet but I'm hopeful I will be soon. Gavin and I are going to visit Katie and Stephen in a couple weeks. They live out in the northwest part of Ireland, the Inishowen Peninsula. We're planning to stay there a few days and then do a bit of sightseeing for a few days. Not a huge trip, but it'll be nice to see them again. I only got to spend a little time with them at the wedding—everything was so busy—but Katie seemed like someone I'd like.

As for your having been left at the altar, I remember it so well. And you were not left at the altar. Ruby Ruby Ruby! What are we to do with you? Yes, you want to protect your heart but what if you lose Ed because you were trying to protect your heart? Trust him. Be a little vulnerable. You can do it, I have faith in you. Love will conquer all, yada yada yada.

Hang in there. I'm going to go chew on some dried ginger.

Love ya!

Pip

From: Erin
To: Ruby
Sent: September 4, 2010
Subject: David

I think I'm going to break up with David.

How's Leavenworth?

From: Ruby
To: Erin
Sent: September 4, 2010
Subject: RE: David

What? What? Why? What happened? Are you sure it's not PMS? I'm not saying your feelings aren't valid, but are you PMSing right now? I know how you can get. I know how I can get. When I have

PMS, I can get so cranky I want to break up with people I don't even know. As Alexandra said to me once, "PMS and Self-Doubt are lovers, gazing on each other whilst strolling hand-in-hand through a mine field of fears, not bothering to watch where they step." Could that be it? What's up?

Leavenworth is fabulous. Such a charming little Bavarian town with such attention to the details of perpetuating the old-world feel; it's probably as close as we can come to being in Europe without having to break out our passports. And the drive to get here is stunning. Literally, there were times when the scenery took my breath away. I made Ed stop at several pull-outs along the road, just so we could breathe in the beauty.

We got here last night and went for a walk, then came back to the condo to experience the giant whirlpool tub in our room. Why do I not have a whirlpool tub at home? Note to self: Get whirlpool tub. Or get Ed to get a whirlpool tub (easier and cheaper!). Then today we went driving along the road by the river, and soon we were on a quest to find a way down to Icicle Creek from the main road. This proved harder than it sounds. It was so frustrating, we could see the river in all its cascading-over-boulders glory, but were never able to find a way to get to it. We stopped at every turnout on the road until finally we found a place where we could scramble down to the river more or less safely (only a few scratches on me). Would you believe it, Erin, there were giant wishing rock boulders all over the place there! It's like a sign. A sign of what, I have no idea, but surely a sign. Some of the wishing rock boulders were embedded in the ground, so we stood on them and made giant wishes. I am hoping that the fact we couldn't then throw the rocks into the river doesn't negate the wishes coming true.

We also found a new oil and vinegar shop down the main street of Leavenworth. The shop featured the most delicious balsamic vinegars ever, and we tried every one. Blackberry balsamic was simply transcendental, but they're all divine. Guess what everyone is getting for Christmas? Please remember to act surprised.

All right, sweets, tell me all about what's up with David. Call if you want. We'll be home Monday. Don't make any rash decisions!

x

From: Erin
To: Ruby
Sent: September 5, 2010
Subject: RE: RE: David

Leavenworth sounds great. Good weather? I should get out there sometime. I should get out more in general. I know I'm off the island all the time for distillery business, but I never really go anywhere. That's not totally true; Scotland was somewhere. Somewhere wonderful. Remind me again why I decided I had to cut that trip short? Did I think the distillery wouldn't survive without me? I do think highly of myself, don't I? Ha.

David. I don't know. I think he's pulling away. I'm scared he doesn't seem interested anymore, not as attentive. Maybe I want to move on before he does. It's easier if it's my decision, you know? I don't want to be hurt. If he's going to dump me, I'd rather dump him first. Story of my life?

From: Ruby
To: Erin
Sent: September 6, 2010
Subject: RE: RE: RE: David

Let me repeat: David's a good guy, Erin, and I really believe he likes you. Is he pulling away because you're pulling away? Self-ful-filling prophesy? Or is that just his personality? He's not the most demonstrative guy, but that doesn't mean he doesn't love you. Have you talked with him about this? Do you know for sure he's going to dump you? Or are you imagining things? You do tend to be the dumper, put up barriers before you can get too close. Maybe it's time to break that pattern.

We'll talk when I get back.

❖

From: Alexandra
To: Erin, Ruby
Sent: September 7, 2010
Subject: Fear and love

Hello ladies,

It seems we have some wary hearts around here these days. I think you two should come over and we should talk. Happy hour at my place. On the agenda: Discussion of fear and love.

Be here Friday, 4 p.m. I'll clear it with your boss.

Now, I need to go find Millie ... something I need to tell her.

I will see you two Friday. Don't anyone go breaking up with anyone just yet.

Love
Alexandra

From: Jake
To: Ruby
Sent: September 8, 2010
Subject:

Hey,

I wanted to say I'm sorry about the art class thing. In retrospect maybe that wasn't my best move. You gotta give me another chance, though, Ruby. We were great together. Can we just meet for coffee or go on a walk sometime? All I want is to talk to you before I go back to Seattle for the next term.

Jake

From: Ben
To: Millie
Sent: September 9, 2010
Subject: Meriwether

Hey Millie!

I've been reading through some of Meriwether's letters and found one from forty years ago where he's talking about you moving in! I scanned it in for you and attached it.

See ya soon,
Ben

October 12, 1970

My darling Maddie,

I can't believe it's three years today since your last breath passed your lips. I miss you still, all the day long; I long for just one last embrace, a chance to say goodbye. Those abominable Fates, not even allowing me the chance to look in your eyes one last time and know you were still in there, looking back. Three years ago today we were gallivanting in Rome, carefree, the world and all our lives ahead of us; then in that God-forsaken moment everything changed. Maddie, I often ponder that idea, the idea that a single minute, a second, can alter the entire course of a life. Or a death. One step off a curb at the wrong moment—a step off a damn curb, Madeline!—and your life was lost, my life was shattered. How many seconds every day are the living changing our lives in such momentous ways, without our even knowing it? What actions of today are changing or creating our paths of tomorrow? Did I just narrowly escape fate in this last second, or this? And how do all the different moments of our lives converge into one?

For example. The moment I decided to build this town was a part of a series of events that have culminated in a young woman named Millicent Adler moving here. Millie. I'd say she's just about Mitchell's age. Never married, but she promised her heart to a young man who went off to war a few years back and has not been heard from since. Millie has been waiting for him but I can see her struggle, wondering when to give up, when to move on. Cruel as those Fates were, at least I knew you were gone. Millie has no such solace. She showed me pictures of herself and her Clive from the week before he left. Even I can see she has shed many pounds since that photo was taken. She is stick-thin now and her eyes are hollow, lost.

Well as it is, my dear Madeline, as you know I believe that there are people in our lives who, when we meet them, we instantly recognize them as a part of ourselves, a part of our souls, people who will be a part of our lives, and this we know even though the person may be a complete stranger. I recognized Millie the day we met, out at the edge of town. She is a blessing to this old man, and I find myself wondering if you sent her to comfort me, to distract me, to give me someone else to worry about so I will stop feeling so sorry for myself for *having lost you. I wonder, if there had been no Wishing Rock, would you and the Fates have finagled a different way to bring Millie and myself together? And what purpose could there possibly have been in taking you from me so early?*

The children miss you too. Meredith, Mitchell. Your grandsons, Mikey and Eddie, who will never know you. Young Mikey is getting into trouble left and right, Mitchell tells me, and the new baby Eddie is doing as new babies do, spitting and shitting and sleeping, but one assumes he'll amount to more than that one day. He's just two months, I suppose, two months a couple of days ago. Mitchell sent pictures last week. They are beautiful children. I see you in both of them. Then again, I see you everywhere.

I wish you were here, always wishing you were here, my sweet Maddie.

All my love,
Meriwether

❖

From: Millie
To: Ben
Sent: September 10, 2010
Subject: RE: Meriwether

Oh, Ben. Thank you for sending that on to me. Meriwether was a good man. I wish you could have known him. I never knew that he was writing those letters to Madeline. It seems strange, because I thought I knew everything about him. He told me everything— I thought. For how long after her death did he write to her? Have you found anything else of interest?

Are you doing your online classes this morning? Come down at lunch and see me. I need to give you a hug.

From: Ben
To: Millie
Sent: September 10, 2010
Subject: RE: RE: Meriwether

Yeah, online classes right now, then self study this afternoon. I'll come by at lunch. Mom says to ask you if you have lunch down there or if you want me to bring something?

From: Millie
To: Ben
Sent: September 10, 2010
Subject: RE: RE: RE: Meriwether

I have soup to reheat in the microwave, and a sandwich. I am good. Bring your own lunch. I'll see you soon, and that thought makes me smile! Now get back to your studies!

From: Ruby
To: Gran
Sent: September 11, 2010
Subject: Love

Dear Gran,

Haven't you been in Switzerland for more than a week now? Where are all your emails to me about lederhosen and alpenhorns and fondue? And about Liam? Don't hold out on me, Gran!

Wishing Rock continues to surprise me. I hope one day you can visit so you get to know all these people I'm talking about. In today's case you already know the person in question: Alexandra.

Where to begin. We've been having trouble in our little paradise. Seemingly out of nowhere, Erin decided she wanted to break up with David, and I've been feeling unsettled about Ed. I think, Gran, if I'm honest, that the crux of it is that I'm feeling more attracted to Ed sooner than I ever expected to, and that scares me.

I worry that Pete … I don't know, that he broke me when he called off the wedding to run off with another woman. I'm scared to let myself get too close to Ed now, because I don't want to be hurt and humiliated like that again. And Ed, he's just amazing. He makes me laugh all the time, and he cares so much. He's observant, thoughtful; he already knows me so well. When we're at a party someone will say something and Ed and I just look at each other and know we're thinking the same thing. He's always trying to find ways to make me happy or surprise me. The other day we went canoeing around the island and he rowed us to a hidden bay on the east side, the "less inhabited" side (if you can really call any of the island inhabited). Earlier in the summer, before we were dating, he'd shown me another little beach that he'd years ago proclaimed "Ed Beach." Just a little beach, enough room for a couple people to pull up a canoe and sit on a piece of driftwood at high tide, not much more.

I'd admired Ed Beach enviously. So, what does Ed do but find another little beach, just for me. He'd gone up earlier, before taking me out there on the canoe, and planted a wooden sign with burned-in lettering declaring it "Ruby Beach." My own beach! I know it's not actually my beach, but could there be a sweeter gesture? He brought a picnic and he'd earlier set up some gnarled driftwood trunks around a wide flat rock, a makeshift table. We sat and had dinner and wine and watched the sunlight dim. (Wrong side of the island for a sunset, but maybe I want my memories with Ed to be sunrises—beginnings—rather than sunsets anyway. Metaphorically, anyway. I like actual sunsets.)

And he's always doing things like that, thoughtful, creative ways of showing me he cares. He is always interesting. He always has something to say. He notices things and thinks about them and comments. You know how sometimes you go to a restaurant and see a couple sitting there in silence, and the whole meal they barely talk to each other? I can't imagine he'll ever be like that. He's too curious about the world, and too excited to share what he's experiencing. Or those couples that bicker and criticize—I was in Moon Bay recently and this woman came into the restaurant, her husband trailing behind her, and she told him she should have parked the car because he did such a terrible job, just kept going on at him, critical and bitter. She said it in such a mean way. Ed would never do that. Ed is so supportive of people. He's kind.

He adores and loves me so much that it scares me. Am I worthy of that much love? Will he one day realize he's been wrong about me and go and break and my heart, just like Pete did?

And then there's Erin.

Erin's situation is worse. She dates all the time but I don't know that any guy has lasted more than—oh, maybe a year at most. She starts to get nervous about commitment and thus starts to find fault with her boyfriends, and they start to sense that, and they try all the harder (why do men like that abuse?), and I think the fear of commitment becomes too much and she runs.

So she's on that path with David, starting to pick at his ways, not because she's mean but because she's subconsciously trying to justify a breakup so she can do it before she gets hurt. Gran, David is fantastic. Sure, he's a little boring … boring's not the right word. Stable, set in his ways, but honestly Erin is too. She likes to think she's spontaneous but the fact is, every morning she's up at six for her run, every day she eats the same yogurt with walnuts and blueberries for breakfast, every evening she does yoga and balances her checkbook. Maybe that's why she is hoping for someone who is more exciting, but I think she needs to realize that not everyone is Hollywood and passion—and not everyone is meant to be or needs to be.

Okay, so that's the background, that's what we had going into our evening with Alexandra last night. I guess I thought we were going there for her to scold and school us (perhaps rightly so) about our own love lives, but as it turns out:

"Ladies," said Alexandra once we'd settled in with our lemon drop cocktails, our little plates laden with goat cheese and fig appetizers and dates stuffed with parmesan and walnuts. We were gathered in true Wishing Rock style—happy hour at Alexandra's home, "dressed" in our pajamas and slippers. Nothing but a walk down a couple flights of stairs and along the hall between us and home; why not be comfortable?

"Ladies," said she, "Let's talk about love. Love, capital L, and Fear, capital F, and what happens if you let Fear rule your heart over Love."

Alexandra, you have to love her. She's more proper than a person needs to be but she's smart and she doesn't bullshit. Letting Fear rule your heart? How would she know about that? I realized I knew nothing about her love life at all. We were intrigued.

"I spoke with Millie earlier today," she said. "Regarding some amends that needed to be made, some truths that needed to be clarified. I never really lied to her, but I did let her make some assumptions, jump to some conclusions. One time long ago she asked me if I ever wanted children. You may know that she always imagined she'd have children, but by the time she heard that the fiancé she'd been waiting on, Clive, had been killed in war, she was in her forties and on the edge of too old to have children of her own. I think she coped with it okay—some people don't really want children but go along with the idea because they think it's expected. Millie may have been one of those. She was born in the forties when most women barely questioned their role in life to be a wife and mother, but by the time Clive's fate was determined in the early eighties, times were changing. I think she made peace with it relatively easy."

At this point, ensconced in Alexandra's ultra lush plum suede chaise lounge, my glass about ready for a refill, I think "Are we here to talk about Millie?" Which is not bad. I love Millie. Who doesn't love Millie?

"But you're not here to hear about Millie."

This is what I'm saying. I think I read her mind, don't you?

"You're here to hear about me. My life. My children."

Her children?! Gran, I know spit takes are just a thing for TV comedic effect, but I just about did a real life spit take there and then. Her children? What??

"My children," said Alexandra.

"Children?!" said Erin.

Alexandra paused for a long time, figuring out what to say next, I suppose. Erin and I exchanged glances but didn't speak. I've never had a psychic reading with Alexandra, but I imagine it's possible that when she works she slips into the there-but-not-there kind of trance that she seemed to go into for a few minutes before she spoke again.

"I was married once."

If Erin and I were paid for every shocked glance we exchanged last night, we would be millionaires.

"Married!" said Erin.

You have to understand, this is a small community. There truly is the sense that no one's business is their own. If you manage to keep a secret for a week, it's a miracle. My not knowing about Alexandra's marriage is one thing—I've only been on the island seven months—but Erin has been here for years. How did she not know? Did anyone know?

"Ed knows," she said. Oh. Of course Ed knows. Ed loves Alexandra more than he could ever love me. Of course Ed knows. My heart dropped for a minute. Trust, Gran; why is it so hard to trust?

My face must have shown the turmoil inside. "Ruby, Ed loves you, he is in love with you. Yes, he loves me completely and unconditionally, and I love him the same way, but that's it."

That's it? Is there more? Something more than complete and unconditional love?

"Ed told me that you found a box of his ex girlfriend's stuff in the basement, and that it bothered you. I don't know the woman or that story but I know Ed. If he says it's in the past, I believe him."

"I talked with him about it," I said. "He dated the woman in Alaska. She broke up with him and some of her stuff was still at his house. By the time he got around to boxing it up, she had moved and he couldn't find out where she'd gone. When he moved to Wishing Rock he didn't know what to do with her stuff so he brought it with him."

"You see," she said, "completely innocent." Whether it's completely innocent or not, I'm not yet sure. Wouldn't it have made more sense to leave the box with someone up in Alaska? He had to have had some feelings for her still. Feelings like that don't just go away.

Alexandra continued. "We all have pasts. You don't have to be jealous of her, and you don't have to be jealous of me." She looked at me pointedly. I hate when Alexandra looks at me pointedly. It means she's right and we both know it. "Ed and I have complete and unconditional love for one another, but nothing romantic. He did pursue me at one point, early on when I was new to Wishing Rock, but I wasn't interested. I was never interested in any man because I was never going to get close to a man again. Ed pursued me, and I refused, and eventually our relationship developed into the intimate, honest, caring friendship we have today. We were never meant for anything other than that. We were meant to be friends.

"But that's not the point," she said. "The point is that I've lived my life making decisions out of Fear, and who knows how many opportunities I've lost because of it. I love you both too much to watch you throw away your time as I've thrown away mine.

"And it's time for me to make a change, too."

"The children? The marriage?" Erin prompted.

… Oh geez, Gran, I just looked at the time! Ed and I are heading over to Moon Bay for dinner, he's coming by to pick me up in five minutes, and I don't have any makeup on! I'll finish the story soon, I promise!! I'll send you the goat cheese/fig and dates/parmesan recipes—they're so simple. But now I gotta go!

I love you! Write and tell me all about your trip! That's an order!

Love,

Ruby

Date Walnut Parmesan Treats

Ingredients
dates
walnuts
good parmesan cheese, sliced into pieces about 1/8" thick by 1/2" wide by 1" long

Directions
Take the pits out of the dates. Into each date insert a walnut piece (about half of a half, or whatever suits you), and a piece of cheese. Serve.

Goat Cheese and Figs

Ingredients
fresh figs, halved
herbed goat cheese
almonds (twice as many as figs)
honey
balsamic vinegar

Directions
1. Preheat the oven broiler on high.
2. Put the fig halves, cut side up, on a baking sheet. Place a small dollop of goat cheese on each fig, and an almond on top of that. Press the almond and the cheese slightly into the fig.
3. Broil the figs in the preheated oven until the cheese is soft and the almonds are turning golden brown, 2 to 3 minutes. Remove from the broiler and let cool for a few minutes. Place figs on a plate and drizzle with honey and balsamic vinegar. Serve warm.

From: Gran
To: Ruby
Sent: September 12, 2010
Subject: RE: Love

Dear Ruby,

My dear, you left me hanging there! The suspense is killing me! The children? The marriage? Write soon!

As for us, we are having a fantastic time. We started up in Zurich and despite its reputation for being somewhat materialistic, we thought it nonetheless had charm. The river running through the city is charming. If a city has a river running through its center I'm probably more willing to forgive it some of its failings. It makes me wonder, though, about the divide of a river. The divide of humanity. On which side did humans first set up homes, and at what point did some others decide they liked the setting but would rather have a river between themselves and their brethren? Or was it two competing tribes, each finding this ideal spot, staring across the running water at one another, wondering? Water unites us but also divides us. What looks like an easy crossing can be deadly if you don't have the right equipment. But we ourselves are eighty percent water, if I remember right from my days long ago in school. Do our water cells pull us to their own kin? Do they have cellular memories of being free flowing, passing by Zurich or Bern or the Columbia Gorge? If our cells do have cellular memories then I am certain mine did not come from the ocean. I have never liked such wide open waters. Even lakes, I suppose. You never know what lurks beneath you. Sharks, coelacanths, the Loch Ness Monster, who knows? No, give me a river any day, rushing by, water with a past and a purpose, going somewhere, something to do. The moods of rivers match my own. Sometimes animated and fierce; sometimes lazy and relaxed. I know, rivers have their dangers too. Some even have their own creatures. Men going to the Amazon undoubtedly will think twice about getting into the river on hearing of the dreaded candiru, a tiny fish known for climbing up the urethra and latching on. But this isn't the Amazon, and there are no candiru. This is Switzerland, where citizens of Bern head upstream along the River Aare at lunchtime on a sunny summer day, dive in and float gently downstream again. I would say the act of floating down a river on a warm day would almost have to lower one's blood pressure significantly. Even living in a place where people do such a thing would lower one's blood pressure. That, and the bells of the churches, chiming on the hour in their soothing, enduring tones. These centuries-old buildings and chapels reminding us that our own time here is so brief; that generations before us have wandered these streets and if we don't destroy it generations after will do the same, and therefore what more do we need to do but live in the moment, this moment that we have?

Yes, Switzerland has its pull, Zurich was lovely for all its high-end shops, and now we have holed up in Wengen. Wengen is a tiny town in the Bernese Oberland, up in the mountains, no cars allowed. We initially planned to stay just a couple days but this town has cast a spell on me and I can't bring myself to leave just yet. We have rented a place through September, up the hill from the railway. Take note, should you ever come to Wengen (which you must): unless you want to add a hill- and stair-climbing regime to your workout, rent your room above the railway. We have met other visitors who made the mistake of staying in rooms down below and they tell us they plan their days so as to avoid having to make the trek up to the main part of town more than once a day. One understands quickly how the Swiss are able to eat so much fondue and chocolate and yet stay slim: Hills, hikes, walking, and lots of it.

And, I love it myself. As I said this town is car-free. The Swiss transportation system is so precise as to be almost magical. One day we had to take the cogwheel train, then a regular train, and then a bus to get to our final destination. You would have thought the schedules had been made precisely for our trip. We hopped off the cogwheel train and the next train—whose platform was just feet away—left only minutes later. Got off the train, made our way to the bus platform, and again in just minutes our bus arrived. One does not find it hard to believe the Swiss were so prominent in the history of clocks. Who needs a car? This is the unencumbered life and we love it. Crisp air, friendly people. Here in Wengen almost all the shops close for an hour at lunch so that the clerks can have a break. These aren't simple people but the way of life is simpler. I find myself thinking often about peace here.

Tomorrow we'll be heading up to the Jungfraujoch, I believe it is Europe's highest railway, and then we'll hike back part way, and take a gondola back from Mannlichen. We can see the gondola from our window and it looks steep, but we're assured it is quite safe.

Liam and I are doing well together. We've proven to be very compatible travel companions, which is always a question that has to be answered. We enjoy many of the same activities but also neither of us is put off if the other wants to do something we do not. At our age, we have learned to entertain ourselves, and I enjoy a bit of time to myself, anyway, to have some tea and a chocolate croissant down at the bakery, watch the people passing by in the gentle Wengen way. I think at my age it isn't quite right to call what I'm doing "dating" but rather it's simply companionship. We have few expectations of each other or of the moment, and as such we are not disappointed. Neither of us expects the other to make us happy. We are simply each glad the other is there. Relationships late in life are much less stressful, I think. Perspective comes more easily. We have loved and lost, and we don't feel the need to spend precious time worrying about who said what or who did what or who didn't. We may both be set in our ways more, yes, but also we're less worried what the other thinks. It works.

However, it sounds as if you young folk are having a much more difficult time on your side of the world. Finish your email when you can; I eagerly await. But remember to keep it all in perspective. You can worry yourself out of a perfectly good relationship, you know, by the simple act of worrying too much. I think you pegged it right when you said you need to learn to trust. Trust that all will be okay. It will.

All my love, Gran

From: Ed
To: Alexandra
Sent: September 12, 2010
Subject: Yo

Lexxxxxxxx!

Lex my love!

Ruby tells me you told her and Erin about your family, your past. She was a bit shaken and very moved. You okay? What prompted your revelation? Not that there's anything wrong with it but you've kept it quiet for so long. How you feeling about things?

Edward

❖

From: Alexandra
To: Ed
Sent: September 12, 2010
Subject: RE: Yo

Signing off as Edward rather than Ed? My, we're formal today; what's the occasion?

Yes, I told Erin and Ruby of my past. I'm fine. I suppose I finally accepted that keeping it all inside could never make it go away, and I want to live life more than I want to keep from ever being hurt again.

I don't relish the idea of people talking about me now as I tell people what happened, coming up to me with their sympathy and wanting to offer me comfort. I would rather comfort myself, as I have done for so long. I am strong.

On the other hand, I've realized lately that a life lesson I need to learn is to be able to receive. I need to learn to let people care

for me. You'd think in a community as tight as ours I'd have figured out long ago that I don't have to go it alone. It is acceptable
to let people carry me sometimes, give to me sometimes.

I suppose maybe I got tired of just holding it all in.

Regarding that, at least, I feel much better now, actually; like
seeing a light when I didn't realize it was so dark.

The strangest thing has happened, though, Ed. The voices in
my head are suddenly quiet. All of them. Gone. They've been
quiet since Ruby and Erin left my home last night. I'm rather unsettled, frankly.

A.

❖

From: Ed
To: Alexandra
Sent: September 12, 2010
Subject: RE: RE: Yo

The voices are quiet? How do you mean?

❖

From: Alexandra
To: Ed
Sent: September 12, 2010
Subject: RE: RE: RE: Yo

I mean the spirits. The voices. Normally I can sort of tune them
in or out as I need to, to go about my daily life without being
constantly disrupted. But now, I can't find them. They're gone.

Maybe they'll come back. I miss them. My children were always in there.

❖

From: Ed
To: Alexandra
Sent: September 12, 2010
Subject: RE: RE: RE: RE: Yo

Oh, Lex. I'm sorry. Maybe it was just the shock of your talking about them? Give it some time. It's only been a few hours. Probably just a glitch in the cosmic transmission.

From: Alexandra
To: Ed
Sent: September 12, 2010
Subject: RE: RE: RE: RE: RE: Yo

You're probably right.

I've been meaning to tell you I'm glad you and Ruby got out to Leavenworth. I do wish you'd take more time off. You're always working, even when you're not working. You deserve a break, and what's more, there's another person in your life to consider these days. Don't let the fact that you work with Ruby and live under our same collective Box roof deceive you into thinking you don't need quality time together away from work. I'll bet you even found a way to do business in Leavenworth, didn't you? You never really get away, Ed. You're always here doing so much for everyone else; maybe it's time you did something for yourself.

From: Ed
To: Alexandra
Sent: September 12, 2010
Subject: RE: RE: RE: RE: RE: RE: Yo

Yes, my lady and I had a wonderful time in the Bavarian village in the mountains; we polka'd around the Maypole, toured the wineries, chatted with the local mountain goats after having putt-putted at the miniature golf course. A good time was had by all. Perhaps there is something to this "getting away" you speak of.

About doing for others, funny you should mention that. I've been thinking I want to do something for Wishing Rock, for the residents. I have a few thoughts but am open to ideas. Anything?

From: Alexandra
To: Ed
Sent: September 12, 2010
Subject: RE: RE: RE: RE: RE: RE: RE: Yo

Ed, you already do so much. The corn maze, for example; you just gave the people a corn maze, and you're employing people there and at the haunted house. What sort of giving do you want to do now? What ideas did you have?

From: Ed
To: Alexandra
Sent: September 12, 2010
Subject: RE: RE: RE: RE: RE: RE: RE: RE: Yo

I'm just thinking, Lex. I've got all this money, I have so much, and times are tough for people, for everyone. I want to do something to help. What good is it to have money if the people I love, the people in my community, are miserable?

I was thinking maybe lectures? I could bring in interesting people from all walks of life, set up some talks down in the auditorium. Free lectures, everyone welcome. What do you think?

From: Alexandra
To: Ed
Sent: September 12, 2010
Subject: RE: RE: RE: RE: RE: RE: RE: RE: RE: Yo

It's a lovely, generous idea, Ed. Be careful with these talks not to get too highbrow. In my opinion, most people don't want to actually go to cerebral, scholarly lectures. People want to have gone to those sorts of lectures—in the past. They want to be the kind of people who go to intellective lectures, without having to actually sit through them. It is an idea, though. Do you have anything else? Keep thinking.

From: Ed
To: Alexandra
Sent: September 12, 2010
Subject: RE: RE: RE: RE: RE: RE: RE: RE: RE: RE: Yo

Keep thinking. Okay then, I'll keep thinking but I'm counting on you to come up with some brilliant ideas!

See you at the bonfire tonight? And we gotta do dinner soon. Look at your schedule and let me know.

And Lex, I'm sure the voices will come back. Don't worry.

Love ya, gal.

❖

From: Alexandra
To: Ed
Sent: September 12, 2010
Subject: RE: RE: RE: RE: RE: RE: RE: RE: RE: RE: RE: Yo

I shall keep thinking.

Yes, see you at the bonfire.

I love you too.

❖

From: Ben
To: Ed
Sent: September 13, 2010
Subject: treasure hunt

Hey Ed, question, do you remember a treasure hunt your grand-dad sent you and Michael on once when you were really young? Either here in Wishing Rock, or somewhere on the island.

❖

From: Ed
To: Ben, Michael
Sent: September 13, 2010
Subject: RE: treasure hunt

Treasure hunt? No, I don't remember that. Bringing Michael in
on the conversation. Michael, does that ring a bell?

From: Michael
To: Ed, Ben
Sent: September 13, 2010
Subject: RE: RE: treasure hunt

Not at all. Why do you ask, Ben?

From: Ben
To: Ed, Michael
Sent: September 13, 2010
Subject: RE: RE: RE: treasure hunt

In those letters we found in the basement that your gramps wrote
to your grandma after she died, I found one where he talks about
a treasure hunt he'd set up for you, but then something happened
and it got canceled or something. I was wondering if he sent you
guys on it some other time. I was wondering what the treasure
was.

From: Michael
To: Ed, Ben
Sent: September 13, 2010
Subject: RE: RE: RE: RE: treasure hunt

Huh. No, that does not strike a bell at all. Can you scan the letter and send it?

❖

From: Ben
To: Ed, Michael
Sent: September 13, 2010
Subject: RE: RE: RE: RE: RE: treasure hunt

Sure. Hang on.

❖

June 29, 1975

Maddie, my beloved Maddie,

I wish you were here. I don't know what to say to our children. I did not know I would have to still be parenting this long after they were, I thought, grown. Did I do something wrong after you were gone? Surely you would know what to do. Help me, Maddie, help me know what to do.

It started with what was supposed to be a special weekend here for the grandchildren, and a chance for Kathy and Mitchell to relax. They've been having challenges in their marriage, you know, just growing apart I think but neither really will confide in me. They would confide in you, I am certain. But I'm just a dense old man, what good am I?

Mitchell, Kathy and the boys showed up in Wishing Rock Friday from Alaska, planning to stay through Wednesday. All was well—a bit strained between Mitchell and Kathy but well enough—until Saturday morning, when some woman named Rita Payne showed up claiming to be Mitchell's lover. In front of the children! Kathy left immediately and Mitchell went off with the woman for an hour, anger rising off him like heat, then stormed back, packed up the children and left soon after. No one answers their phone when I call. I can only assume everyone got home safely.

The Rita woman did not stay around either. After talking with Mitchell she went straight to the ferry dock and waited there for two hours, staring intently at the water as though she were reading it, until the next ferry came. Who she is, whether she actually was Mitchell's lover, where she came from or where she went to, I have no idea. She has caused chaos in our family's world, though, and I hope never to hear the woman's name again.

Before Mitchell and Kathy and the kids arrived I'd spent hours preparing a treasure hunt for Mikey and Eddie for Saturday afternoon. There's a cave up north, the mouth of it shaped like a tilted egg. I put together a "treasure" I thought the boys would like, gifts and goodies and random whatnot that I thought they would enjoy, plus a couple special treats I bought specifically for them, wrapped it all up in a big envelope within several plastic bags, put it in my old toolbox. After I had it all assembled I took the toolbox to the cave and half-buried it under the edge of a boulder. The kids left before I even had a chance to tell them about it. I'll need to go back and get it, though I'm hoping they'll be back soon to visit again so maybe I will leave it for now.

I miss you, Madeline. You would know how to fix this. I miss you.
Forever yours,
Meriwether

From: Ed
To: Michael, Ben
Sent: September 13, 2010
Subject: RE: Meriwether's letter

Whoa! Whoa whoa whoa! Treasure hunt smeasure hunt, we'll get back to that … What about Rita? Who is this Rita? Michael, did you know a Rita? June of 1975, I would have been five. Michael, you would have just turned eight. You have a better memory than I have, too. I didn't realize Mom and Dad's troubles started that long before the divorce.

Do you suppose grandpa ever went back to get that toolbox? Maybe it's still there. David explores caves around here all the time. He might be able to think of a cave with a mouth like a "tilted egg." I'll ask him.

From: Michael
To: Ed, Ben
Sent: September 13, 2010
Subject: RE: RE: Meriwether's letter

No clue who Rita was but I do remember Dad was gone a lot around that time. We came down here with Mom, but not Dad, during Spring Break in 1975 and then again in June with both of them. That must have been the time grandpa was talking about. You might have been too young to remember that Mom and Dad had separated for a few weeks in 1974, and then again in the summer of 1975. They got back together for a few years, then Dad moved out and they were separated for a good while until the final divorce in 1982.

I wonder about the treasure. I don't think we ever went on a treasure hunt but that doesn't mean grandpa didn't go retrieve the tool-box at some point. I may have to take up spelunking now! Ed, let me know what David says. If he has an idea of some possible caves I'd like to go out with him to see if we can find anything. Whatever "trea-sure" is out there is at least 35 years old, if it's still out there. It could be worthless, or decomposed, or worth some real money.

From: Ben
To: Ed, Michael
Sent: September 13, 2010
Subject: RE: RE: RE: Meriwether's letter

Like you guys need more money! If you go looking around in the caves I want to go too!

From: Ed
To: Michael, Ben
Sent: September 13, 2010
Subject: RE: RE: RE: RE: Meriwether's letter

I'll talk with David and get back to you guys.

From: Ruby
To: Gran
Sent: September 14, 2010
Subject: RE: RE: Love

Dear Gran,
    I am so sorry to have left you hanging the other day! Ed took

me out to dinner and we had a great time, wandered around the streets of Moon Bay afterward to walk off the meal a bit, dipped our toes in the waves at the beach before heading back to our own town-in-a-box. Lovely!

The way you talk about Switzerland I can almost see it. You sound so at peace there, Gran. I definitely am adding Switzerland to my list of places I want to go.

Okay, where was I? Talking about Alexandra. And even more has happened since I wrote! This has been an eventful week to be sure.

So, Alexandra, children … Erin, me and Alexandra in our pajamas drinking cocktails and noshing on appetizers, Alexandra talking with us about fear, and love, and her past.

"And it's time for me to make a change, too," she had said.

"The children? The marriage?" Erin had prompted, expressing the eagerness we both felt to hear the details of this bombshell.

Remember? Okay.

"The children? The marriage?"

"Yes." Alexandra took a deep breath, let it out slowly. "I'm not sure where to begin. My childhood, I guess. I wasn't psychic then. Or if I was, I didn't have a clue that my experiences were any different from anyone else's. I was just an ordinary kid, growing up in Mt. Vernon. My parents were poor, very poor, and Dad was prone to both depression and violence. I never knew his parents, my paternal grandparents. He barely talked about them. I knew they were alive and that they had beat him regularly and that he both loved and hated them intensely, and that was about it. Looking back, with the wisdom of age, I feel sorry for him now. I think he never learned to love, never felt loved, never believed in love, never understood what love was meant to be. I'm sure he either never knew unconditional love or never trusted it. Hitting people and pushing them away was his way of being sure people wouldn't like him. Being violent with people allowed him to justify it in his mind if people didn't like him, I suspect. One time he was at a bar, thought a guy looked at him funny so knocked out two of the guy's teeth. Dad didn't know how to be kind, didn't know what kindness was. He was in a lot of emotional pain. Back then of course he didn't seem young to me, but he was; both my parents were very young. I was born when my mother was nineteen and Dad was twenty. Mom worked two jobs just to be out of the house, and Dad would beat me and my brother, so once I got a bike I would ride all day, just to be away from home. It didn't matter if it was raining, which it did a lot. I didn't care. I would ride all the time, for hours, this was before the tulip festival started but there were fields of tulips already, and I'd ride up and down the rows, imagining myself a fairy in Tulip Land, where everyone was kind and loving and everyone's clothes and gowns were made of tulip petals, and no one ever hit me. I'd come home and sneak in the back door, dripping from the rain, take off my clothes in the bathroom and wrap an old towel around me so as not to get the house wet. Getting the house wet would get me a beating. I learned quickly to stay away and to be careful.

"In later years, Dad became less violent and more apathetic. He'd sit in his chair and stare at the TV and not talk to anyone. Some nights he wouldn't move all night and we'd find him there in the morning. He lost his job, Mom had to take a third job just to make ends meet." Alexandra spoke and we barely breathed, entranced, imagining her as a little girl with curly blond hair streaming behind her in the wind as she conjured up her own reality amongst the tulips.

"So as you can imagine, I couldn't wait to get out of there. When I was seventeen I met a young man, a dentistry student named Jimmy Sparks. Barely a man! He was nineteen but I thought at the time that he was so old and wise and sophisticated.

He treated me like a precious gem. All the regular chivalrous stuff—holding open doors and walking on the street side of the sidewalk and all that—but also, he hung on my every word. Everything I said was fascinating to him. He'd pay attention to the little trinkets I noticed in stores, and then later, when he could afford it, would surprise me with them as gifts. He bought me little chocolates, wrapped up like presents. One day after we'd been dating for about six months, he asked me to marry him. I said yes without hesitation. We were married on Halloween, the day after I turned eighteen."

"You became Alexandra Sparks?" asked Erin. I don't know if I've mentioned this, but in the whole time I've known Alexandra, she's never given a last name for herself. She just goes by Alexandra. At first I thought it was because of her career, some sort of celebrity psychic thing, but in fact she legally doesn't have a last name. She dropped it at some point and I never knew why. Questions were swirling in my head, more questions with every sentence Alexandra spoke. There was a last name. There was a husband. Where is the husband now? And the children, where do they come into the picture … and where do they leave it?

"No. Alexandra is my middle name." She sighed again, but didn't offer any more information. Alexandra wasn't even her first name? Who was this woman?

"Does anyone else need another drink?" she asked. Erin held out her glass. Alexandra took it and hers to the kitchen for refills.

"Did you know she had been married?" I whispered to Erin, though I knew she didn't. "How could we not have known any of this?"

"I suppose if a person doesn't want to tell something, there's no way for anyone else to know. What is past is past. If no one is around to contradict something, especially from a few decades ago when it was easier to hide, then I suppose anyone could be anyone.

Anyone's history could be anything. We just assume we know people but … we don't. Maybe we never really know anyone."

Alexandra returned with the drinks. She sat down and immediately returned to her story, clearly having decided if she was going to tell us all there was no point in stopping.

"Jimmy and I were young but practical. I took a job as a secretary and he worked nights while he went to school during the day. I hardly saw him, but still we managed to get me pregnant not once but twice. The first, a boy, was born a year after we were married, between Jimmy's birthday and mine, all of us in October, and then the second, a girl, in May a year and a half after that. Charles—Charlie—and Chloë. Apples of my eyes, loves of my life, the physical manifestation of my heart and all the joy in my world. In all my years I had no idea how much love I had in me until the moment I laid eyes on Charlie. Before he was even born, I knew I would die for him. And then again with Chloë. I was filled up with love as bright as the sun. I could not contain my bliss."

Here she stopped, for a long time. I wasn't sure she was going to continue. She put her chin in her hands, staring off through the air into the past. Tears crept from the corner of her eyes, but I'm not sure she noticed. She was lost in time. Erin and I were afraid to speak and break the spell. We waited.

Finally, she continued. "It was over far too soon. 'Over' doesn't begin to describe it. Charlie was four and Chloë was two and a half. January, the cold of winter. I had gone away for the weekend to a friend's wedding. Jimmy stayed home with the kids. I was driving to the church when suddenly I got the deepest chills I'd ever felt. Far beyond the chill from the cold of the day but rather, a chill through my soul. I felt nauseated. I knew without a doubt that something was wrong, something that involved the children.

"I knew they were dead," she said. "I just knew it."

"I couldn't concentrate on the wedding ceremony and didn't

stick around for the reception. This was before cell phones, of course, so no one had any way to contact me. When I got back to the hotel the clerk at the front desk handed me a note to call my mother."

"You will recall that I did not have the closest relationship with my mother. A note to call my mother was as good as a confirmation that my fears were correct, but I called anyway. Jimmy had been driving the kids to a restaurant for dinner, a place the children loved that serves pancakes for dinner. It was freezing and he didn't see the black ice on the road. The car spun out of control, another car hit them and flung them into a metal pole that sliced the car in half. Chloë was killed instantly, and Charlie and Jimmy died on the way to the hospital."

She stopped.

"I'm so sorry, Alexandra," I said after a while. "I'm so sorry. I had no idea."

She looked up, dazed, looked a little surprised to find herself in 2010 in her home in Wishing Rock with Erin and me. I'd broken the spell.

"No, of course not," she said, shifting in her seat. "You couldn't have. No one did. Only Ed knew part of it, but not all of it. I never told anyone because it was too painful. People would ask me if I had ever wanted to be married, ever was married, ever wanted kids, and I'd just say 'no' to end the conversation. But there you have it, that's the truth of it. I was married. I had the most beautiful boy and girl and husband in the world, and they died.

"Interestingly," she continued, "that's when my psychic powers kicked in. The night they died, Charlie and Chloë visited me. I thought it was a dream, but I was wide awake. They told me they were okay. The told me they loved me and not to be mad at Daddy, it wasn't his fault. Because, you see, later the police would say they weren't sure who was at fault in the accident. I already knew, though, because Charlie and Chloë had told me. They came to me all the time in those first months, and Jimmy, too. They wouldn't necessarily talk; they'd just let me know they were there with me and that they were okay. At first they visited me only when I was alone, then when I was out. Then they started bringing friends." She laughed. "And then I became a psychic. People found out, started asking me to do readings. It paid better than being a secretary. I quit my old job and took on a new life. Moved to Wishing Rock a few years later, in 1994, where no one knew me or my past, and started fresh, dropped my first and last name. I didn't have to be this tragic woman whose family died in a horrible crash and who people had to look on with sympathetic eyes and mounds of pity. I was just Alexandra, the psychic.

"And that's also when I very carefully started to protect myself from ever being hurt again. I got close to people, certainly, but I maintained a distance of sorts. I numbed myself. When Ed moved to Wishing Rock, I think it was 1996?, anyway, he took a liking to me I suppose, but I would have none of it. Eventually our relationship mellowed into what it was always supposed to be—a very close friendship. I declined advances from all other men over the years as well. Better lonely than to be hurt again, and I was never really lonely; I could close my eyes and talk to Jimmy and the kids again. They'd sometimes tell me to move on but I wouldn't listen."

She stopped again. Erin and I sat there, silent. What do you say when someone reveals to you this horrible past? It was nearly twenty years ago but still, I can't imagine a person ever gets over the loss of her entire family. I can't imagine. And this Jimmy. A person in her life who had her whole heart, and then was gone. It made me think, I know it's obvious but so often we take people for granted. Any of us could die tomorrow. Would we have said all the things we need to say? Gran, you know how much I love you, right? It's easy to tell you, though. There are people in our lives who we love, but who it's harder to tell. Like Ed. I mean, I love Ed. If he were gone tomorrow, I would be devastated. All this time and energy I've been putting into worrying about whether he loves me, when in reality I need to simply and completely love and enjoy him in this day, this moment.

As I thought those same thoughts Friday night, I came to understand that was the point of our being there. Alexandra wanted to remind us to live now, love now.

"I know you girls are having troubles with love. And who am I to lecture anyone about love? I haven't let anyone in my heart for twenty years. If you tell yourself often enough that you don't need anyone, that you can't handle the hurt again, then you become numb inside. That's what I've become. Numb inside. But the fact is, if you spend all your life protecting your heart from any possible hurt or harm, you can never win. It's time for me to risk again. I'm scared and I don't even know where to begin, but it's time for me to jump in with both feet. I'm worth that.

"And so are the two of you. I can't tell you how to live your lives or who to love. But just keep in mind that making choices out of fear will never get you to love. You have to make choices out of love. You have to be willing—we have to be willing—to be vulnerable. It's so easy to preach it, so hard to live it, but I'm going to live it again and I hope you will to. Be willing to be vulnerable. Be willing to open our hearts to being broken and devastated. We have to be willing to be the one to say 'I love you' first, and without thought for whether it's returned. We have to be willing to trust that the people we love, love us, rather than pushing them away or running away ourselves before they can hurt us. We have to be willing to let people in.

And what's even harder is that if we really want to jump in with both feet, we have to have the courage to compensate for the fact that everyone else is acting out of fear, too. Other people make choices based on their fears that they won't get the love they want, and that makes us want to run away from them before they run from us. The greatest challenge is to hold in your heart the knowledge and trust that even if others' actions are based in fear, they do want to love you, they do. If they push you away it may be because they're afraid you'll push them away. Do you see what I mean? You have to decide to hold firm, to refuse to do anything but love. To fill yourself with compassion for that person and know that they want the same things you do: To be loved and accepted for who they are. Not to fight fear with fear but instead to fight fear with love. And even if they can't love you back due to their own fears, the only real way forward is to love anyway. When we're all the quivering messes of uncertainty that humans too often can be, having the fortitude to trust our way through our own fears as well as everyone else's can seem impossible. But I believe that it's the only way forward. I do. Replace every cell of fear with trust. That's my path from here on out."

It's a tall order, isn't it, Gran? I know exactly what she means, though. I know Pete loved me completely. When he left me, it wasn't because he didn't love me. It was fear. Did I have a choice at that time to refuse to give in to his fear? Could I have refused to believe he didn't love me anymore, and where would that have landed us? Would we still be together now?

On the other hand, I don't know if everything happens for a reason or if we give reason to everything that happens, but I am infinitely grateful that Pete left me because I would never have left him. And if he hadn't left me, I wouldn't have found Ed. Whatever convoluted messed up path I may have taken to get here, it brought me to Ed. Despite all my reservations and fears, he's the one I want. I love him. I do, and I am renewed in my decision to love him, to let him love me, to travel through this life together.

Erin, on the other hand, was not as convinced.

"Alexandra," she said, "I am so sorry for all you've been through. I admire the person you've become, having come from such a childhood, and it makes me love you all the more. I can't imagine losing my children and I don't know how you got through that pain. And I do understand that we need to love people when they're here with us because we never know when they'll be gone. But that doesn't mean that every person is right for every other person, that every relationship must be worked on until it works, does it? I shouldn't stick with David if I don't love him. That seems cruel to him and to me. Shouldn't the uncertainties of life be all the more reason for me to move on to find someone who is right for me?"

"But why is he not right for you?" I asked. "He's a perfectly pleasant man. He's smart, he's funny in a quiet way, he loves this, his adopted island, as intensely as you do, he has a stable job, he's handsome enough, he's good at carrying on a conversation once he feels comfortable, he doesn't act out in embarrassing ways. He's kind and compassionate. What don't you like about him? Do you not have chemistry with him?"

"We have chemistry," she said.

"No compatible interests?"

"No, we do. That's not it."

"What is it then?"

But Erin was silent. Not everyone's problems can be solved in one night, I suppose. I do think she's thinking about it, though, and isn't going to just break up with him like she was going to before. I think they're a great match, Erin and David. They're both a bit more emotionally restrained, maybe, than I am, but they both have good, kind hearts. But timing, you can't fight timing, and maybe this is simply not their time. I hope she gives him another chance. We'll see.

Anyway, that's about it from that night, except the strangest thing,

Gran. Alexandra says she isn't psychic anymore. All the energy is gone, she says. It just left her that night after we went home. Gone.

She doesn't know if it will ever come back. I think she's pretty distressed, actually. She said she talked with her kids a lot, got comfort from their being there. Maybe their leaving is their way of saying she is strong enough to go it on her own now.

Well then. That's all from Wishing Rock for now. Pass on my love to Liam, tell him thank you for raising a son as wonderful as Gavin, who takes such good care of my beloved Pip. I love you, Gran, I love you with the love of a thousand suns.

Ruby

From: Gran
To: Ruby
Sent: September 15, 2010
Subject: RE: RE: RE: Love

Oh my goodness, Ruby. Poor Alexandra. I'll need to write her. I know it was so long ago but you're right, I can't imagine a person ever fully gets over such a tragedy. It's good she finally feels strong enough to move on.

That is tremendously strange about her psychic abilities disappearing. I hope it's temporary. In the meantime, you all keep her busy. Erin and Millie and the others will have to just be there for her. I'm so glad you all have each other.

We're off for our nightly walk through our lovely car-free Wengen. Liam sends his love back. I love you with the love of a thousand suns too, Ruby, more than that, all the love of the universe, all the universes there may be.

Gran

From: Ed
To: Alexandra
Sent: September 16, 2010
Subject: idea

To begin, my love, you never told me that Alexandra is your middle name! First you keep your last name hidden from me, now your first? What is your first name? Inquiring Eds want to know.

Secondly. Since you nixed my brilliant lecture series idea I have continued to ponder other possibilities. What about scholarships? Scholarships would help people.

From: Alexandra
To: Ed
Sent: September 16, 2010
Subject: RE: idea

Hm. Maybe I'll tell you my first name one day. Maybe. We'll see. Any guesses?

I did not nix your other idea; I merely encouraged you to continue to brainstorm. Scholarships. Certainly a noble idea. Limited in scope, as we have a small number of children in Wishing Rock or even on the whole island, though you could expand it to include anyone else interested in going back to school or furthering their education. How many people do you want to include in your giving? One time only or on a continuing basis? What is the goal, the vision, the dream? I think you're headed in the right direction—keep pondering, my friend!

From: Ed
To: Alexandra
Sent: September 16, 2010
Subject: RE: RE: idea

Hm indeed. I shall continue to think. Thank you ... Persephone?
Belinda? Ariel?

From: Alexandra
To: Ed
Sent: September 16, 2010
Subject: RE: RE: RE: idea

None of the above. Don't worry, my love. The times, they are
a'changin. One of these days I'll tell you my birth name, probably
sooner than later. All a part of embracing the wholeness of life and
moving on.

From: Ed
To: Alexandra
Sent: September 16, 2010
Subject: RE: RE: RE: RE: idea

Don't tell me just yet. And also, dinner party at my house on Friday. See you there, Evita? Fern? Sabina?

From: Alexandra
To: Ed
Sent: September 16, 2010
Subject: RE: RE: RE: RE: RE: idea

Keep guessing. I'll give you a hint: It's a completely normal name. Friday, your house, six o'clock? Let me know what to bring. See you then, my love!

From: Ed
To: Michael, Ben
Sent: September 17, 2010
Subject: cave hunt

Men! We have a mission! We are going hunting! Treasure hunting! David has some ideas of what cave could be our cave. He tells me there are many many caves on this island. He does not guarantee we will find grandpa's treasure cave on the first trip out. However, he will lead and we may follow. Saturday morning, we will leave Wishing Rock at nine. Which of you is man enough to brave the cavernous depths with us?

From: Ben
To: Michael, Ed
Sent: September 17, 2010
Subject: RE: cave hunt

Count me in!

From: Michael
To: Ed, Ben
Sent: September 17, 2010
Subject: RE: cave hunt

I'll come along, of course. Carolyn says she'll pack a good lunch for us all.

From: Ed
To: Michael, Ben
Sent: September 17, 2010
Subject: RE: RE: cave hunt

Carolyn, my favorite sister-in-law! Tell her we accept her offering of robust sustenance. Don't forget, dinner party at my house tonight. Come and eat heartily, for tomorrow our quest begins!

Text from Ruby to Erin
Sent: September 17, 2010

Hey, Erin. You going along on the treasure hunt tomorrow?

Text from Erin to Ruby
Sent: September 17, 2010

No. David invited me and I thought about it, but it's really Ed and Michael's thing, I think. Are you going?

Text from Ruby to Erin
Sent: September 17, 2010

I thought about it too but I think that's a few too many cooks in
the kitchen. Only so many people fit in a cave! Are you coming to
dinner tonight then?

Text from Erin to Ruby
Sent: September 17, 2010

Yup.

Text from Ruby to Erin
Sent: September 17, 2010

Try to contain your excitement. Still thinking about things with
David?

Text from Erin to Ruby
Sent: September 17, 2010

Yup. I don't know why my brain is so muddled over all this. It just
shouldn't be so hard.

Text from Ruby to Erin
Sent: September 17, 2010

I know. It shouldn't. Don't wear yourself out thinking. We'll talk later. Love you!

Text from Erin to Ruby
Sent: September 17, 2010

Yup. Love you too.

From: Alexandra
To: Millie, Erin, Carolyn, Claire, Ruby
Sent: September 18, 2010
Subject: spa weekend

Good morning, ladies!

As you all know by now, my world has been a bit shaken as of late. No, the energies have not returned yet. Yes, it is still unsettling me.

I think a poker group spa weekend is in order, and it's my treat. I had next weekend in mind, at a spa in Bellingham. We could head over Friday afternoon and return Sunday, or Monday if people would rather and are able. Hot stone massages, seaweed scrub facials, mud baths, whatever you like. In addition we could go on some scenic drives, walk around Bellingham and/or Fairhaven, explore cozy little tea shops and dusty bookstores and such, see if there's a show on one night, or just in general enjoy ourselves.

As I said, I'm paying. Let me know if you'd like to come along. Who's with me?

From: Erin
To: Alexandra, Millie, Carolyn, Claire, Ruby
Sent: September 18, 2010
Subject: RE: spa weekend

That's generous of you, Alexandra, thank you. I'd love to come along. I may have to come back Sunday night; I'll check my workload and see. Hot stone massage, here I come!

From: Carolyn
To: Alexandra, Millie, Erin, Claire, Ruby
Sent: September 18, 2010
Subject: RE: spa weekend

I am definitely up for a spa weekend. That sounds divine. Stone massage for sure, and I've never tried a mud bath! But Alexandra, you don't need to pay. I can certainly chip in.

From: Millie
To: Alexandra, Erin, Carolyn, Claire, Ruby
Sent: September 18, 2010
Subject: RE: spa weekend

That sounds just lovely, Alexandra. You are so generous and I know you've been having a rough week. I think a weekend away with the girls is just what the doctor ordered. I can be away through either Sunday or Monday, whatever the group would like. Ben's been wanting a few more hours in the store to make some money so I am sure he'll have no problem with it. He's around next weekend, isn't he, Claire?

I do have a question about the mud baths. How often do they replace the mud? I don't want to be sitting in someone else's left-over mud sludge.

From: Claire
To: Millie, Alexandra, Erin, Carolyn, Ruby
Sent: September 18, 2010
Subject: RE: RE: spa weekend

Millie: Yes, Ben is around. I'm sure he'd be more than happy to take on the store and such for you, and Tom can help out if needed as well with the mail or anything.

Alexandra: Absolutely I am in! It's been a busy summer at the Inn and I'd love a weekend away for once! I just checked the reservations and we only have one couple booked. Ben and Tom can handle that. Tom's a master chef at the Inn breakfast, don't you know! Haha! And Ben is learning, too. He's quite good at scrambled eggs. Low heat and slow cooking, that's the way to do it! As Carolyn said, though, you don't need to pay. I can pay my bit.

As for Millie's mud bath question, I had never thought of that. I've never had a mud bath either. But I can't imagine they're not clean. I mean, regulations being what they are!

From: Millie
To: Claire, Alexandra, Erin, Carolyn, Ruby
Sent: September 18, 2010
Subject: RE: RE: RE: spa weekend

I'm just saying, imagine what all could be in that mud. That's all I'm saying.

From: Ruby
To: Millie, Claire, Alexandra, Carolyn, Erin
Sent: September 18, 2010
Subject: RE: RE: RE: RE: spa weekend

Yes, yes, yes! So much fun!

Erin: Ed's out in the caves right now trying to find their ancient treasure. I'll tell him to call you when he gets back about your (and my) taking that Monday off. Based on what I know of workload I think it'll be fine, don't you? Ed can handle the shop for a day.

Millie: What all does that active imagination of yours think could be in that mud?

From: Millie
To: Claire, Alexandra, Erin, Carolyn, Ruby
Sent: September 18, 2010
Subject: RE: RE: RE: RE: RE: spa weekend

Skin cells. Fingernails. And, I'll be blunt, pee. Certainly in the history of time and spas at least one person has to have peed in a mud bath. It's just the law of averages or some other equally unbreakable law. The law of drinking too much wine when on a girlfriend spa retreat and then going to a mud bath. Law of something. It's happened, for sure.

And Ben! I'm so glad you mentioned Ben. It's his birthday today! I almost forgot! I need to get his present to him!

From: Erin
To: Ruby, Millie, Claire, Alexandra, Carolyn
Sent: September 18, 2010
Subject: RE: RE: RE: RE: RE: RE: spa weekend

Millie, are you planning to pee in the mud? Is that what you're trying to tell us? If that's the case, I would like to schedule my mud bath before yours.

❖

From: Millie
To: Erin, Ruby, Claire, Alexandra, Carolyn
Sent: September 18, 2010
Subject: RE: RE: RE: RE: RE: RE: RE: spa weekend

I am not planning to pee in the mud, thank you very much Miss Erin. I just think of these things. And I'd like to know. I can't imagine people don't ask all the time. How often is the mud switched out? Is it switched out completely, or is it like Amish Friendship Bread, where there's always some cells from the original batter in it?

❖

From: Claire
To: Millie, Alexandra, Erin, Carolyn, Ruby
Sent: September 18, 2010
Subject: RE: RE: RE: RE: RE: RE: RE: RE: spa weekend

It is, indeed, Ben's birthday. And I forgot Carolyn's birthday! Three days ago. Happy birthday, Carolyn! I'd meant to get a note out earlier—we'll be having cake and ice cream tonight at seven. You all are welcome of course. Come on by. Maybe the boys will all have tales to share of finding lost treasure. Tom wanted to go on the hunt but I told him the caulking in one of the guest room bathrooms would not wait one more day!

From: Alexandra
To: Millie, Claire, Erin, Carolyn, Ruby
Sent: September 18, 2010
Subject: RE: RE: RF: RE: RE: RE: RE: RE: spa weekend

First of all, I am paying and that's all there is to it. This is my treat. You all can put your wallets away.

Millie, I'll call the spa and ask them about the mud.

So it sounds like everyone is willing and able to go. I'll tell you what, I'll reserve rooms for everyone through Monday and if you have to leave early that's no problem.

Claire, I will gladly come by tonight at seven. Happy birthday, Carolyn! Happy birthday, Ben!

Good, I'm delighted you all can join me. Being surrounded by friends is a spa treatment for the soul.

From: Carolyn
To: Alexandra, Millie, Claire, Erin, Ruby
Sent: September 18, 2010
Subject: RE: RE: RE: RE: RE: RE: RE: RE: RE: spa weekend

Thank you all for the wishes! Claire, we'll be there tonight too. See you all soon.

From: Ed
To: Alexandra
Sent: September 18, 2010
Subject: Let's start at the very beginning

Anna? Abigail? Amy? Alice? Adelaide? Agatha? Astrid?

From: Alexandra
To: Ed
Sent: September 18, 2010
Subject: RE: Let's start at the very beginning

You're home from cave explorations, then?

No, no, no, no, no, no, no. Move on. It does not start with an A.

Thanks again for a great dinner party last night, as always. I can't wait to hear about today. Are you going up to the Inn for cake and ice cream for Ben's birthday?

From: Ed
To: Alexandra
Sent: September 18, 2010
Subject: RE: RE: Let's start at the very beginning

Such a silly question, Beatrice, you know where there's cake and ice cream involved, I'm there!

From: Alexandra
To: Ed
Sent: September 18, 2010
Subject: RE: RE: RE: Let's start at the very beginning

Keep guessing. See you at seven.

❖

From: Jake
To: Ben
Sent: September 18, 2010
Subject: birthday

Happy birthday punk!

❖

From: Ben
To: Jake
Sent: September 18, 2010
Subject: RE: birthday

Eighteen! I'm so old!

Ma's having a party for me in an hour. Wish you could be here.

Went with Ed, Michael, and David through a bunch of caves up on the north/northeast end today looking for that treasure. I thought we knew all of the caves but David took us to some I'd never been to. He's really obsessed with caves. We weren't sure what we were looking for—a cave with a mouth shaped like a tilted egg? When you start to look at them, they all look a little like that. Thanks, ol' Meriwether! That helps a lot! I think we went to five or six caves before Michael said he had to get back, but it was fun anyway. I wish Meriwether had said in one of his letters what the treasure was. I'll have to keep reading. I'm not through them all yet.

We're going to go out again next weekend. Ed won't be here but David, Michael, and I will go. Maybe Tom.

Ed and Michael talked some today about the Rita that their dad supposedly dated or something. Weird to think how much we don't know about people sometimes.

Have you talked to Ruby lately? You over her yet? She and Ed seem pretty tight, dude. I think you gotta move on.

From: Jake
To: Ben
Sent: September 18, 2010
Subject: RE: RE: birthday

Yeah, eighteen, you're ancient and full of wisdom. May as well get a walker and start writing your memoirs.

Haven't talked to Ruby for a bit. Still don't want to talk to Ed. Still nothing to say. Why won't Ed be there next weekend?

School's good, classes starting soon. Good to get moved in over here again. Getting to know the first year students. Some cute girls there who could be worth getting to know.

From: Ben
To: Jake
Sent: September 18, 2010
Subject: RE: RE: RE: birthday

Sounds like the healing has begun. You're a good man, Jake.

Ed's going to some conference for distillery owners or something. I think Ruby is going to go over too, but also all those ladies are going on a girl weekend first. People are going places and didn't invite me, that's the gist of it.

From: Jake
To: Ben
Sent: September 18, 2010
Subject: RE: RE: RE: RE: birthday

Must be nice to have all that money Ed has to buy a girl's love. Good for Ed.

Have a good time at your party, buddy. Talk to you later.

From: Ed
To: Alexandra
Sent: September 19, 2010
Subject: RE: RE: RE: RE: Let's start at the very beginning

Connie? Cathy? Clarice? Donatella? Daria?

From: Alexandra
To: Ed
Sent: September 19, 2010
Subject: RE: RE: RE: RE: RE: Let's start at the very beginning

So close and yet so far.

From: Ed
To: Alexandra
Sent: September 19, 2010
Subject: RE: RE: RE: RE: RE: RE: Let's start at the very begin-
ning

I will figure it out. Don't you doubt me. I will.
    What's up with the voices? Anything yet?

From: Alexandra
To: Ed
Sent: September 19, 2010
Subject: RE: RE: RE: RE: RE: RE: RE: Let's start at the very be-
ginning

Nothing yet. Maybe it's their way of telling me it's time for me not
to be alone anymore. If you should find any eligible bachelors at
your conference, be a dear and let me know, will you?

From: Ed
To: Alexandra
Sent: September 19, 2010
Subject: RE: RE: RE: RE: RE: RE: RE: RE: Let's start at the very
beginning

Will do, my beloved Eunice.

From: Alexandra
To: Ed
Sent: September 19, 2010
Subject: RE: RE: RE: RE: RE: RE: RE: RE: RE: Let's start at the very beginning

Ed, you warm my heart. Keep guessing.

Text from Ruby to Ed
Sent: September 20, 2010

Hey good lookin'. Just wanted to say I love you.

Text from Ed to Ruby
Sent: September 20, 2010

An amazing but unexpected message from the world's most pulchritudinous woman? To what do I owe this pleasure?

Text from Ruby to Ed
Sent: September 20, 2010

Pulchriwhat? Going to have to look that up. I've been thinking about what Alexandra said the other night. I don't tell you enough. I don't trust you enough. I get scared because I fancy you so much and I'm scared you'll go away. But I really like you, Ed. Also, you never know what could happen to you or to me. If something were to happen to one of us, I'd want to be sure I told you. I love you.

Text from Ed to Ruby
Sent: September 20, 2010

Pulchritudinous: alluring, bewitching, ravishing, fascinating, enticing, gorgeous. My darling Ruby. Don't you worry. we are going to live long lives, and we'll live them together, grow old and bald together. And I love you too. You amaze me every day. I love you.

From: Ed
To: Alexandra
Sent: September 21, 2010
Subject: community dreams

Lex. Okay, so I'm moving on from the lectures idea. You talked about dreams which got me thinking. I want to help people fulfill their dreams. When I talk to people, it's always money that gets in the way of their fulfilling their dreams. Every time. I want to give them money for their dreams. What do you think?

From: Alexandra
To: Ed
Sent: September 21, 2010
Subject: RE: community dreams

Ed. I think it's the start of a wonderful idea, definitely admirable and definitely on the right track. I'll tell you my thoughts and concerns. How are you going to decide who gets the money? Everyone will want money; that's just the way it is. If you're not careful you might end up starting some fights and stirring up ill will (and even if you are careful you might start fights and stir up ill will). How are you going to decide how much money? Does everyone's dream cost the same? How often are you going to give it away?

Besides all that, there's the question of what people do with wealth they didn't work for. I tend to believe that people appreciate gifts more when they have put some effort into them. Dreams, too, are a tricky subject. People have ideas of their dreams, but I think dreams are like our proverbial horse being led to water. You can lead people to their dreams but you can't make them live them out. Giving someone money for their dreams won't make them actually go out and pursue those dreams. If they really wanted the dreams, wouldn't they already be working to make them happen? I don't believe money is the only obstacle in some cases.

What if you had an application process? You could even make yourself a foundation of some sorts, I'd think. Require that a person has to live in Wishing Rock. Maybe you could even have some sort of "sweat equity" be a part of the agreement. That is, in the same vein of the way other charities that build homes require the homeowners to put in a certain amount of work toward the building of the house. You could require people to do some work toward the goal before getting the money. Just so you and they both know they really want what they think they want, and that they understand dreams don't come easy. People may think it's just about the money but there's a ton of hard work and dedication involved. Living a dream is just that: living it, every day, all day, the ups and downs, being inside it and a part of it. It takes commitment. It takes courage, and it takes believing in oneself, and persevering, and never giving up. If people don't have it in them to believe in their dreams, then all the help you can give them, all the money in the world, will be of absolutely no use to them.

❖

From: Ed
To: Alexandra
Sent: September 21, 2010
Subject: RE: RE: community dreams

Whoa, Nellie! Wait, is that it? Nellie? Slow down there, Lex! So many thoughts, so little time!

You're probably right, people need to buy into their dreams to really have a chance at making them come true. I love the distillery but it's a lot of work. You've got some good ideas, there, lady. I like the idea of their putting some sweat equity into the dreams before getting the funding.

All right, I think we're onto something here.

I think I'll call them ED Grants: Everybody Dreams. ED. Because my name is Ed. Get it? Too much?

Keep thinking, darlin'! If you know anyone who knows anything about setting up foundations let me know.

So, Genevieve: What is your dream?

❖

From: Alexandra
To: Ed
Sent: September 21, 2010
Subject: RE: RE: RE: community dreams

Your question took me aback. I suppose I always thought I was already doing what I was meant to be doing, helping people connect with their loved ones who have passed. Now that that's gone, I don't even know anymore. I'm hoping that having some "me" time at the spa this weekend will give me some clarity. I also have a psychic friend in Bellingham and I'm planning to visit her while we're there, to see if she can shed any light on my new spiritless developments. It seems so strange to me that the spirits would turn on and off like that. I've always sort of suspected that people could all be psychic if they just knew how to "tune in" better. We all have intuition; many people simply don't trust it or know how to use it. I still feel in tune with my intuition, but the connection with people on the other side is simply gone. I don't know whether to make peace with that, or wait for it to return. Or beg for it to return. So maybe right now my dream is simply to figure that out. Unfortunately, nothing an ED grant could help with.

Come by later, bring Ruby if she wants to come too. We'll have cocktails and we'll toast to dreams.

From: Ruby
To: Erin
Sent: September 22, 2010
Subject: Checking in

Just checking in, I know you're out on a distributor run today. Are you gone overnight?

Ed's talking these days about finding a way to give people money, to help them reach their dreams. Suddenly I feel inadequate. Do you know what your dream is? What do you want from life? I'm not even sure I know what I want. To be loved and appreciated for who I am. To be with Ed. But now I feel like I'm supposed to want more than that. Am I supposed to want more than that? Do I have to have a dream to be valid? Can't I just enjoy living?

So how are things with you and David? Have you had a change of heart? Have you talked with him? What does he think?

Love you!

From: Erin
To: Ruby
Sent: September 22, 2010
Subject: RE: Checking in

Hi, yes, I'm heading over to the coast today, back tomorrow.

I talked with David about it a little bit but didn't really do a good job of explaining myself and what the problem is. I think he's confused; I confused him. He's not too communicative, he thinks a lot but doesn't say as much. Maybe that's part of the problem, neither of us knows how to talk each other.

I hear you about the dreams. I don't know what my dream is either. I think it's harder to see long-term when the short-term feels so messed up. Maybe I dream of inner peace. It's like world peace, only more personal.

I'm glad you and Ed are doing well. After Pete I was worried your heart would be broken forever. I mean, I know in reality very few people's hearts are broken forever, but sometimes it seems that way. Seeing you with Ed does make me wonder if I messed up in letting a good one slip away, but he and I just didn't fit together the way you two do anyway. You say all the time how great he is, but you know, you're wonderful too, Ruby. You are as good for him as he is for you. It's a good thing he and I broke up or you two would never have gotten together! Hindsight, so interesting to see how all the pieces fit together, when we had no way of knowing at the time. A magic ball would be very nice to have sometimes, but we're stuck with just having to feel our way through life, making the mistakes and then learning from them, trying not to let regrets paralyze us from moving on. Anyway, my point is, it's so great to see you happy. I know you still get scared about your heart, but you are a fantastic person, Ruby, and you're strong. I have complete faith that you can get through anything. You deserve all the joy in the world.

From: Erin
To: Pip
Sent: September 22, 2010
Subject: Gavin

Hey Pipsqueak,

Question for you, since you're a little more uninvolved in my love life than Ruby is (or anyone in Wishing Rock is): How did you know Gavin was the right guy for you? Did you have any doubts? How did you know the others weren't right? I can't figure out if my doubts are doubts or fears. Or just good instinct that it wasn't meant to be.

Hi to the Captain,

Erin

P.S. Alexandra sat us down the other day to tell us we should tell the people we love, that we love them. There was more to her lecture, of course, but that was part of it. Love you, Pipsqueak. I mean it.

❖

From: Pip
To: Erin
Sent: September 23, 2010
Subject: RE: Gavin

Hi Erin,

I'm sorry to say, or not sorry to say but sorry for you, I never had a doubt with Gavin. All those people who say "you just know when you find the right one," you know how that is? And until it happens you think, "How do you 'just know'?" Because that's ridiculous, right? That's judging a book by the cover, that's ... I don't know. It's not logical, and we humans are supposed to use our logic, isn't that the whole point of not being chimpanzees? After meeting Gavin, though, my whole perspective changed. We both knew from the start that we were going to be in each other's lives for a long time. Past lives? Chemistry? I don't know. But we knew. I never had doubts. I definitely had fears—mostly about the fact that I didn't have doubts. But I didn't have doubts.

Now, that's not to say that I don't think you can grow to love someone. You can also meet the right person at the wrong time, or meet the right person but be too scared or closed off to see it. What I think: There's no mistaking love. The trick is that love can be so gentle and quiet. All the other emotions—most especially fears—are loud and demanding and aggressive. If you're not careful, they might drown out the clear voice of love. Look at Ruby. She thought Pete was the one, but he wasn't. Then she thought Jake was the one. I don't think she ever thought Dan was the one. Now Ed is the one, but she didn't think that when she first met him. Different people have different experiences.

So I know that doesn't help.

What's up with you and David? Not feeling it? There's nothing wrong with taking some time away to clear your head. That whole absence making the heart grow fonder, that's a saying for a reason. We want what we can't have, we don't know what we had until it's gone, etc. Maybe if you spend some time away it'll help you know if you want him back?

I love you too, Erin. That Alexandra, she's a keeper.

Pip

From: Erin
To: Pip
Sent: September 23, 2010
Subject: RE: RE: Gavin

Thanks, that helps loads. If only people came with tags. "This one will grow on you." "This one should be taken with a grain of salt." "This one not to be mixed with good company." "Erin Paige Anderson, this one's for you!" That would help. It's a guessing game and I have never been comfortable with uncertainties. I want to know. I like things settled. I don't want to make mistakes with my heart.

All right, thanks Pippers, I appreciate the thoughts even if you couldn't give me the one definitive answer to resolve all my issues. Work on that, will you?

E.

❖

From: Ruby
To: Gran
Sent: September 24, 2010
Subject: Bellingham

Gran,

Well, we've made our way over to Bellingham, the poker ladies and I, for our spa weekend. We all took off from Wishing Rock around noon so we would get here while it was still light. Wouldn't you know it, being island people, first thing we did after checking in at the inn was find ourselves a little beach. I went straight into beachcombing mode; I do it so much at home that

I don't think I can go to a beach anymore without instinctively looking down to see what treasures are beneath my feet. I found a wishing rock after a few minutes, and then, Gran, once I looked more closely I realized the beach was sprinkled with a smattering of wishing rocks. More than a smattering. Lots of wishing rocks, all over. This has become a theme in my life: wishing rocks, everywhere I go.

A while back I started telling you my wishing rock theory of life, the ways wishing rocks are like life. I have to add this to the list: I firmly believe that in everything in life, what you focus on increases. If you start looking for wishing rocks, you'll start to see wishing rocks everywhere. If you start to focus on all the amazing, helpful, kind people in your life, you'll start to attract more amazing, helpful people into your life. If you focus on petty trivial things, you'll attract that instead. If you're not awake to life you won't feel its buzz around you. If you're not aware of wishing rocks you may not notice them at all. I started looking around this beach and my beloved rocks were just everywhere, wishing rocks left and right. A bit of home.

It was such a nice little beach, tucked away from the main drag. There's something about beaches that draws me, a magnetic pull. I don't know what it is, but it's primal; I feel it. That peace—both melancholy and joyful at the same time—that comes with staring at the waves, the meditative state I got into by writing messages into the sand and then watching as the waves reclaimed the words. I used the sharp end of a shell to write some wishes into the sand near the lapping waves, and then wished hard as the water washed them away, vanishing my hopes into the elemental deep. I wrote some thoughts farther back from the edge of the water and left them there, hoping someone else would come along and be surprised with a message of kindness from the universe. "You are amazing, just the way you are," I wrote, and also

"Everything will be all right." I imagined some questful soul who had come to the beach seeking the solace of the ocean, randomly stumbling across those words in the sand, and it felt good. I hope someone found them before they were gone.

All in all, the weekend is off to a good start.

Love, Ruby

❖

From: Gran
To: Ruby
Sent: September 25, 2010
Subject: RE: Bellingham

Ruby,

What a delightful find, discovering your wishing rocks away from home. Everything on this Earth is connected, and wonderful treasures reveal themselves everywhere to souls who are paying attention. We must go through life and the world with our eyes open.

Liam and I are certainly keeping our eyes wide open in this magical land. We left Wengen the other day though I don't know if it can be beat for mountaintop allure. Now we're down in Vevey, on Lake Geneva, and it too has a beauty and appeal I couldn't have imagined. On the other hand, I sometimes remind myself that for some people this glorious place is simply home. Part of the joy of travel is the mystique of being somewhere new, the enchantment of unmet people and undiscovered places.

That said, I am enjoying Vevey. The Swiss, reserved as they may be, I love them more and more every day. A place known for chocolate and cheese and efficient transportation must be doing something right, mustn't it?

From our base this time we are exploring the area on foot and train. Yesterday we took the Chocolate Train—Chocolate Train!

—to visit a chocolate factory and then a cheese factory. With the train meandering through picture-perfect countryside, the side trip to a castle, the fascinating insights into the making of cheese, and the chocolate tour topped off with as much chocolate as we could eat, the day could not have been more charming.

Tonight we have our feet up after another lovely train/foot day. We caught the Wine Train up to the top of the hill, hopped off at a tiny nondescript village (I thought surely there would be a sign, "Disembark here for the Vineyard Trail" but as far as we could tell there was not), wound our way through a few roads hoping to find ourselves on the right track, and sure enough found the trail we'd been wanting to walk. It's a long downhill ramble through acres of vineyards with vines clinging to every inch of the hillside, and it's stunning. As we ambled along down at our pensioner's pace, we watched the Swiss ferries gliding gently below us along Lake Geneva, taking travelers to and from the dock at Rivaz. Our path led us to the town of Saint Saphorin, where we waited a half hour or so for the train back to Vevey. Upon our return we went in quest of a bottle of Swiss wine and some bread and cheese for the evening meal. The Swiss make delicious wines, but not much of it, so you'll rarely find it outside the country. We are enjoying it now. Liam is writing to Gavin and I am writing to you, so the circle is complete.

Tomorrow there's a farmer's market at the square in town. Few things bring me more joy than the colors and flavors and cheer of a local farmer's market. If only we had a kitchen in our little room. But, we'll make do with what we can buy and eat on the spot. After that we may head down the road to the Chateau de Chillion, which I hear is spectacular.

Tell everyone hello for me and enjoy your weekend away. I'll have to get in touch with Alexandra to find out how she's doing with these new developments in her world. Life does like to throw us curve balls. She is strong; I'm sure she will get through.

All my love,

Gran

From: Ed
To: Alexandra
Sent: September 26, 2010
Subject: Yo

Hey Lex! I hope you ladies are all having a good time at that spa there. Can't believe you didn't ask me along. Don't I look like the kind of guy who would enjoy a nice mud bath and facial?

So Lex. With you all gone I've had too much time to think. I've had Jake on my mind and it's bugging me. He and I used to be buddies, doing buddy things like Gavin and I are doing here. I know he's off in school now so things would have been different anyway, but he's really turned from me. Ben says Jake says Ruby only wants to date me for my money and that it was a cheap move on my part to take her from him. None of which is true. She broke it off with him before we started dating, and I really don't believe Ruby wants me for my money. (Clearly it's for my rock-hard abs and my hearty infectious guffaw.) I'm a guy, sure I know the "man code" but I'm also an adult and I know things aren't that simple.

How do you see it? Should I have told Ruby I couldn't date her since Jake was my mate? Asked him first? Neither of those sits well with me. But I miss the kid. I wouldn't give Ruby up for anything, but I miss the kid.

How are you doing? Still silent up there in your spirit noggin?

Ed

From: Alexandra
To: Ed
Sent: September 26, 2010
Subject: RE: Yo

Darling Ed, we can't control our hearts. Would it have been nice for you to follow the man code and not date Ruby? Well, it would be nice if Jake would follow the adult code and not be annoyed with you for wanting to find true love. No, I don't believe you did anything wrong. We can't limit others, begrudge or deny others their happiness, simply because we haven't found it ourselves. That leads to nothing but bitterness and loneliness. Jake needs to grow up. And wasn't that the problem all along? He's a mature young man but he's young. He needs to grow up.

Time heals all wounds, my love. More than that, love heals all wounds. You and Jake were good friends and will be good friends again. Just give it time.

I'm doing all right. Our spa weekend has been a welcome diversion and we're all having a great time.

Today when everyone else went to lunch, I went to visit my psychic friend. She told me my family are all still around me. I knew that, logically, from my own past experience and having seen how the spirits work, but it was good to know she validated that as well. She said they wouldn't say too much other than what I'd figured out: They want me to stop using them as comfort and crutch, and to go out into the world, live life and find love. Cruel little buggers. So out into the world I'll go. Pretty scary stuff.

It's strange, Ed. I always thought that by this age I'd have life all figured out, that I'd have all my issues resolved and be completely at peace with myself and the world. Apparently that's not the case.

Apparently we continue to learn and grow throughout life. Apparently we are all onions after all, layer after layer after layer.

My love,
Alexandra

From: Millie
To: Adele
Sent: September 27, 2010
Subject: Spas

Adele,

Forgive me for not having written for so long! Ruby has been telling me about your travels as you've been sharing them with her. Switzerland sounds just fabulous. I'll add it to my list. Maybe Walter and I will have to travel there sometime. As I said before, we've been taking the slow route and enjoying it. We go on dates and he takes me to dinner, the way things should be. He's a bit of a musician, actually, and if I'm lucky he'll pick up his guitar and strum me a tune every now and then. Makes me feel young again. Have you heard of those "slow" movements—slow food, slow travel? It's what you and I used to call "food" and "travel" back in our day, but with the fast pace of the world these days the younger generations have to remind themselves to slow down. Anyway, being with Walter reminds me of those slow movements. I savor the moments and take them each in one by one with him. The story of Millie and Walter is unfolding slowly but beautifully.

So maybe one day we'll have to visit Switzerland together.

At any rate, I just have to share with you the tale of this past weekend I spent with my Wishing Rock "poker group"—the girls: Ruby, Alexandra, Claire, Carolyn, Erin, and me.

Poor Alexandra, she's in such an inner tizzy these days. I think to keep herself busy and fill up all the quiet in her head she's been active as a rooster in a chicken coop lately. She decided to take us all on this luxury trip just to make sure we'd all come along and force her to relax. I had never been to any sort of spa before, so I didn't know what to expect. The hot stone massage was nice enough but I do find it a little strange to be naked around strangers, even if you're usually more or less covered up by a soft sheet.

The mud bath, though, Adele, was a different story. It is this story I bring to you today, and I bring it to you as a warning that should be passed on to the generations.

Let me tell you about the mud bath.

Going in, I had no idea what to expect. I'd had a conversation with the girls about how often the mud gets changed, since for purposes of practicality it obviously can't be changed out after each person. The girls looked at me crazy for wondering, but as it turns out, only about half the mud is changed out daily. Between you and me, the way the spa worker sort of hesitated on answering that question made me a bit suspicious that it's not even that often. However, I was told that a mud bath was an experience I must have, and so have it I would.

Perhaps you've never thought much about mud and the differences between mud and water. Water, being of a cellular structure that is, by definition, liquid, is something a person can just slip into and it will part and make way for the body being placed into it. You step into a bath and your foot goes straight to the bottom of the tub, and you don't think another moment about it.

Not so with mud baths.

No, Adele, mud baths are, by definition, not liquid, and this was something I had not partially much less fully considered. For some reason the mud baths in this particular spa were not in completely isolated areas. There were two baths next to each other, so

Erin and I paired up for our bath time, but on top of that there were workers all around. (Possibly fewer than it felt like, but it felt like dozens. Two or three at least. I have no idea what they were doing as I was practicing the two-year-old's belief that if I didn't look at them, they would not be able to see me. Because you see at this point we were naked and had to drop our robes to get into the baths, and while I am not a prude I do not in general wander around naked in front of strangers, much less strangers who have been hired to do a service on me.)

I stepped in and wriggled my foot a bit to find the bottom of the tub. Found it, then carefully—we are not as young as we used to be, you know, and we have to be careful, always, not to fall—carefully held the edge of the tub, lifted the other foot, dug my toes through the mud. I was at this point crouched over a bathtub full of mud.

Then I sat down.

I sat down on top of the mud, that is, but did not sink in.

This, my dear Adele, was the moment when I realized just HOW solid mud is. And how ludicrous my situation was. A sixty-something-year-old lady, naked as a jailbird, and a wrinkled and saggy jailbird at that, sitting on top of a pile of mud in a room full of strangers.

So I did what any self-respecting woman would do in an attempt to salvage her dignity: I started digging with my hands to create a hole in the mud in which I could sit. Wriggling and scooping and moving the mud from under me to on top of me.

I've never felt so dignified.

I need to note that the mud was not just wet dirt. I'm not sure what I expected but there were tiny twigs in this mud, even. This becomes important later in our story.

Well, I finally got myself situated underneath the mud instead of on top of it, and at this point OF COURSE I had an itch on my face. I scrunched my nose and wiggled my face as much as I could but to no avail; the itch would not go away.

And so then, in the natural course of things, I had mud on my face as well.

And what, Adele, what pray tell is a person supposed to do once she is sitting in a mud bath? I didn't want to lean back and get mud in my hair too. I couldn't read—didn't bring anything to read and my hands were covered in mud anyway. So I sat there. Waiting for someone to come along and tell me it was time to get out. I finally looked over at Erin—I'd avoided her gaze during my whole ordeal—and we looked at each other with eyes that said "Really? People do this for fun?"

Finally, we decided we'd had enough, gotten our money's worth—whatever that might have been—and were ready to get out.

You know that sucking sound that is made when you pull your foot or a boot out of a deep pile of mud?

Well, anyway, all in all, the mud bath was not really what I would label "relaxing."

But there's more, Adele. The worst was yet to come. Just as the baths themselves were in the open, where onlookers could look on, so were the post-bath showers. The shower heads were attached high on the wall; no detachable wands here with which a person could direct the flow of the water, but merely a shower head coming up from about a foot above my head. Now I don't know about your body, but on mine there are parts that water coming from above does not hit, unless I contort my body and aid the water with my hands. And there are natural folds and creases in the private areas that need aid as well, if one wants to fully remove any mud that may have gotten into all one's crevices. And even if the onlookers were not looking on, I nonetheless felt quite exposed and opposed to lifting legs or spreading cheeks amidst this audience. I spent my time in the post-bath cleansing shower in awkward contortions trying to remain ladylike. It didn't work.

The next morning, Erin came out of the hotel room shower and said "There were still twigs in there." She was not alone.

But, as I said, the hot stone massage was nice.

And, all joking and mud baths aside, we had an absolutely wonderful time, full of many thought-provoking, candid, honest conversations. As the younger ones would say, "we bonded."

We went to dinner one night at a cozy intimate bistro, and were emotionally nestled in that friendship zone, that zone where you're all relaxed and know you're in a place where it's safe to say what's on your mind, and you have all the time in the world to solve problems or chew on challenges, and so we did. It's fascinating what conversations come up when people let down their guards, even old friends and good friends. We never really can fully know another person, can we Adele? There is always more to learn.

Midway through our third bottle of wine (there were six of us, after all), Carolyn, who more often than not is content to observe conversations rather than start them, piped up.

"The other day, I saw a notice that someone was building the world's largest something or other, a restaurant or store or some such thing. While I've never really had an opinion about the world's largest anything before, in this case I suddenly had a visceral reaction. What purpose does it serve us to have a world's largest whatever? I'm perfectly happy with some of the world's smallest things. Our town, it's tiny, small enough that we're all in one building, but I wouldn't have it any other way. Millie's store is miniscule. We don't have a choice of thirty different kinds of toothpaste, but I don't need that choice. We don't have to have the exact right toothpaste. Isn't it just enough to brush our teeth?

"Anyway, somehow thinking about all that somehow got me

thinking about this culture of perfection we've created over the past ... oh, I don't know, thirty years? We've developed this idea, this belief that there's one right, best way to do things, and that if you don't do a thing in this right, accepted best way, then you're doing it wrong and really shouldn't be doing it at all. There's one best way to do things, and anyone who is respectable will do it that way or at least try to do it that way and have the proper amount of shame if she doesn't manage to reach that arbitrary perfection.

"This just crushes people's creativity, crushes their spirit, and what does it do to innovation? If people are afraid to try doing things in new ways, nothing new will ever be invented. Brilliant people may have their ideas squelched because society's firm disapproval is so strong.

"That figure drawing class we took got me thinking. We were the only people there who really had no clue how to draw. I wouldn't have gone if it weren't for Alexandra's prodding, because I 'know' I 'can't' draw." (Carolyn wiggled her fingers in the air around the words "know" and "can't"; Erin tells me we call those finger movements "air quotes," and that is how I know Carolyn spoke those words with quotes around them. Air quotes! Who ever thought of that!)

"...I 'know' I 'can't' draw," said Carolyn, "but I've always wished I were an artist. There are times when I wish I could express my emotions in some real way. I can't draw, I can't sing, I can't paint, I am completely devoid of all artistic talents.

"But then I think about all the people who make a living as artists. And, frankly, some of them aren't creating what I would call 'art.'" (More air quotes.) "But the thing is, they're expressing themselves, and I can't fault that. Too many of us avoid creating anything because we're so worried it won't be 'right' or 'acceptable,' but what does that do to the human spirit? If we're afraid to express ourselves because we're worried about others' judgments on our efforts, if we stop before we start because we believe our attempts will be rejected, then what happens when we lose those outlets of expression? What do we become? Do we lose ourselves?"

"But what about you, Carolyn," said Erin. "You're perfect. Your house is perfect, your husband is perfect. You make perfect meals. There's never a coaster out of place on a table or a speck of dust in place on a counter. You do everything the way we all only wish we could."

"I never have expected that anyone else should things the way I do them," said Carolyn. "I do things the way I like them, because I like it that way. I don't judge anyone else's home or housekeeping. There are far more important things than caring whether someone has all their books brought out to an even edge on the bookshelf."

"Am I supposed to have my books brought out to an even edge on the bookshelf?" said I. I didn't know that was something people paid attention to!

Carolyn shook her head. "No, Millie. You're supposed to do it in whatever way makes you happy. That's the point; doing it some way that satisfies someone else but not yourself is worthless. Do what makes you happy, even if other people don't approve. Within reason, of course … I think it was John Stuart Mill who said that my liberties end where yours begin. Meaning, you have to take into account the public good and others' rights. If what makes you happy is spreading raw meat on my front door, that's not okay. And of course that's an extreme example, but you get the idea. We live in a community and you have to take the community health and happiness into account as well as your own. It's part of the social contract; no man is an island and we must consider each other in our choices. However, I think there's much room for people to express themselves, in ways that we don't because we're afraid of that judgment. I want to paint watercolors. I don't think I'd be any good at it but I want to do it. I don't do it because I think people would judge my efforts; because I would judge my efforts. But if a child came up to me with a watercolor painting I wouldn't say 'What is this you're giving me? This is crap!' I'd be delighted that she thought of making a painting for me.

"That's what I'm saying, I guess. When we were kids, it was okay not to be perfect and to try new things and to practice and experiment. Now that we're older, we're just so trained to judge and to expect to be judged that we don't even try anymore. I think that's a shame. I think we are losing something as a society when we start to think we have to be perfect at something before we can even attempt it. The Internet doesn't help. If you mess up, there's someone, somewhere, with a website dedicated to screw-ups like you, and they're drooling at the thought that there's someone else out there to mock, someone else's attempts they can publicly ridicule. People like that irk me. I don't see the value in mocking someone for trying. At least the person tried, and that is far better than never trying at all."

She had a good point, and we continued to talk about it for a while. These days there's always someone on TV telling you how to do things, and I haven't seen all those shows or websites that make fun of people for their efforts, but Ben confirmed to me that it's all out there. What a shame that we've come to that: People who do nothing with their own time, making fun of people who are at least out there trying to live life, learn new skills, do something. It's ridiculous. It's not the way it should be. But what does one do about it?

All this emphasis on doing things "right" gets us nowhere and does us no good, it seems. People need to worry far less about doing things "right," and start worrying about whether they're doing things at all.

Well then, Adele, that's about that. We did not solve all the problems of the world on our spa weekend but we did grow closer to each other, and give each other time and attention, which I think is largely what the world needs more of, so maybe we did some good in the world after all.

I will keep you up to date on Walter, as I think he may be around for a bit. Tell Liam I said hello. And Adele, you really must come visit us here sometime!

Love,

Millie

❖

From: Adele
To: Millie
Sent: September 28, 2010
Subject: RE: Spas

Dear Millie,

Liam and I just finished reading your description of the mud bath and are still rolling. I can't believe it! I would never have thought they'd only clean out half the mud. I don't think I would have thought to ask. You have effectively cured me of any desire to ever have a mud bath. Did you enjoy any other spa treatments? I've never been to a spa either. Those things became trendy far after my time. I wonder if our generations just didn't get as stressed, or if we managed it differently, or if we were less likely to think of indulging ourselves, or if we didn't have the money to spare, or if we simply never thought that immersing ourselves in mud sounded like a viable, marketable idea. It's a good thing the spas don't have to rely on me for their livelihoods. A nice walk in the Alps does as much good for my body and soul as any massage ever would, I should think. That and a nice cuddle with Liam.

I am so glad to hear that you and Walter are doing well. It's good to be able to be alone and to enjoy one's own company, but I do think we humans were meant for companionship. Among other things, it keeps the mind lively. After Gerald died the house was so quiet. I was used to turning to him with little comments: "Did you see that hummingbird go by?" "The neighbors seem to be having a party." "I think it might snow." The kinds of things that aren't worth a phone call to someone but which we notice and like to comment on nonetheless. I missed having someone there to listen to my trivial observations. I think in some ways it may have made me stop noticing things as much, when there was no one there to share it with. Having Liam by my side, I feel the world has come alive again. I didn't really know it had gone— that's the way it is, isn't it, things slip away so quietly that we aren't aware we miss them—but having someone with whom to share my wonder at the world is something I am grateful to have back.

We are now in Vevey, Switzerland. I have taken to this free-spirit life better than I would have imagined. We don't know how long we'll be here but we'll leave when the time is right, move on to the next place. There are still so many places to visit in the world.

Keep me up to date on Walter and yourself, and absolutely come visit us if you have the time and inclination. Tell us where you'd like to meet up, and when, and we'll be there.

Love,
Adele

From: Erin
To: Ruby
Sent: September 28, 2010
Subject: Laurel Payne

Ruby—

Not to rush you, since you just got there, but when do you guys get back from that conference again?

I'm at work and the weirdest thing just happened. A woman came in, looking for Ed. Very abrupt. No hello, just "Is Edward Brooks here?"

"He's away from the office for a few days," said I. "Can I help you?" She pursed her lips. "I doubt it." She looked agitated.

"Can I leave a message for him?" I suggested.

"Yes." Hands on hips. "Tell him Laurel Payne is here and she'd like to claim her third of the town."

I was so confused by her comment, I didn't know what to say. Before I could speak, she asked where she might find Michael. I was pretty sure he was up at Claire and Tom's earlier, but I didn't know if he was still there. Either way, I sure as hell wasn't going to make it that easy on her. Small town; she'll find him soon enough.

I shrugged my shoulders and said nothing. She left without another word.

I texted Michael that a woman named Laurel Payne was looking for him. I didn't hear from him but a few minutes later got a text from Ben: "Payne? Are you sure? That's the last name of the woman M & E's dad had an affair with. I read it in one of Meriwether's letters." Michael must have been with Ben and read my text to him.

I texted back that I was sure, as the woman wrote it down for me to make sure I got it right.

Haven't heard anything else since. Has Michael been in touch with Ed yet? So bizarre. Wanting to claim her third of the town?

And she has the same last name as the woman their dad had an affair with? You don't think …?

Miss you, write soon.

Love, Erin

P.S. Broke up with David.

From: Ruby
To: Erin
Sent: September 29, 2010
Subject: RE: Laurel Payne

Erin—

"P.S. Broke up with David"? Is that really P.S. material? Okay, well, I know you've given it lots of thought. I can't tell you what to do (or I can but it doesn't really matter what I think). I just worry about you sometimes. You seem less happy these days than you used to. I worry.

Ed talked to Michael, and you're right, though by now you probably already know all this through the Wishing Rock grapevine express. The woman is the daughter of Rita Payne, a woman Ed and Michael's dad apparently had an affair with back in the mid '70s. This woman is saying she's the love child of that relationship, and since Meriwether left the majority of his estate to his grandchildren, she's claiming that she should get a third of the town and everything in it, as well as anything else Meriwether left to them. Michael is insisting on a blood test but the woman is threatening to expose their dad if they don't comply immediately … It doesn't really make sense because it seems their dad will be exposed either way. She said she won't take a blood test and is going to have her lawyers serve some papers or other. I would think her lawyers would want a blood test too, wouldn't they? To prove that she is the rightful heir?

Michael has a call in to their lawyer to get a copy of the will. He and Ed are torn about what to do about telling their dad (and mom). They have a good enough relationship with him but aren't really what you would call "close." Do you suppose they have to tell him? I guess they probably should. I wonder if he would know if he had another child? He would have told them at some point, don't you think? They're not kids anymore; they know even parents aren't perfect. They know people sometimes do things they later regret. They can handle it. On the other hand, it isn't really the sort of thing that's easy to bring up in casual conversation. "I'm heading into town to get some groceries, and by the way you may have a half-sibling somewhere." And Mitchell (their dad) never told them about the affair, either; they only know about it through Meriwether's letters. So who knows. It's a mystery. Ed is anxious to get back home now to deal with it all. The main part of this conference really just started today, though, and it's important for Ed to be here too. We'll get home as soon as we can.

Last night we went to a concert, something arranged by the conference people to entertain those of us who arrived yesterday. At the theater while we were waiting to go in to our seats, I was talking with an usher about the show and the conference and life in general, the state of the economy, the hard times we're all facing around the world. A few minutes into our conversation he said "My son committed suicide seven years ago." He said it with as much emotion as one might say "I bought milk at the store this morning." I was taken aback, to be honest. "He was such a happy fellow," said the usher. "To this day we have no idea why he did it." So now I want to ask you, you've never thought about suicide, have you? You're not there now, right? I know, but I just have to ask. I don't want not to have asked. That usher, he said they all wished they could have known to ask. It didn't even occur to them. So, I'd rather have asked. Like I said, I've been worried about you lately. Are you okay?

Keep me up to date on anything you hear about the Payne lady, and I'll do the same. And you know I'm here any time, no matter where I am in the world, you know that.

Ruby

❖

From: Erin
To: Ruby
Sent: September 29, 2010
Subject: RE: RE: Laurel Payne

No, you don't need to worry. I've never considered hurting myself. But I can understand the path that takes a person there. Sometimes, I don't want to be dead but being alive seems like such a struggle. The other day I was watching a show on TV about how the world might end, and the thought crossed my mind that if there were a global catastrophe and the world ended, it would just make things easier, you know? Life gets so complex sometimes. Relationships are so complex, figuring out who I am, figuring out who the right person is, knowing without doubt that you've found someone you can live with the rest of your life. And the rest of your life, that's so complex too. Like you were talking about, I don't know what my dream is. What do I even want to do with my life? People with dreams— where do they get them? I want one.

I feel like something is broken lately, and I don't know how to fix it.

Okay, I'll keep you updated on the Payne happenings on this end. I'll see you soon.

x

E.

From: Ruby
To: Erin
Sent: September 29, 2010
Subject: RE: RE: RE: Laurel Payne

Thank you for letting me know where you are. I know, life gets hard. Those dreams. Sometimes it feels like everyone else has a dream, and it's hard to feel directionless. But you know you're not alone. We'll figure this out.

I am going to talk with Alexandra when I get back. I think it's time to call in the troops.

❖

From: Erin
To: Ruby
Sent: September 30, 2010
Subject: RE: RE: RE: RE: Laurel Payne

The troops, ha. I am very lucky to have troops. I love you guys. See you soon.

❖

From: Ed
To: Jake
Sent: September 30, 2010
Subject: DNA

Hey Jake,
    Do you know, does that clinic you worked at this summer do paternity or DNA or that sort of tests? Michael and I have a bit of a conundrum at home.

Hope you're good. I'd love to hear from you.
Ed

❖

From: Jake
To: Ed
Sent: September 30, 2010
Subject: RE: DNA

Yeah, Ben told me about your situation. Crazy stuff. First Meriwether's letter about your dad having that affair, then this woman shows up claiming the town. Does Michael think she's legit? Like, does he think she looks like you guys? Hopefully not quite as ugly.

DNA testing never came up when I was there but I'm sure he can take care of it for you. The lab he works with might need him to use a specific kit, so just give him advance notice to make sure he has it on hand. Want me to give him a call?

❖

From: Ed
To: Jake
Sent: September 30, 2010
Subject: RE: RE: DNA

Thanks, buddy, that would be great.

P.S. Thanks for accepting the olive branch.

❖

From: Jake
To: Ed
Sent: September 30, 2010
Subject: RE: RE: RE: DNA

Dude, I am not touching your olive branch. But yes, we're good. Whatever, it's just life. It happens. I hope you and Ruby are happy, I really do.

I'll give the doctor a call. Take care and let me know the DNA results, and also if you find that treasure Ben's out looking for. See you soon.

J.

OCTOBER

From: Ben
To: Ed
Sent: October 1, 2010
Subject: treasure hunt

Hey Ed,

Going treasure hunting again with David tomorrow, Sunday too if we still don't find anything. Michael might come along. He's not sure yet. He's still dealing with that chick who claims to be your sister. Mom refused her a room at the Inn once she found out what was up, so she's staying over in Moon Bay.

It feels like we've been in every cave on the north and east sides of the island but David says there are some obscure ones he knows about. We're going to try those first. Your grandpa sure hid this thing well. Either that or it's long gone. I hope whatever is in it is worth it!

David's pretty bummed so I hope the treasure hunt cheers him up. Erin broke up with him. Sucks, dude. I told him "Buck up, little camper." I'm going to start a relationship talk show where I give advice.

See you soon.

Benjamin

October 2, 2010
Wishing Rock News
Millie Adler, editor
Guest Editorial from Ed Brooks

Hello, attractive and intelligent people of Wishing Rock,

Edward R. Brooks here. Millie has let me take over the news-letter reins for a quick message to you all. Some of you know about this already but I've been using all this extra space in my noggin to have some thoughts lately. It's no secret, Michael and I have been blessed with far more money than goofballs such as ourselves deserve. What are we to do with all these greenbacks? We can only build so many corn mazes before things start to get a little ridiculous.

And my people, what I want isn't money (I enjoy the money, don't get me wrong, but two months with ol' Ruby have brought me far more happiness than all the zeros in the world at the trailing end of a savings account ever could). What I'm saying is, happiness is people. More than that, happiness is happy people doing what they love. I want happy people around me, I want people to be fulfilling their potentials and being creative and innovative and finding what makes them happy and following their dreams. That, I think, makes for a better world. To paraphrase a quote I heard once, the world needs more people doing what makes them come alive.

I've been talking with a lot of people and I've come to believe that there are two major things that stand in the way of people following their dreams. The first is not knowing what those dreams are to begin with. The second is funding: having the money to make those dreams into realities.

Therefore, I hereby officially announce that I am introducing ED grants: "Everyone Dreams" grants, for the purpose of helping further the dreams of the people of Wishing Rock. I'm working on the application form now and hope to have it done by the time I'm back from these meetings and this never-ending conference. I'm not going to just give away money; you'll have to show that you have a plan and that you're willing to do the work to make it happen. Money isn't everything. You have to have the ideas and the drive, and be willing to put in the time and effort. All will be explained in the forthcoming Explanation of Application form.

And for those of you who don't yet know what your dreams are, don't worry, ol' Ed hasn't forgotten you. I'll be looking into bringing some people to the island to give a lecture or workshop or something that might help you find that passion that's inside you and figure out what you want to do with it. My suggestion, though: If you don't know what your dream is, start by doing more of the things you like, or even love. It can't help but get you pointed in the right direction.

Watch this space for news as it happens. I want to get started right away with this, so the first deadline is … get this! … October 15. Yes, you read that right. October 15. This is a head start for those of you who have had a dream percolating in your brains for a good time now. You already know what you want, where you want to go, what you want to do, how you want to get there. I'll send the application form on to Millie as soon as it's ready and she'll have them on hand in the store. Get ready. Dreams: COMMENCE.

In the meantime, I invite you all to ponder the question: What would you do if you could do anything? If everything were possible? What would you do?

Ed

From: Ed
To: Ben
Sent: October 2, 2010
Subject: RE: treasure hunt

Benjamin! My man!

I hope you find that treasure, I really do. Seems like a little of the good kind of excitement could be good for Wishing Rock right now. We'll see that your time and efforts are rewarded, don't you worry. If there's bubble gum in that toolbox, my friend, I'm giving you my half! No, no, don't refuse. That's just the kind of generous guy I am.

Don't stress yourself out over finding it, though. It could be that gramps went back and got it. Did he mention it in any later letters?

We'll be home soon. I got some good business done before the conference started, and we've had some great sessions here, but I am ready to be home. We're getting in the car now and will be home late. Get the welcoming party ready!

Ed

From: Ruby
To: Ed
Sent: October 2, 2010
Subject: ferry

Two seconds after we sat down on the ferry, and you've already fallen dead asleep. That was a long week. Your face looks so gentle when you're sleeping. I think maybe you carry lots more worries in you than anyone knows. We'll get all this Laurel business sorted, don't worry. I'm here for you. Everyone is here for you.

I'm going to snuggle into you now. You've been warned.

I love you,

Ruby

From: Ed
To: Ruby
Sent: October 2, 2010
Subject: RE: ferry

Ah, who's sleeping now? We're about ten minutes away from home. Almost time to go down to the car but I hate to wake you. I'd say you look beautiful when you're asleep but there's never a moment when you're not beautiful. Well, when you're angry at me and your right eye twitches, that's not so pretty. But even then, I love you.

xxx Ed

From: Erin
To: Ruby
Sent: October 3, 2010
Subject: Welcome home!

Hey, I'm assuming you guys got in safe last night. Let me know when you're awake.

Word on the street (via Ben) is that Michael and Ed are going to the clinic this week to get DNA tests. I guess Michael must have finally gotten that woman to agree to it. We need to have a dinner party with the gang once the tests are back and get the scoop on all this business. I have been moping a lot and running a lot and am out of the loop. You must get me back in the loop. Come by when you're up!

I'm so glad you're home. Missed you.

E.

From: Ruby
To: Erin
Sent: October 3, 2010
Subject: RE: Welcome home!

I'm awake!

Michael has been in touch with their lawyer and has a copy of Meriwether's will. Even if this woman is related, the will clearly states that the land and town and everything that Michael and Ed received were "to be evenly divided by my grandsons Edward and Michael," which is different from "to be evenly divided between my grandchildren." Interesting, isn't it? Sort of makes a person wonder if Meriwether worded it that way because he knew about Mitchell's affair and wanted to be sure there was no confusion if any other grandchildren ever showed up. We get the feeling from Michael that if the DNA test comes back showing they're all related, this woman will absolutely contest the will. I don't get why people do that. Greed, nothing but greed. What people pass on to the people they leave behind is purely a gift. No one is owed anything, no one deserves anything. It's a gift. Contesting a will just seems like nothing but greed to me.

It all seems so unfair. But I suppose if I were her and thought my biological father had run off on my family or something, and then because of that I was struggling to make ends meet while my half brothers swam in cash, I would probably think that was unfair.

We'll know more soon.

I'll come by before dinner and say hi. I'll bring wine.

I missed you too.

From: Erin
To: Ruby
Sent: October 3, 2010
Subject: RE: RE: Welcome home!

Want to stay for dinner? I feel like having a good chat.

From: Ruby
To: Erin
Sent: October 3, 2010
Subject: RE: RE: RE: Welcome home!

I would love to. Just me, or Ed too?

From: Erin
To: Ruby
Sent: October 3, 2010
Subject: RE: RE: RE: RE: Welcome home!

Just you. I love Ed but I love you more! Girl time. I'll see you
soon.

From: Jake

To: Ruby
Sent: October 4, 2010
Subject: Sorry

Hi Ruby,

I think I owe you an apology. I'm not sure where to start here. There's so much I want to say and I don't know how to say it all.

I'm sorry for having shown up at your figure drawing class. I wanted your attention and I got it but that's not how I wanted it to go down. In retrospect it wasn't my most brilliant idea ever. Funny how the desperate things we do to get people's attention often do just the opposite. I wanted you to love me again and now you hate me instead.

This isn't me begging you to take me back; this is me just asking so I can know. What was it? What did I do wrong? I've always had this fear that people will figure out I'm a fraud, and I think maybe you did. Everyone always says how I'm so perfect, but I know I'm not. I'm absolutely not, and I have this fear that people will find out and when they do they'll turn away from me. And you did.

Do you know, people always assume I must be turning away girls left and right but lots of times girls don't even look at me. But you did. I thought you really loved me. I really loved you.

I'm sorry, Ruby. I know you've moved on and I'm moving on, slowly, but I'm sorry I wasn't good enough for you, and I'm sorry I made a mess of it afterward. I hope you and Ed have a happy long life together. He's all right.

Love always,
Jake

❖

From: Ruby

To: Jake
Sent: October 4, 2010
Subject: RE: Sorry

Oh Jake. That's not it at all. Of course you're good enough. It just wasn't right, you know? Some people have one rebound relationship but I had two. It's not that I didn't love you. I loved you then and I love you now and I'll always love you. Sometimes it just doesn't work out. I don't know why. I mean, I thought for sure Pete and I were right for each other and as it turns out I was wrong. Now that I have some perspective on it I'm really glad he broke up with me. It taught me that if I can get through that, I can get through anything. I'm still scared, sometimes, of loving Ed so much because I have this fear that he'll leave too … and I have to get past that or he just might leave me after all. But if for some reason he ever did leave me, I know I could survive.

There's this saying someone told me about once, something like "If you want to curse a man, give him forty years of good luck." The idea being that our challenges make us strong and help us learn to cope with life. A man who had forty years of good luck would crumble on the first stroke of bad luck. Sometimes we're in each other's lives to help each other learn to be strong, I think. It's painful but in the end I've always been so grateful. Once I get past the pain.

As for people finding out you're a fraud, you're not a fraud, Jake. No one actually thinks you are perfect. What is perfect, anyway? One person's perfect is another person's flawed. I remember my twenties, so many friends had that exact same fear. That someone would find out they weren't what everyone thought they were.

But then, you hit thirty, and I swear to you it all just gets easier and you start to realize that you are who you are and what other people think just doesn't matter as much. In your twenties you still think you're supposed to fit other people's definition of "good enough" but by your thirties you just don't care anymore, and then you get to start living your own life.

Jake, you're not perfect, and neither am I, but the thing is, we don't have to be. You are wonderful and lovable just as you are. I know there's a woman out there for you who you will love and who will love you back as much as you deserve. With a guy as great as you, you need a woman who's just as great, so she may be harder to find, but you'll find her.

Thanks for writing, Jake. I know it's hard to be friends after having been more than friends, but I hope we can eventually find that space. You mean a lot to me, and especially to Ed. We want you in our lives. I hope we can find our way.

Love you,
Ruby

❖

From: Ruby
To: Alexandra
Sent: October 4, 2010
Subject: Erin

Hey, friend! I'm home!

Jake wrote me. What a surprise! I thought he was going to hate me and Ed forever. Ed wrote him the other day to find out if the clinic in Moon Bay does DNA testing—and also to just try to reach out to Jake and see if he'd reply. He wrote back. And then wrote to me. We're both so relieved.

Strange how someone who you once loved so much can become someone you can't be around anymore. What makes that happen? Are we deluded at first, and then we come to see the light? Does too much intimacy ruin the possibility of friendship? I think sometimes people give up too soon. They start to worry about being rejected, and so they do the rejecting first. Not just in intimate relationships but even in friendships. It's like you were saying the other night, we're ruled by fear. Doing the work to become friends with Jake again—for either me or for Ed—might be really hard, and he might reject us time and again in the process. Not because he wants to be mean but because he was hurt. If we want to be friends with him again we may have to suck it up and be prepared to bear the brunt of his hurt and fear. Not always an easy choice to make.

Regardless, I'm glad he wrote. I want to try to be friends with him, or at the very least I want to see him and Ed be friends again. Even if he never speaks to me again, Ed loves him and wants him back in his life.

Our hearts. They're so fragile. Why is putting up walls so much easier than opening doors? It makes no sense.

Speaking of friends, I went over to Erin's last night. Alexandra, I'm worried about her. How do we fix her? She seems so down. How do we help?

❖

From: Alexandra
To: Ruby
Sent: October 4, 2010
Subject: RE: Erin

Ruby my love,

First, before I forget, the usual suspects are all invited to my house for dinner on Friday. Come at six. I'm making breakfast for dinner (I got the recipe for that spinach quiche I love so much from the Moon Bay cafe—recipe below) so bring some sort of breakfasty appetizer, whatever that means. I want to hear all about Ed and Michael's situation with the Payne from the past! Michael is more tight-lipped than Ed and getting information out of him while Ed was away proved less than satisfactory. Ed plus some wine equals a recipe for satiating my curiosity. A recipe which must be utilized frequently, as I am a very curious woman!

Now then. Erin. I've talked with her a bit and while she's definitely down, I don't think she's in danger of harming herself. With that in mind then, we can't "fix" anyone. Everyone must fix themselves. In the end, none of us can make anyone else's mistakes or live their lives for them, and even if we could, it wouldn't do them any good. We may see someone going down a path that we know will lead to pain and despair, but we know that only because we've been down that path ourselves. Some lessons—too many lessons, it seems sometimes—have to be learned the hard way. And sometimes we have to be the object of someone else's life lessons; we have to be a part of their mistakes, even if we can see it coming. But even if someone else's mistakes hurt you, it is often the case that there's simply no way through the mistakes but through them. This is where kindness and compassion and forgiveness come in. Knowing that we have done wrong ourselves in the past, not intentionally but wrong nonetheless, is a reminder to forgive others for having to learn their own lessons.

No, none of us can save anyone but ourselves. We can offer all the help in the world but it's up to each individual to decide whether to accept it and then act on it. How nice it would be if someone else could do the work for us. There are far too many people out there, playing the victim, refusing to take responsibility for their own lives, crying "woe is me" and saying "no one will help me, why will no one help me?" They think the responsibility for fixing their lives lies outside themselves. But that isn't the case. Fixing our lives requires our stepping up and claiming our own futures. It requires doffing the victim hat and donning the hat of determination. Getting out of a funk unfortunately can sometimes require a solid decision to do so, and that requires that we go against the inertia of feeling sad. It's far easier to slump into self-pity than it is to get up, get dressed, and get out. But no one can do this for us. We each must do it for ourselves.

That said, we can certainly provide a nudge to get Erin facing the right direction again. I firmly believe that boredom and loneliness are the enemies of happiness and the accomplices of depression. Having too much time to oneself to think and wallow never does a person any good. Therefore, I have a proposal for the poker gals, which I will send out soon. Stay tuned.

As for Jake, I'm so glad you and Ed have heard from him. He and Ed were always so close. You may not have seen that as much; things changed once you got here. But they were great friends. You are exactly right about fear and rejection. Fear causes people to take instead of give, to hoard instead of share, to judge rather than be compassionate, to sabotage rather than support. We don't trust ourselves to be able to cope with the pain of not being loved, so we destroy our relationships before we can be destroyed. The irony being that if we simply learned to trust, we could have everything we hoped for in those relationships. Trust that we are loved. Yes, be gentle with Jake as he opens up again. He does love you and you do love him, and the same goes for Ed. It would be a shame for that love to be lost due to fear.

As for me, I suppose I need to start thinking about what sort of job I'm good for, if my psychic abilities never come back. I never really prepared myself for this possibility. I'm heading in to Seattle tomorrow for an appointment with a career counselor. Spending the day doing career testing and aptitude assessment and whatnot. A new chapter of my life awaits. Wish me luck.

Love

Alexandra

Moon Bay Café Spinach Quiche

Note: The Café sent me their recipe that makes two quiches. Since I'm serving so many people I'm making two for dinner. If you want just one, halve everything!

Ingredients
2-3 Tbsp butter
6 cloves garlic, chopped
1 onion, chopped
2 (10 oz) packages frozen chopped spinach, thawed and drained
6 oz herb and garlic feta, crumbled
6 oz package blue cheese, crumbled
6 oz sharp Cheddar cheese, grated
6 oz white Cheddar cheese, grated
salt and pepper to taste
2 (9 inch) unbaked deep dish pie crusts
6 eggs, beaten
1.5 cups milk
salt and pepper to taste

Directions
* Preheat oven to 375°.
* In a medium skillet, melt butter over medium heat. Sauté garlic and onion in butter until lightly browned, about 7 minutes.
* Remove from heat and pour into a large bowl. Stir in spinach, feta, blue, and 1/2 cup of each Cheddar cheese.
* In a medium bowl, whisk together eggs and milk. Season with salt and pepper, if desired. (Note: cheeses are probably salty enough and recipe won't need much extra salt.)
* Pour egg mixture into spinach and cheese mixture. Mix well. Evenly divide into the two pastry shells.
* Bake in preheated oven for 15 minutes. Sprinkle tops with remaining Cheddar cheese, and bake an additional 35 to 40 minutes, until set in center. Allow to stand 10 minutes before serving.

From: Millie

To: Ed
Sent: October 5, 2010
Subject: Grants

Ed,

What a wonderful idea your grants are. This has people talking about their dreams and I am in heaven, hearing about these passions people have that I never even knew about! Take my Walter, for example: I have discovered that he would like to put together a community band. He's a wonderful guitarist and musician, which I knew, but what I did not know is that when he was much younger he taught music at a high school. He now has dreams of conducting and performing. We're going to put together a proposal just as soon as applications are open. Hurry up and get those applications open! Walter has a twinkle in his eye and a song in his heart! Let's make this happen! Tell me more about the grants and I'll spread the word.

You're a gem, Mr. Brooks!
Millie

From: Alexandra
To: Erin, Ruby, Millie, Carolyn, Claire
Sent: October 6, 2010
Subject: Erin

Hello, my beloved friends! I'm back from my brief sojourn into Seattle to figure out what to do with myself if the voices don't return. The counselor suggested possibly psychology. I'd have to go back to school, obviously. It would be quite a life change, but I suppose I have to do something. If the voices ever do come back, it might not be for a while (the counselor didn't tell me this; this

I figured out on my own). Or they may never return. Forward we look, onward we go, new adventures ahead, forging on. It could be quite interesting, actually, to do work associated with the brain. Though I don't have my magical powers anymore I do have somewhat unusual insight into other dimensions of knowing. I've also always been intrigued by Ed's synesthesia. All these things could make for a fascinating field of study. I've brought home loads of materials to read and look up online. If you don't see me for a while that's where I'll be.

But! But you will be seeing me, and lots of me, because we, as a poker group, have a new mission. Our dear Erin is struggling a bit, and as am I, so I'm calling on us all to rally together again. This time, adventure is our goal. As I was telling Ruby, I believe that boredom and too much time to think can be our enemies. I also believe that stepping outside our comfort zones is a direct path to happiness. As they say, you don't regret the things you did; you regret the things you didn't do. With this in mind, then, I propose that we all take on some adventures that stretch our minds, challenge our hearts, enrich our souls. Anything that takes us at least slightly out of our cocoons of inertia will do.

I have some ideas but would be interested first to hear what you all propose?

❖

From: Erin
To: Alexandra, Ruby, Millie, Carolyn, Claire
Sent: October 6, 2010
Subject: RE: Erin

1. FYI I'm not depressed or anything. Just a little down. Seriously, you guys don't need to worry about me.
2. But that said, sure, a little adventure sounds fun.

3.   No mud baths. Brilliant idea! And we (you) paid for it!

From: Millie
To: Erin, Alexandra, Ruby, Carolyn, Claire
Sent: October 6, 2010
Subject: RE: RE: Erin

Alexandra, wonderful ideas as always. But first, Ed's synesthwhatsia? I've never heard of this. What in the world are you talking about? It never ceases to amaze me that there are still things about each other that I don't know. However, I agree with your counselor, you would be wonderful at psychology or counseling or anything that involves you talking with people to help them feel better and make sense of the world. You don't have to be psychic to do that, just wise and compassionate, and goodness knows you're both in spades. If I can be of any help in your quest to figure out your next phase in life, just let me know.

Do you know what I've always thought would be fun? An archaeological dig. Can we do a dig? To go out and unearth what's been earthed, discover what's been covered, bring history to life! Wouldn't that be absolutely fascinating?

From: Ruby
To: Millie, Erin, Alexandra, Carolyn, Claire
Sent: October 6, 2010
Subject: RE: RE: RE: Erin

Yes, Alexandra, Ed's synesthwhatsia? You'd think I'd know about this too! Do I need to get immunized for this? What is that? I don't pretend to know everything about anyone yet but if he has a strange condition I would like to know! After all I've just the other day found out that he likes to do laundry naked. (He hates having dirty clothes on when everything else is clean.) Now this. So much more to learn about the man.

Back to Erin, though. Do we ALL have to do these adventures? We couldn't just cheer you on sometimes? I mean, I've been out of my cocoon a lot the last few months. I'm rather enjoying having a cocoon for once.

I'm kidding, of course, haha, anything for you guys. But if anyone suggests eating bugs or other such exotic cuisine, I am OUT.

Millie, I think an archaeological dig sounds fantastic. I'd love to go. That is, I'd love to go, if you took away the sweltering heat, the dirt and dust and lack of showers, the backbreaking tedious work with a toothbrush, and so on. If you can find an opportunity for us to go on a dig and have shirtless men bring us exotic cocktails, in glasses that are glistening with condensation, while we rest our weary bodies on wicker chaise lounges covered with pillows from an overpriced trendy home furnishings store, then yes, I am one hundred percent in on that idea!

From: Claire
To: Ruby, Millie, Erin, Alexandra, Carolyn
Sent: October 6, 2010
Subject: RE: RE: RE: RE: Erin

Um, what about pole dancing? That pole dancing exercise is very popular, I hear.

I don't know what else. Paint ball? The boys love paint ball but I've never done it.

From: Carolyn
To: Claire, Ruby, Millie, Erin, Alexandra
Sent: October 6, 2010
Subject: RE: RE: RE: RE: RE: Erin

Claire! Ha! Does Tom know you want to learn pole dancing? I … I don't even know if I could!

Ever since we did that figure drawing, I've been thinking I'd like to do more visual arts. Any sort of drawing class, painting, even sculpting could be fun. I'm sure if we wanted to learn some woodworking Michael would be more than happy to help us out and let us use his wood shop.

From: Erin
To: Carolyn, Claire, Ruby, Millie, Alexandra
Sent: October 6, 2010
Subject: RE: RE: RE: RE: RE: RE: Erin

1. I think Claire should learn to pole dance.
2. I veto paint balling. I have paint balled. There is nothing worse than getting a paint ball in the ass. And once you've gotten a paint ball in the ass, you spend the rest of the hour paranoid, wondering who is going to shoot you in the ass next. No.

From: Claire
To: Erin, Carolyn, Ruby, Millie, Alexandra
Sent: October 6, 2010
Subject: RE: RE: RE: RE: RE: RE: RE: Erin

What? Have you never wanted to learn to pole dance? You don't think Michael might enjoy that? I'm just thinking, both boys will be out of the house soon, maybe it's time to spice things up a bit! Maybe I'll add a special suite at the Inn: the Pole Dance Suite. I think I could market that, what do you think?

From: Alexandra
To: Claire Erin, Carolyn, Ruby, Millie
Sent: October 6, 2010
Subject: RE: RE: RE: RE: RE: RE: RE: RE: Erin

Synesthesia, what Ed has. Nothing contagious, I assure you. It's a condition in which a person's senses sort of get mixed up or blended. I am, actually, surprised none of you knows about it but I suppose Ed only recently found out about it himself. Last winter sometime I was at dinner at Carolyn's, Michael was there of course and Ed too. Michael had just heard of synesthesia. Most commonly it manifests with colors and numbers/letters. People see the letter "a" and it is always red, for example, or the number "4" might always look green. I don't have the condition so I don't quite understand it, but for every person the colors are different. Michael was going on about how he thought it was all a load of baloney, when suddenly Ed piped up. "You mean you don't see letters that way?" he said. We thought he was joking at first but he was serious. He has always associated colors with numbers and letters, and it never occurred to him that not everyone does. At first he thought it must have to do with those little letter and number refrigerator magnets we all played with as children, but then he looked into the phenomenon and learned there's far more to it than that.

The color/letter association is, as I said, most common, but any of the senses can be mixed in any way. People may "taste shapes," as in a soup might taste round, which to that person might mean it is salty. Or some people hear colors. Going to a symphony would be quite an immersive experience, I'd imagine, for those people. Can you imagine?

At any rate, I of course believed Ed, having an unusual brain myself. Michael said he was not inclined to believe the original source from which he learned about the condition, but even though Ed may be known for his practical jokes, he believed him. We had Ed go online and perform some synesthesia tests and sure enough, he has inherent color/letter associations. It helps him remember, he says. While each letter or number has a color, words too might have associations. A person's birthdate might be orange, for example, or their name might be blue. I wonder, Ruby, if your name is red to him when he sees it written? There's a question. You might ask him. Fascinating stuff!

And so you see, even if my psychic powers do come back I just might take my life down a path of studying the brain. I can't help but be interested and could go on at some length about it all. But for now I won't. For now, we are focused on Erin! And on our impending adventures.

Claire, I don't know if you're serious or kidding about the pole dancing, but if you want to do it I think you absolutely should.

I'll tell you some of the other things I thought of. I'd like to try dancing (without a pole), for one thing. As a psychic I've lived my whole life more or less inside my head, out of my body, figuratively and sometimes literally. Dancing might get me back in touch with the fact that I actually have arms and legs and a torso and everything associated with all the above. (Yes, pole dancing would do the same but I'm not quite sure I'm ready for that just yet.) Ballroom dancing, line dancing, any of that would be fun. Too bad there isn't a bar that has line dancing on the island. (Maybe someone should open one, with an ED grant!) I missed that hoedown this summer and it sounded like such fun. Ruby's escapades aside, of course.

We could also try archery or photography. Martial arts. We could do a comedy improv night. Pottery. (After which, Claire, you and Tom could re-create that scene from that movie, right? With the pottery wheel, you know the one!) Rock climbing. Star gazing.

Anything sounding good?

From: Millie
To: Alexandra, Claire Erin, Carolyn, Ruby
Sent: October 6, 2010
Subject: RE: RE: RE: RE: RE: RE: RE: RE: RE: Erin

Alexandra, that is absolutely fascinating about Ed. Now I'm intrigued. I'm going to have to talk with him about it. Fascinating stuff indeed.

Your mention of symphonies gave me another idea for our adventures. What about playing instruments? Did I tell any of you that Walter is thinking of applying for one of Ed's grants, to start a community band? Maybe we all should join! I've never played an instrument but I can learn! I think that would be great fun.

Dancing sounds good too. I do know there's a dance studio over in Moon Bay. I don't know how often they're open, but I'd be all in for dancing. Ballroom sounds more fun. I like to hold and be held.

From: Claire
To: Millie, Erin, Carolyn, Ruby, Alexandra
Sent: October 6, 2010
Subject: RE: RE: RE: RE: RE: RE: RE: RE: RE: RE: Erin

Walter is starting a band? That's wonderful. I played flute in high
school. I was second chair! My sister Dee was first. Marching
band, too. With the big funny tall hats and stiff polyester uni-
forms and everything. Millie, tell Walter that if he starts a band I
am definitely interested.

I would be in for dancing, too. Can we bring the men along?
We might overload the room with women if we all go alone.

❖

From: Erin
To: Claire, Millie, Carolyn, Ruby, Alexandra
Sent: October 6, 2010
Subject: changing the subject line

Note: I did know about Ed doing laundry naked. Did not know
about the color/letter thing. Sometimes I think I just know far too
much about all you people.

I am not sure about dancing. I mean, I'm just not sure I want to
hold and be held right now. I just broke up with someone. I realize
I'm the one who broke up with him but I just don't feel like being
held right now. And besides, as Claire said, if we all went we'd totally disrupt the male/female balance, which very possibly leans too
female as it is. My vote is that we postpone dancing until later.

Also, I changed the email subject line because it was getting
weird seeing my name in every subject line. It was starting to
make me feel like I was talking about myself in the third person.

❖

From: Alexandra
To: Erin, Claire, Millie, Carolyn, Ruby
Sent: October 6, 2010
Subject: RE: changing the subject line

Erin: Good point. We don't want to rub salt in any wounds and if you're not up for dancing yet then we can postpone it. I do think I might like dancing for my own purposes so I may go on my own, but as a group we can certainly find dozens of other things to do before we need to subject you to something that will make you feel uncomfortable. We're just out to have fun and distract ourselves until we start to feel better again.

I tell you what, you all e-mail me dates you are available in the next two weeks, and I'll pull something together. A surprise. It's an adventure, after all! Get ready! We are about to have an inordinate amount of fun.

❖

From: Millie
To: Adele
Sent: October 7, 2010
Subject: The happenings in Wishing Rock

Dear Adele,

Greetings from Wishing Rock, where the days are getting shorter but intrigue fills all the hours! Where to begin—with Erin's love woes and Alexandra's psychic disappearance and subsequent decision that we all are going to have grand dangerous adventures to lift our collective moods? With Walter, who charms me more every day, and who is putting together a proposal for funding to create a community band? With a report of Ruby and Ed, who I am so pleased to say seem to be doing just beautifully?

Or with the latest Brooks family drama? Of course, we begin with the drama! These Brookses, right or wrong they're my Kennedys, my royal family. I adore them all and can't get enough of the Meriwether/Maddie family story and all the comings and goings. My own family is so sedate in comparison, just getting along happily and contentedly day to day. But these Brookses! You just never know what's going to happen with the Brooks family—alive or dead.

Laurel Payne, the woman at the center of the scandal, has been largely absent since she first disrupted our happy hamlet (and was sent away by Claire, who got a bit of a bee in her bonnet and refused Laurel a room at the Inn). As I was kneeling on the floor in the store yesterday, though, rearranging jars on the shelves to make room for some raspberry and blueberry jams Carolyn made, who should walk in but Ms. Payne herself. I hadn't seen her the previous time she was in town, so it took me a minute to figure out who she was. In fact, my powers of perception are sorry to report, I didn't clue in until she said, "Are you Millie? I'm Laurel Payne." At that moment, Adele, I thought to myself, "This is Laurel Payne!" And I was correct.

After that, she didn't speak for a bit and neither did I. I studied her, scanning for a family resemblance. Meriwether's eyes, Ed's nose, Michael's chin, did she have any of it? I couldn't see any connection but that means nothing. Long ago I knew a woman with dark hair, brown eyes, who married a man with dark hair, brown eyes. Their first child was a beautiful daughter, dark hair, brown eyes. And then a son came along. Hair the color of a red-orange sunset, eyes the blue of a turbulent ocean, skin as fair as a spring day. Recessive genes, of course, but by a very young age the boy had already heard the question "Where did you get that hair?" one too many times. A bright summer day he was out on a walk with his mother and sister, and a new neighbor saw them, stopped them. "Where did you get that hair!" she proclaimed, and the three-year-old sprang forth with a new answer: "The dentist." His mother reported that once she got her own jaw back in place, she merely smiled and winked at the neighbor, turned, and continued the walk with her children. The dentist! Clever boy. I suppose even with his incongruous coloring he did share bone structure with his father, and also the look in both their eyes of quiet, amused observation of the world. This Ms. Payne bore no resemblance in either coloring, physique, nor attitude with any of the Brooks family, but then the world will do that, living life will do that; time and hardships will chisel themselves into one's face as surely as genetics. Her face looked hard but not necessarily unkind; her eyes had a steel wall behind them. No one would be let in without earning their way in, I could see. Her stance, tense. Ready to fight if she had to.

Once I realized I was staring at her, I tucked onto the shelves the jam jars I still was juggling in my arms, and slowly straightened myself to standing.

"Yes, I'm Millie." Now, I know she's supposed to be the enemy, but frankly, Adele, I'm too old to put time and effort into having enemies. What I am at this stage in my life is curious, leaning to indifferent in this case until the situation demands otherwise. After all, we all have pasts. We all have stories. We all, I will add, have made mistakes, and what's more, the mistake in this case was her mother's and Mitchell's, not hers. The sins of the mother need not be borne by the daughter. I was determined to give her a fair hearing.

I extended my hand and she took it in hers. You can tell a lot about a person from their handshake, and I think she was judging mine as much as I was judging hers. Her shake was both hesitant and firm, like she was expecting to be rejected and was preparing herself for it. I wrapped my other hand around hers in what was intended to be a gesture of compassion and understanding.

After half a second, she pulled away. So much for that.

My store is not always busy, as you may have guessed. Therefore in one of the corners I have a small love seat, a comfortable but not-quite-matching overstuffed chair, and a small coffee table, so people can visit with me when they come in. (I like the company, and work can usually wait!) I invited Laurel to sit down.

She sat at the edge of the chair. I settled into the love seat. "You've been causing quite a stir around here," I said.

"I just want what's mine," she said quietly. "We never had anything. My mother told me my father was dead. That's all she ever said. 'He's dead.' 'How did he die?' 'Never mind that. It doesn't matter. He's gone.' And now she's gone, too."

Her eyes scooted over to the water cooler and back. "Would you like some water?" I asked.

She nodded the slightest consent so I got up and poured some into two mugs, handed her one.

Laurel took a sip, continued. "She died eight months ago. Lung cancer. She never even smoked. It made no sense. She was perfectly healthy, and yet somehow ..." A deep breath, a long sigh. "We didn't have good insurance. I have medical bills coming out my ears, and the funeral costs to add insult to injury. I'm a single mom. I have two hungry teenagers to feed and clothe.

"After Mom died, when I was cleaning out her house, I discovered old diaries. I never even knew she kept them. She must have stopped when I was young. I started reading from the year before I was born to see if I could find out anything else about my father. The only man mentioned the whole time was this Mitchell Brooks. He has to be my father. There's no one else it could be.

"I tracked him down. Took me a while to find the right guy, but when I did I learned about Meriwether Brooks, and this town, and how he left it all to his grandchildren."

"To Ed and Michael," I said gently. "He specified Ed and Michael in the will. He left it just to them. Specifically."

Laurel hadn't met my gaze since she sat down, but with this news she looked at me. For a moment she seemed frazzled, but she regained her composure. "It doesn't matter. That confirms that I'm legitimate, doesn't it? Obviously Meriwether knew about me or he would have just said 'my grandchildren.'"

Ruby had had that same thought, as you may know. Myself, I don't believe it proves anything either way, so I just shrugged.

"There's no one else who could be my father," she repeated with an edge of despair. "It has to be him. And a third of this town is mine."

"Are you sure there was no one else?" I asked. It seemed a bit naive to believe her mother couldn't possibly have been with more than one man.

She glared. "Are you suggesting my mother slept around?"

I shrugged again. How was I to know? I know nothing about her mother except that she seems to have produced an angry daughter. Then again, when life takes so much from us, it's hard not to be bitter sometimes.

"I want my third. I need it. It's only fair," she said.

I nodded. There was no point arguing with her, and besides, it wasn't my fight to fight. "Are you going to take the DNA test, or have you already?" I asked.

She shook her head, pushed her hair behind her ears; her hair that is dark but not as dark as Ed's or Michael's. "I know I'm right. I can't afford to spend that money. If they want it so bad they can use their riches to pay for mine."

They will, I thought, but did not say. Money is no object to Ed and Michael. Such a contrast to this woman. Who knows, were circumstances different, were she not in debt and worried about her present and her future, maybe she wouldn't even be here. I scrutinized her face again, still looking for any resemblance, but her demeanor was so unlike any Brooks I ever knew that I just couldn't see it.

Then again, I have only ever met Mitchell a few times. And he always seemed to lean a bit toward bitter himself.

She put down her mug, stood.

"I came here to buy some tea," she said. "Do you have any?"

What, they don't have tea in Moon Bay, where she was staying? I thought this but again said nothing. On the other hand, what in the world could she have wanted from me? And did she get it? I couldn't imagine that she had. "Certainly," I said, and pointed down the second aisle. "Not too many choices, I'm afraid. I generally stock what the people in town like most. Earl Gray, mint, chamomile, a few others. Hopefully you can find something that will suit you."

I situated myself behind the cash register while she perused her choices. She paid for a box of mint tea, turned to go, turned back. Maybe I am mistaken but her eyes seemed just the slightest bit softer. She looked at me and opened her mouth.

And then closed it without a word, and walked out the door.

That would have been all I had to report to you, Adele, and you and I both would have had to wait in hopes dear Laurel would take the DNA test. But! I got a text—ha, a text!—from Erin about half an hour later. (I haven't a clue how to send a text, but I manage to find them to read them on the rare occasion people send them to me, which I really wish they wouldn't, it's so complicated!) "You'll never guess who has showed up at Ed's!" she wrote. And then the next text, all capital letters: "MITCHELL BROOKS!!!!!!!!" With that many exclamation points.

Mitchell. Well! And completely unannounced, at that. He has some explaining to do, I should say. One way or another, he has some explaining to do.

And so, a dinner party planned for tomorrow night has grown by one person, and I strongly suspect every other person who was invited will be there with bells on to hear this one.

In other news, as hinted at above, Alexandra has decided we are all going to stretch outside our comfort zones, leave our little boxes (and I suppose our Box!). Erin has been feeling low lately so we are all rallying to lift her up. Truth be told, though, I think Alexandra is doing it as much for herself as she is for Erin. There's still no change in the voices in her head, or the lack thereof. She told me she's still talking to her children and husband every day, but no one's picking up the phone. Poor woman. Having the foundation of her life pulled out from under her like that.

At any rate, I'm eagerly anticipating the fun to be had. I've a renewed thirst for learning and for art and for trying new things. It could be Walter who has brought this out in me. He's been giving me piano lessons—I never learned. Carnegie Hall won't be calling me anytime soon but I very much enjoy sitting beside my handsome friend on the piano stool and picking out a tune. Walter has the most wonderful idea about art and artists. He says everyone is an artist whether they know it or not. Someone who loves to cook and puts her heart into it is an artist. A gardener who tends her garden with care is an artist. He might even say that an accountant, for whom there is beauty in a well planned spreadsheet, is an artist. We have such limited ideas of what constitutes art, and thus we feel we ourselves are not artists, and so we don't believe in our own creative potential. But it's in us. When we were six years old, finger painting with abandon, we had no such doubts of our skills. It was learned out of us, but we can learn it back in. And I am doing just that.

Yes, I'm enjoying myself. This new chapter in my life may be the best one yet.

I will write again soon! I cannot wait to find out what all I will be telling you!

My best to you and Liam both,

Love,

Millie

From: Adele
To: Millie
Sent: October 8, 2010
Subject: RE: The happenings in Wishing Rock

Dear Millie,

Wonderful as always to hear from you. Just heading off down to Montreux for a late lunch with some new friends we met at the Vevey farmers market earlier this week. Can you believe it, turns out they used to be neighbors of one of Liam's children. The more I travel the more I realize the world is not nearly as large as I thought it was. There isn't enough fondue in the world to satisfy Liam, it sometimes seems. I can't wait to hear the story of Mitchell Brooks!

Love,

Adele

Text from Ben to Jake
Sent: October 8, 2010

Hey—any chance you're home this weekend? Still haven't found the treasure. No one else can go looking this weekend. Want to come?

Text from Jake to Ben
Sent: October 8, 2010

Hey. Sorry, gotta study. Haven't you guys looked at every cave on the island by now?

Text from Ben to Jake
Sent: October 8, 2010

Not quite. Meriwether mentioned in a later letter that he still hadn't gone back to get the treasure so I think it's still out there. The riches will all be mine and mine alone! Have fun studying, dude!

Text from Ben to Jake
Sent: October 8, 2010

PS Almost forgot—guess who's in town? Ed and Michael's dad! I wasn't going to go to dinner with all the old fogies tonight but I think I'll go after all. Could get interesting!

Text from Jake to Ben
Sent: October 8, 2010

Mitchell Brooks? Is that woman who's claiming to be his daughter still there? Is she going to dinner too?

Text from Ben to Jake
Sent: October 8, 2010

She's still on the island but I seriously doubt she's been invited to dinner. I'll call you when I'm back from treasure hunting tomorrow to let you know the scoop from dinner.

Text from Jake to Ben
Sent: October 8, 2010

I'll be waiting by the phone for your call. Talk to you soon, little buddy.

From: Ruby
To: Gran
Sent: October 8, 2010
Subject: Hello!

Hi Gran!

How are you? Are you still in Switzerland? Where are you going next? Or will you go home to Scotland for a bit in between countries? I wish I could be everywhere at once. The way you describe Switzerland, I want to be there with you right now among the vineyards and at the castles and on the trains. But I love my Wishing Rock, too; more than I ever thought I would. So quickly it has become home.

At any rate, I think I'll stay put for a bit. The suitcase is now tucked away in its closet for a while, and the travel underwear is tucked away too. Oh yes, travel underwear! Did I tell you about the travel underwear?

On our Scotland trip, as you may know, we had to wash out our delicates in the sink all the time. Every night, almost. Socks and underwear. It was a drag. I perfected the art of using the hairdryer to dry my clothes, but at one point I sort of burned out a B&B's hair dryer when I had it shoved down the tube of a sock (oops). (I did tell the owner and they said not to worry about it.) Nonetheless, more than once we had to put on clothes that seemed dry but once they were on our bodies were revealed to be slightly damp. As I'm sure you can imagine, this was unpleasant, especially with the undies.

On our return home, Erin investigated quick-dry clothes for her next trip, and bought a few pairs of travel undies. Being the great friend she is, she bought some for me too. (You know you're close friends when someone buys you underwear!) I thought it sounded like a fantastic idea and for some reason decided to try them out at the conference last week. What was I thinking!

As it turns out, travel underwear is not the panacea of all undergarment woes as I'd hoped (and, frankly, expected). Certainly they did what it says on the tin—that is, they dried fast—and I never had to go out with wet drawers. But I have a question for the manufacturer of these goods: did they have to design them with a cut and stretchy fabric that ensure that they hang out the top of your pants no matter how you try to tuck them in? Seriously. The "regular" style is pretty much quick-drying granny underwear (um, no offense, Gran! I'm sure your underwear is lovely!), with a waistline that goes up to your neck and enough fabric to serve as tent in case of a weather emergency. The "briefs" style, well, you'd think those would be better, but all they have done, really, is cut the leg holes higher. Which means that the upper part of one's thighs is not covered—thank goodness, because I wear so many outfits that are cut up to my hip and the lower part of my underwear was always showing! (Or not.) But the top of the underwear, the waistband, STILL can be comfortably pulled up to meet the lower edge of one's bra. When you get dressed, you may artfully arrange your drawers so that they're under cover of your pants, but any movement at all, and once again the top of the undies is hanging out the top of the pants. Sexy!

And while this travel underwear was awful—throughout the conference I kept checking my waistband to make sure my underwear wasn't hanging out—I've heard of worse: disposable paper underwear. Can you imagine? This instantly offers itself up as inherently problematic. While I am not fond of paper cuts in general, there are just certain places that I especially do not want to get paper cuts, and these places also happen to be the parts of the body that are generally covered by underwear. Perish the thought! Paper underwear? Who ever thought that was a good idea?

So as it turns out, regular, quick-dry travel underwear that reaches up to one's armpits, that's the "best choice." You'd think it might have a negative effect on the romantic hopes of some travelers. If a woman were traveling with idea of meeting a hot dude, for example, the travel underwear would undoubtedly kill the deal. I imagine this scenario:

Hot dude to woman: "Well hellooooooo gorgeous!"

Woman to hot dude: "Helloooo handsome!"

Woman turns to the bar to get her drink. Hot dude sees woman's travel underwear peeping out the top of her pants.

Woman turns back around: "So are you from … hey, where'd he go?"

And by the way, why is it called a pair of underwear? It's only one garment. A pair of leg holes, but not a pair of anything else. Not like a pair of socks, which makes sense, but more like a pair of pants, which is equally baffling. My shirts have a pair of arm holes, as well as a neck hole and a torso hole, but I don't call them pairs of shirts. I don't call my bra a "pair of bras" even though that would seem much more apropos. Pair of underwear? Is it the same in other languages? Now I'm going to lie awake at night wondering.

So annnnyway, the luggage and the undies are all packed away for the time being, and good riddance to them. I'm happy to stay home for a bit, sleeping in my own bed, washing clothes in my own washer and drying them in my own dryer, not wearing travel underwear.

Well, I'd better go. Alexandra was going to have the gang over for dinner, but Ed and Michael's father showed up, so now he's coming too and the whole shebang has been moved to Michael's house. I'm going to go over and help Carolyn get ready, since Michael and Ed are out talking with their Dad. I'm hoping we get to hear the whole story at dinner, whatever that story is! The people who are coming are all basically family—Michael, Carolyn, Ed, me, Alexandra, Claire and Tom Stewart (I think Ben is coming too), Erin. Oh, and Millie! Of course. Millie. I don't know if she's bringing Walter. Millie told me that she'll be sending you a report of the evening's discussion. I'll be interested to hear her account of it as well!

I'm off! Have a great day, Gran!

Much love,

Ruby

Text from Ben to Ed
Sent: October 9, 2010

I'm off for one last try on the treasure. Back in a few!

Text from Ed to Ben
Sent: October 9, 2010

Thanks, kiddo! Does anyone know where you'll be? So we know where to look if you're lost? Not a lot of cell phone signal out that way. David can't go along? Can you wait until tomorrow when I could go?

Text from Ben to Ed
Sent: October 9, 2010

Dude, I'm eighteen and I know this island as well as anyone does. I'm fine, my man! But yes, mom knows where I'll be.

Text from Ed to Ben
Sent: October 9, 2010

Good on your mother. Don't spend too long out there. If we don't find it we don't find it. Thanks, Ben.

Text from Ben to Ed
Sent: October 9, 2010

This is me rolling my eyes. Later dude! I'll bring back the booty!

Text from Ed to Ben
Sent: October 9, 2010

Make us all proud, son! Check in if you can! Come by when
you're back home.

❖

From: Millie
To: Adele
Sent: October 9, 2010
Subject: Mitchell

Well, Adele!

Oh my, what an evening we had last night! I don't know where
to begin. Some skeletons from Mitchell's closet were let out, or
ghosts from his past, whichever you prefer. Whether these things
were still haunting him I don't know but I don't think the boys
had previously known everything he revealed. Mitchell, Michael,
and Ed had all gone off yesterday afternoon to talk, so by the time
the rest of us converged at Michael and Carolyn's house, they already knew whatever there was to know. Better than springing it
on the boys in front of everyone.

Having known Meriwether so well, I already knew some of
what was told last night. The boys probably did, too.

Well, I'll just jump in.

When I got to Carolyn and Michael's, Ruby and Erin were already there helping and chatting and setting the table and mixing
drinks. Michael and Ed weren't back yet with Mitchell. Everyone
slowly filtered in and we sat down to a lovely dinner: Caesar salad
made with kale, garlic green beans, sweet potato biscuits, chicken
cordon bleu, and a berry pie with ice cream for dessert. (We of
course didn't eat all that at once. Just letting you know what was

served over the course of the evening.) Ed served some of that delicious Wishing Rock Brose that he makes from the recipe you sent over earlier in the year; it's become a favorite around here already. Thank you for that, Adele! We are all quite grateful.

Dinner conversation was simply conversational. Catching Mitchell up on all the people and happenings of the town, telling him more about Meriwether's letters that Ben found, discussing the changes at the distillery, that sort of thing. After the last course but before the pie, however, we all retired to the living room to hear what Mitchell had come to say.

I'll remind you of a few of the basics, which Mitchell did not mention. He was born in Alaska in the early 1940s. He met Kathy, who was to be his wife, when they were in college together. They were married in 1965, I think, and he found work as an engineer and she as a teacher.

"Kathy was a good woman," he said, sounding as if she were dead rather than just far away in Iceland, where she lives now. "I was drawn to her independence when I met her. Reminded me of my own mother, who could not be caged." A twinkle in his eye divulged his fond memory of Madeline. "I liked it at first, and that's why I married her. But as it turned out, we were both pretty independent, maybe a little too alike in ways that mattered too much, and over time we started to clash. After just a few years of marriage we started fighting. The boys were both young. We tried to hide it, tried not to fight in front of the kids, but at some point I suppose we just gave up trying. They're smart kids. They knew."

I looked over at Michael, who was holding Carolyn's hand. He would have been older during all the fighting, would have remembered it more. And his reflective, more introspective personality may have led him to think too much about it, dwell on it too much, perhaps blame himself too much. The dynamics of the older child, trying to protect the younger and also create peace in the household. Very possibly he took on a role that was not his to take at that young age. The look he gave Carolyn suggested they have had discussions about this very thing.

"Now I will say that Kathy is a smart woman too. I do not fault her intelligence or her independence; as I said, we just clashed. I found myself wanting to be challenged less and appreciated more. She was all edges, no softness. Right or wrong with no room for anything in between. Part of that, I'm sure, was age. We married quite young, before we knew who we were. As we started to figure out who we were, we started to learn we weren't as compatible as we'd thought we were. We just grew apart.

"In 1974, we were ready to give up. I moved out of the house for a bit for a trial separation, down to Anchorage where I was on site at a project for work. That's when I met Rita, in a bar in Anchorage."

You will remember, Adele, that Rita, Rita Payne, is the cause of this whole brouhaha. The woman Meriwether mentioned in a letter to Maddie, one of the letters Ben uncovered in the basement.

"Rita. Waves of dark brown hair flowing over her shoulders, her hair styled and coiffed, not just combed wet and left to dry. A severe contrast to Kathy's utilitarian hairstyle, cut by the neighbor so Kathy wouldn't have to waste time and money driving into town—her frugality, not mine. Rita wasn't glamorous or dressy, but she was beautiful. Classy. The kind of woman I never thought would look at me. She saw me alone at the bar and scooted over to talk to me. Smiled at me and listened to my woes, and we became friends.

"Bush pilot, turns out. She was a bush pilot. I would never have pegged her as one—she was too pretty. Nothing against bush pilots, mind you. Her plane had broken down so she was in town for a few days waiting on some parts and a repair.

"I saw her at the bar the next night and the next. She got her plane fixed but she kept coming back. We grew close in our loneliness. I started going out with her on her plane on weekends, whenever she didn't have to fly somewhere."

Mitchell's gaze was lost in his past. His face was washed with a smile to himself of a memory from long ago.

"The look she'd get in her eyes when she was in the air …. Raw passion. Passion for life, and a wonder at the world. She wasn't jaded. She'd seen it all before but every day it was new for her. She drank it in. I saw her joy and bliss and I wanted that back. I'd had that before but the years of arguing with Kathy and trying to hide it from the boys and of trying to pretend everything was okay, of trying to fix things but never being able to appease Kathy or do anything right, the years of being beaten down …. Rita filled me up in a way I didn't even know I'd been empty."

He shook his head and looked at Michael. "The whole time, though, we were nothing but friends. Sure, I wanted more, craved more, but I wasn't ready to give up on my family and my vows just yet. Then, after a couple months, Kathy called one day to say she wanted to talk. She knew she had been in the wrong, too, that she'd been part of the problem, and she wanted to try to make amends. Well, that was the first time she ever acknowledged her role in our issues, so I listened. Would I come home and try again? Yes.

"So I went home. Lost touch with Rita and tried to heal my family. And it worked, for a while. But then one day I found out that while I'd been in Anchorage, one night when the kids were out of the house, Kathy had taken up with a bachelor neighbor. She didn't tell me this; I had to learn it through the grapevine. But when I confronted her with it she didn't deny it. Looking back, I'd say I wasn't even angry, really, or hurt. It was if I knew something like that would happen, and it was just a matter of when. I didn't move out again, but I did stay away on business more often. And I found Rita again. And this time, we were not just friends."

He nodded his head, acknowledging the indiscretion to himself, remembering. A deep breath, a long sigh. "We continued like that for a short time, but then I came to my senses. I didn't want to live a life like that. I broke things off with Rita and never saw her again. Kathy and I never did manage to work things out, and finally were divorced when the boys were teenagers. I had no other affairs; Kathy had one. That was the one that ended us, though really we'd been ended years before."

Mitchell looked at Ed and Michael. "I know we messed things up, boys, and I'm sorry. I am sure your mother is too. We married too young and didn't know ourselves, and we messed up. But I look at the two of you and I think, you are such exceptional young men. Despite all the ways your mother and I screwed up, look at you. You're the best young men I know, and I'd say that even if you weren't my own. You're kind and generous and thoughtful, you give so much to this town and to the people you love. It doesn't surprise me that dad bypassed me and your Aunt Meredith and willed it all to you two. He knew we'd just make a mess of this as well, but you two, you two are the pride of the family. I could not be more proud of the men you've become, but I can't take any credit for it. You decided what kind of people you want to be, and became those people. I don't know how you did it, coming from me and Kathy, but I hope you know, we are both so proud."

We all continued talking for a good while after that, but that's the crux of Mitchell's story. Interesting, Adele, how something that is a scandal in one moment becomes simply a story with the passing of time. Michael and Ed were undoubtedly challenged by all this as children, and likely would not have taken well to hearing of all the affairs. But as adult men they were able to see it all with a bit more perspective, forgiveness, compassion, and even humor. As adults we understand better the mistakes others make, because we have made so many mistakes ourselves. It was beautiful, actually, to see these men coming together and sharing in a way I don't think they have for a very long time. There was no judgment there last night, only compassion, only seeking to understand.

When he was younger, I never saw much of Meriwether in Mitchell. I never knew Maddie, of course, so I can't say whether he resembled her in look or attitude, or if he was simply a rogue gene. However, time has perhaps distilled Mitchell's personality, and I saw more glimpses of Meriwether this time. The kinder eyes, the more introspective approach to life. His hair, once dark and curly, now is peppery, like Meriwether's was until his later days when it turned mostly gray. Ed is very unlike Mitchell, I think, but Michael is more similar. Inquisitive, observant, quieter.

The question to be answered now, of course, is Laurel's parentage. Mitchell is going to get the DNA test himself so there can be no argument that Michael and Ed's tests aren't conclusive enough. The boys both went in for their tests earlier in the week. Apparently the test takes three to ten business days to be returned; this being Wishing Rock I'd bet on fourteen. Hopefully soon.

And with that, I am off for the day. Walter and I are heading into Moon Bay for an evening out, to share our own stories and make new memories, enjoy each other's company, and simply be grateful to be alive and together.

All my best,
Millie

Text from Ben to Ed
Sent: October 9, 2010

I'm home. Nothing, dude.

Text from Ed to Ben
Sent: October 9, 2010

No worries. We'll stumble on it when we least expect it. If it's meant to be found, we'll find it and if not, no harm no foul. Thanks for looking.

From: Erin
To: Alexandra
Sent: October 10, 2010
Subject: don't worry

Hey Alexandra,

Yes, I know it's the middle of the night. Can't sleep.

I wanted to say thanks, for worrying about me. But really, you don't have to worry. You don't have to make the gals go off on crazy adventures for my sake. I'll be fine. But thank you.

E.

❖

From: Alexandra
To: Erin
Sent: October 10, 2010
Subject: RE: don't worry

Erin,

I'm awake, too. What else is new? I just finished a very long and calming meditation and was checking email before bed.

Do you want to come over? It would be good to talk.

❖

From: Erin
To: Alexandra
Sent: October 10, 2010
Subject: RE: RE: don't worry

Tempting, but no thanks. I'm all cozy, snuggled in my blankets, electric mattress pad warming me up, pillows piled around me. I'm good.

❖

From: Alexandra
To: Erin
Sent: October 10, 2010
Subject: RE: RE: RE: don't worry

I completely understand. Well, here's what I wanted to say then.

I know you say not to worry about you, Erin, but that's what friends do. They look after each other, watch out for each other, take care of each other. You are always so strong, independent, self-sufficient. I never for a moment doubt that you can take care of yourself, go it alone in this world if you have to. That's the thing, though, Erin: You don't have to. You have to remember that sometimes it's okay to lean on people. Sometimes it's okay to let others carry some of the load. Care for you and give to you. You have to learn to receive. Life is about give and take—note that: give AND take. It may feel selfish to take, but in order for some to give, others must receive. We have to allow the Universe its balance.

Receiving graciously is a gift to the giver. If you give something to me, give with great love and care and thought, and I react by saying "No, I don't need this, take it back, I'm fine without it," then how does that feel? You'd feel rejected, spurned, foolish for having extended a gift where it wasn't appreciated or wanted. What's more, it's not just material gifts that need to be received well; the intangible, the emotional must be received too. Letting others love you. Letting others love me. I think we both have some work to do on letting people in.

Actually, that's just what I was meditating on earlier, as I think I face this challenge too. Letting other people give to me isn't a skill I've learned so well in life either. It's time for me to learn it, I think, and maybe time for you too. As for me, I've resisted letting anyone in since Jimmy and my children died, obviously because I didn't want to feel that pain again. Knowing it is far different from living it. I've gotten by just fine; I have wonderful friends around me whom I love unconditionally, and who return that love. But it's time for more. As I said the other night, if we live our lives trying to protect our hearts from all possible hurt or harm, we will lose. If we are to participate in love and life, we are going to be hurt, and what may be worse to deal with, we will hurt other people. Take Jake and Ruby—Ruby didn't go into the relationship intending to hurt Jake. Or Pete, Pete didn't ask Ruby to marry him knowing that shortly thereafter he'd break off the engagement and break her heart. If we are going to be in the game, as it were, we have to be prepared to lose sometimes, chalk it up to growth. The alternative, to risk nothing, is to lose for certain. And so, all these years later, I'm screwing my courage to the sticking place, as Lady MacBeth advised, and I'll not fail. I am diving in to love. Whatever that might mean.

But back to you. Be honest with me, Erin. How concerned should we be about you? What's percolating over there in your mind?

From: Erin
To: Alexandra
Sent: October 10, 2010
Subject: RE: RE: RE: RE: don't worry

I'm fine. Seriously, don't worry about me. We all go through dark phases, don't we? Ebb and flow of life. It's not linear and much as I may hate life's unruliness, it's not meant to be easy going all the time. Ups and downs, that's the way it is. Sometimes you just have to make the decision that you're not going to fall apart.

That's what I've been thinking about a lot these days (though not meditating on—aren't you supposed to clear your mind when you meditate?)—how our modern culture is afraid of the dark places in our minds and lives. Yes, I'm struggling. Yes, I feel like there's something wrong, and I don't know what it is. But I've been down before and I got through it before. Sometimes the only way through it is through it. I don't want to suppress my emotions just because they're uncomfortable. That's how a person ends up drinking too much, shopping too much, doing anything too much—it comes, I think, from not letting the emotions just exist, from trying to numb pain. Pain is real. Pain is part of life. A fish doesn't know it's in water; water is all it knows. Without the dark times we couldn't really appreciate the joy in our lives. That's what I'm trying to focus on right now: the moments, the smallest things that bring me joy, and to be really present in those moments, before the dark slides back in.

So I'm angry a lot of the time right now because I'm ... because I'm just angry. I'm in a dark place, and that's the way of life. The tide goes out and the sun sets and the cup feels empty, but then the tide comes back in and the sun comes up and your cup runneth over again. That's the way of life. I'll be happy again, I know, even if I can't really feel it right now. That's what I keep telling myself, over and over.

What's most frustrating, I suppose, is not really knowing what's wrong. If I knew what was wrong I could fix it. But I'll be okay.

That's the long answer. The short answer is: You don't need to worry.

❖

From: Alexandra
To: Erin
Sent: October 10, 2010
Subject: RE: RE: RE: RE: RE: don't worry

All right. Well, you know if you ever need me or any of us, we are all here for you.

I agree with you about the ebb and flow of emotions. Some people are fairly stable, never too high nor too low. Others swing far, high highs and low lows. With each person it seems it balances out. Maybe the reason we're worried about you is because you've always been one of the more stable types. It's not the swing that's disconcerting; it's the disruption of the pattern of the Erin we know. On the other hand, if the Erin we know isn't the fully authentic Erin who is inside you, then sometimes a disruption is what is needed.

At any rate, thank you for sharing your thoughts with me. Ruby and I were talking about the usher at that concert she went to with Ed at that conference, the man whose son had killed himself, and that also got me thinking. I think our society has evolved … no, evolved isn't the right word; that implies progress. We've morphed, perhaps, into a people who have lost our sense of control over our own lives. These days, people so often seem to feel either entitled or victimized, both of which hand over the reigns of control to something or someone outside themselves. Either "the world owes me" or "the world ruined me," but whichever it is, it relieves a person of having to take responsibility for his or her own life. People then see happiness as completely external: if so-and-so loves me, I will be happy. If I receive the thing I want, the acknowledgment from outside myself that I am worthy, the phone call, the job, the external whatever, I will be happy. After long enough without taking (or realizing) responsibility, a person almost loses the ability or knowledge of how to do so, how to take charge and make changes. People no longer know how to reassure themselves, how to validate and affirm their own worth, and they look to someone else to give them that reassurance and affirmation. No one can give us these things but ourselves, though, and all the reassurance in the world from an external source cannot actually reassure. Give a man reassurance, he feels good for an hour. Teach a man to reassure himself—you see where I'm going with this. But because people have come to believe everything is outside their control, they feel powerless to fix things when things aren't going well. They lose hope, while waiting for someone else to step in, something external to change, when in fact as we all know, change must—can only—come from within. Absolutely no one can in any way fix our lives but ourselves, and we can fix no one's life for them.

The opposite of the two extremes of entitlement and victimhood is, of course, claiming the authority and obligations and encumbrances and power of directing one's own life. "I make my own future. My choices and my consequences are mine." It's a radical and challenging truth to comprehend. In some ways, it's difficult because we want so much to help others. Take Ed and his grants, for example. He wants to help people live their dreams but he has had to realize that only the dreamer can live the dream. He can give them all the means in the world, but in the end they have to take it on and own it themselves. Said our dear friend Walt Whitman, whose barbaric YAWP I greatly envy: "Not I, not anyone else, can travel that road for you. You must travel it for yourself." And he continues: "It is not far. It is within reach." Too many do not believe that last bit, that what they want—happiness, love, success, their dreams—just might be within reach, if only they would keep going.

Where I was going with this is, I wonder if an increase in depression and even suicide rates follows from this entitlement/victim trap. People have unlearned or never learned that they do have the power within them to make their lives better. They feel hopeless, perhaps, because they don't realize they can change. That nothing from yesterday has to be a predictor of tomorrow. That we all are granted the right and ability, at every moment, to start anew. And in this moment. And this moment again. Over and over until we have it "right." People give up too soon, and I think they give up because they feel hopeless and helpless; and I think that is because they don't believe their life is theirs to guide. It is sad.

Well, it's very late—or is it very early? I suppose it depends on whether one has been to sleep yet. I'll let you go. Enjoy your electric mattress pad. For years I would only warm up my bed for an hour or so with a blanket turned on before I got in, but then I'd turn it off as soon as I was under the covers, as I once read that women who want to have children should avoid the blankets for some reason or other. I've long since graduated to keeping the blanket on low all night. Few inventions seem as wonderful as a warm blanket on a cold night.

Sleep well.

A.

From: Erin
To: Alexandra
Sent: October 10, 2010
Subject: RE: RE: RE: RE: RE: RE: don't worry

I'm not tired yet. Stay up with me.

Now, wait. Didn't you just say you want to find love, and then right after that you say that we can't look outside ourselves for happiness? Aren't you looking to someone else to make you happy, then? I want exactly what you said: To be able to find that happiness within myself. Looking to someone else contradicts that, doesn't it? David couldn't make me happy; only I can. Isn't that what you were saying?

You mentioned kids. Enough about me; what about you? Do you ever think you might still want kids? It's not too late. There are ways.

❖

From: Alexandra
To: Erin
Sent: October 10, 2010
Subject: RE: RE: RE: RE: RE: RE: RE: don't worry

Kids. Hm. It was easier to avoid this question when everyone thought I was just a cranky old spinster and destined to stay that way. Well. The late-night, early-morning honest answer then. I, too, am fine. I know they're still here. I miss them but I still talk to them. I believe things happen for a reason so I have to believe there is reason to this as well, though in some ways this feels like losing them all over again.

Do I want more children? No. For the longest time after my children died, I didn't even think of having more. For one thing, it seemed like it would be trying to replace them, which seemed cruel and ridiculous. For another, their death marked the beginning of my ability to talk to people on the other side. They were always with me. In the same way I convinced myself that I didn't need a companion again, I was sure I was plenty fulfilled with the children I had, even if they weren't exactly here with me.

My mind was, once again, in contradiction of itself in its multitudes. On the one hand, a part of my brain always had that open question: Will I have children again? If so, when? With whom? The question never resolved but also never grew. It sat there in its chair in a corner of my thoughts, waving at the room from time to let me know it was still around, but never insistent, never coming out to join my predominant thoughts.

And then on the other hand, from the moment I learned my children died there was a part of me that knew that was it, I wouldn't have children again. Certainly I was plenty young enough but this other part of my brain knew that phase was past. Do you know the saying that you can never step in the same river twice? The reasoning is that the water molecules that are at any point in the river in any given moment are different from the ones you stepped in before or will step in later. The river is the same but different. It can never really be the same again. I don't know if this makes sense but that's how it felt about children. They were a part of the river of my life when I stepped in the first time, but stepping in again, they were no longer there and none others would come to take their place. I always knew that. Self-fulfilling prophesy? Maybe. I can never know.

When I moved to Wishing Rock, I still had all their belongings, plus all the paraphernalia of my own life I'd been saving for my children as they grew. When I was a kid, one of my favorite things to do was to play with one of my friends' parents' old toys, read their comic books, sort through their school memorabilia. It was always such fun imagining these parents—who seemed so very old—in their youth; to get insight into the children they used to be, the things that shaped their world growing up. Anticipating the same for my kids, I'd saved a lot of my own history. From toys to report cards to books I'd loved, high school sweaters and programs to dances; anything that I thought my kids might enjoy one day, I'd saved it all. Along the way I'd also collected some other knick-knacks, things my children were too young to play with yet, but I imagined them playing with some day. A giant box of building bricks I'd bought at a garage sale. Old purses and gloves I'd saved for future games of dress up or Halloween costumes. All of it, neatly labeled and boxed up for "later."

Fast forward to several years after I moved here, October of 2002. I was turning thirty-five. Octobers are infused with thoughts and memories of my family. Jimmy, Charlie, and I were all October babies, and Chloë was born in May. I always worried she'd feel left out of the October fun, but hoped that instead maybe she'd feel unique and special. Anyway, October 2002, I looked at the stacks of boxes in my closets and down in storage and realized my life and my closets were filled with the past and with broken hopes and expectations, with things I was holding onto for a someday that deep down I knew would never come.

The part of me that knew I would never have children again decided it was time to give it all away. At the time, I knew it was still theoretically possible that I would meet someone and marry and start "another" family. Anything's possible. I didn't want faded dreams to hold me back anymore, though. So one rainy day I sat down with all my boxes and a pile of tissues, and sorted through the memories I'd saved for children who never lived to see them. It felt almost impossible to let go of some of it—the things we save aren't just about our past, but about our legacy. To know that no one would ever care to see the letter books from my kindergarten years, in which I'd learned to write; that no one would wonder what comments teachers had made about me when I was eight; that no one would ever pore over yearbooks looking for my name, to come running to me, pointing at my old pictures and laughing … there was a sense of loss of self that I can't describe. It made me feel very very small. I looked at old carefully drawn family trees with a new light. Rather than seeing generations branch off after me, leading to the future, I saw the blunt end of my own line. Branches snapped short. There would be no one to whom I would pass on my cherished recipes; no family reunions with screaming grandkids chasing after each other or eating at the kids' table; no Christmases where I had to figure out how to share my children with my children's spouses families. My home was as full as it was going to be.

Giving away all these things brought into clear focus a future that theretofore had been cloaked in denial. I felt in some ways like I had lost my family for a second time. For a while, I was reminded constantly of this reality I was facing. It was hard even to let go of the struggles and challenges I would never have to deal with. Not only had I collected toys and dress up clothes, but I'd spent a good deal of time musing over how best to raise a child. I had ideas filed in my brain, ready to be pulled out at the right moment. How I would deal with a non-talkative teenager. What I would do about homework expectations. My theories on the right balance between discipline and permissiveness. Watching other people parent for years while I was still waiting for my turn, I'd spent hours thinking, How would I do it differently? I'd watched friends with rowdy kids and friends with calm kids, and I'd dissected what made the difference between the two. I'd seen parents spoil their kids by giving in to every whim, and I'd vowed never to do the same. Well, I had my wish, I suppose: intentional or not, I would never do the same. For better or for worse, I was leaving a world of concerns behind.

Having had enough of lingering nebulous grief, I made a choice to consciously grieve for a bit. While I still had my family with me, of course, and could still talk with them, they weren't and would never be here on earth with me to travel through the physical world with me. I went away to Thorp, over in the mountains, for a week and spent time talking with them and writing in my journal and planning out my future. Worked through all my anger and sadness and fears. I thought.

I don't know if having them always with me made it harder or easier to let them go. In theory, after that week I decided I would no longer dwell on what I didn't have, but instead look to what I did have. In theory. Now that they're completely gone from inside my head, though, I realize I never really did let go. I always used them as a crutch and an excuse not to really go forward with life. Their presence masked the fact that I am, I've now realized, lonely.

So that's where I am these days. Thinking about the lessons I was supposed to learn, thought I'd learned. Thinking about finally moving on and living a full life, a life in which I practice what I preach about being a participant not just a spectator. Which is why I am subjecting the poker gals to whatever wonderful out-of-the-Box activities I may think up. Not just for you. For me, too.

Which brings us to whether I must find happiness within myself, or whether I am allowed to say that having a companion is key to my happiness. To quote our dear Walt Whitman again, "Do I contradict myself? Very well, then I contradict myself, I am large, I contain multitudes." No, actually I don't think it's a contradiction. It's a complexity, certainly, but not a contradiction. One can want companionship without losing the ability to take care of oneself. Humans are social creatures. Look at the popularity and evolution of cell phones. It's not as though the five billion of us with cell phones are living our lives in such critically important ways that we must be reachable at every moment. No, it's about connection. The desire to share. A phone used to be just a phone, but look at all the things it does now. I can send you a picture or even a video of what I'm doing right in that moment. I can answer emails the moment they come in, from anywhere. None of that is necessary; it's simply a result of our intense desire to connect with each other. If I send you a picture of a cloud it's not because I think your life will be incomplete without a picture of a cloud. Rather, it's a way of saying "This is something I want to share with you; a moment where I want to connect." The cloud is immaterial. The photo itself is immaterial. It is merely a means to an end.

Our whole lives and society are built on that urge. While we have to find happiness within ourselves, at the same time I firmly believe that happiness is rooted in our connections with other people. Not independent or dependent but interdependent. You finding the courage and confidence to be fully you, me finding the courage and confidence to be fully me, and in the meeting of the two, a bond.

Maybe this is the answer to your question: Happiness is intertwined with our connections with other people. Connecting with other people is inherently dangerous business; it requires us to be vulnerable, to risk rejection over and over again. Surviving that vulnerability and those rejections demands a confident core; we have to be confident in who we are, enough so that we don't feel we have to change ourselves to please someone else or fit another's mold. Confident enough in who we are that we know if someone doesn't like us, that doesn't make us bad people. It's simply an indicator of an ill fit. Not everyone will like everyone else. So that inner confidence, that comes from loving oneself, from being strong and from facing adversity and conquering it. So! I've solved it! Happiness comes from our connections, which come from our ability to be vulnerable, which comes from our confidence in our own worth. There you go.

So that is what I am seeking. Both the happiness within and the happiness with another. I believe it is time for me to have it all.

There, have you fallen asleep while I've been writing?

From: Erin
To: Alexandra
Sent: October 10, 2010
Subject: RE: RE: RE: RE: RE: RE: RE: RE: don't worry

Ha! Actually, yes. The "new message" ding woke me up.

Well there, you have solved the secret to happiness. Deep late night thoughts with Alexandra … did Ed ever figure out your given name?

That's intense about your kids and cleaning out your old stuff. I know, "intense" is lame. I'm so tired I can't think. I'll react appropriately tomorrow.

On that note I think I will tuck into my bed and go to sleep. What sorts of dreams will I have with all this churning in my head? I doubt I'll remember; I never remember my dreams.

Anyway, thank you, Alexandra. Go to sleep. xx

E.

From: Alexandra
To: Erin
Sent: October 10, 2010
Subject: RE: RE: RE: RE: RE: RE: RE: RE: RE: don't worry

I think Ed has forgotten that he was trying to figure out my name. You needn't remind him! He gets a bit compulsive.

No worries about not reacting appropriately. I understand being so tired you can't think.

And you're welcome. Goodnight.

October 11, 2010
Wishing Rock News
Millie Adler, editor
Letter from the Editor

Well hello, Wishing Rockers!

A few quick notes for you all today. First, a reminder on behalf of Mr. Edward R. Brooks that the first deadline for the first round of ED grants is October 15—that's this Friday! If you know your dream, put it down on paper and maybe Ed will help fund it. Applications are here at the store. Come down and say hello and pick one up. Grants will be given out bi-monthly so if you're not ready to submit for this round you have a couple more months to work it out. Deadlines will be posted on the lobby bulletin board. Get dreaming!

Second, Alexandra in her mysterious ways has asked me to tell you this: "If you like to laugh, wear loose clothing and come to the fifth floor Commons room on Saturday, October 16, at 3:00 p.m." To which I say: Bah! Laughing! Who needs it! You won't find me there!

Third, don't forget our annual Cider Press Party, Saturday, October 23. We'll be out on the lawn. We'll have the tents up and fingers crossed for good weather, but be sure to dress warm. Pressing starts at 2:00. Bobbing for apples will take place under the tents while the pressing is going on. Potluck afterward in the second floor Commons, starting around 4:30, so if you're planning to bring an appetizer, be prompt! Claire will be setting up a caramel apple station, caramel and apples provided. Ed's working on a new apple brandy and will bring some for tasting by the adults. By the end of the day we'll have kept a hundred doctors away! No offense to Jake, our resident doctor-in-training, who I'm told might join us if he can. Full moon is October 23 so I'm expecting crazier than normal antics. From myself that is! I hope you'll join me! I just may dust off the line dancing moves I learned earlier this year. Watch out!

Fourth, the Haunted House and Corn Maze are ongoing. Great fun, so if you haven't been yet, get yourself over there!

Fifth, get ready, it's almost Halloween! Trick-or-treat floor schedule posted down at the store.

I think that about sums it up! Except that I'm still waiting on a great corn bread recipe. Where are you people when I need you?

Millie

From: Ruby
To: Erin
Sent: October 12, 2010
Subject: Seattle

Heya,

We made it over to Seattle. Got Ed and Michael's dad off on a taxi down to the airport to fly home, and then the remaining four of us found our hotel, settled in, and went down to the hotel restaurant for happy hour. Caipirinhas, baby! Yum. Tomorrow Ed and Michael will meet with the lawyer. Laurel's test results were supposed to be here by today but it sounds like the lawyer didn't get them. I'm not sure. Anyway, she's supposed to be there too. Carolyn is still deciding whether she wants to join in on the meeting; as for me I don't think it's quite my place yet since Ed and I have only been dating a couple months. I'll probably head to the market and see what I can see. I need to find something for Alexandra's birthday at the end of the month.

Thinking of you. Let's get together for an official girl's night out, not just dinner in. You and me, when I'm back, okay? We haven't done that in forever. It's time.

xx Ruby

From: Ed
To: Alexandra
Sent: October 13, 2010
Subject: results

Lex! I mean … Kelly? Emily? Stacey? Rhonda? Maria? Paula? Susan? That Erin, gotta love her, reminded me I'd forgotten my mission. I'm back on it! Veronica? Yvette?

Quite a day we've had here.

The long and short of it: Laurel isn't related to us.

Ruby's going home tomorrow, and I think Carolyn is too. Maybe Michael. I'm going to stick around for a day. I want to talk to Laurel. She doesn't seem like a bad person, really. She's fallen on hard times, had a hard life. She doesn't expect much of the world. Dad talked about her mom, Rita, as a woman with such sparkle, though, and after spending a little more time with Laurel yesterday I feel like I see some glimmers of that in her. I'd like to talk to her, anyway, just to talk, I guess.

I'll be home Friday. See you then! Louise? Evelyn?

From: Alexandra
To: Ed
Sent: October 13, 2010
Subject: RE: results

I'll give you a hint: None of the names you suggested this time has the correct first letter. Getting cold, Ed. Try again!

See you this weekend.

Love,

Me.

❖

From: Gran
To: Ruby
Sent: October 15, 2010
Subject: Switzerland!

Hello, Ruby!

How are you, darling? I hope everything is going well. I talked to Pip yesterday and she sounds good. Starting to feel a bit better, thank goodness. That nausea is just no fun at all.

We had a bit of excitement around here the other day. I told you about the couple we ran into here, who Liam knew from back home? We've gone on a few outings with them and have had a lovely time. A couple days ago the time came for them to head on to Zurich, and we were going sightseeing that day ourselves so we decided we'd all take the same trains until our ways parted.

These friends were carrying a good bit of baggage, and the husband, Ian, insisted on wearing a fanny pack (Liam tells me a "fanny" is something different in Europe and I shouldn't call it that, but that's what it's called!). He had it turned so the pouch was to his front, and it was chock full of maps and money and passports and every piece of paper he could possibly ever need. Well at any rate, as they were getting onto the train with all their bags, a man almost forcefully tried to carry Ian's big suitcase for him. Ian wasn't going to let go, though, so there was a bit of a struggle. Standing at the train platform, Liam and I watched this commotion with confusion until finally the man released Ian's bag, and we waved as Ian and his wife went off on the train on their merry way. Well! We got an email from them the next day: as it turns out the fracas was merely a distraction. Ian sat down on the train and realized his fanny pack had been unzipped. Lucky for him he had it so tightly packed that no one could get anything out quickly, but can you believe that when we all were watching this, someone else slipped in under the baggage and tried to pickpocket him! In Switzerland of all places! We thought we were so safe here, the country of neutrality, who would try to steal from some nice old tourists? A lesson learned the easy way, thank goodness. Liam and I are certainly going to be a little more careful with our belongings than we have been, especially on those trains that can get quite crowded sometimes. You hate to think there are people like that out there but there just are. All we can do is be a little more careful.

Other than that, we've been going along on our pleasant way but I think we're nearing our fill of fondue and yodeling. We may move on soon. Possibly home (Scotland) for a bit to check in on the house and the children. Don't be scandalized, Ruby, but when we left Scotland I moved my things from the cottage to Liam's home. No need to pay rent on a home I wasn't going to be using for an indeterminate amount of time. Don't worry, I promise, we've done nothing you haven't done yourself.

On that note, we're heading out for a romantic dinner, cheese and chocolate and love.

Please give my best to all the Wishing Rock gang.
Much love to you,
Gran

❖

Text from Ben to Ed
Sent: October 16, 2010

Dude! Where are you?

❖

Text from Ed to Ben
Sent: October 16, 2010

Impromptu beach picnic. Carolyn wanted to get rid of leftovers.
Probably we'll have an impromptu bonfire soon. What's up?

❖

Text from Ben to Ed
Sent: October 16, 2010

I found it!!!!!!!!!!

❖

Text from Ed to Ben
Sent: October 16, 2010

…..?? It? IT?? THE TREASURE????

❖

Text from Ben to Ed
Sent: October 16, 2010

FOUND IT!

Text from Ed to Ben
Sent: October 16, 2010

Get over here! You're kidding! Where are you? Get over here! Do you need help carrying it? Get over here now!!

Text from Ben to Ed
Sent: October 16, 2010

Naw, it's not that big. I'm just getting in the car. On my way!

From: Ruby
To: Gran
Sent: October 18, 2010
Subject: RE: Switzerland!

Gran! Pickpockets! Be careful out there! And I thought Switzerland was so safe. I guess hard times hit people the world 'round, or maybe they're feeling a bit chafed from the lederhosen. Tell Liam I said he'd better keep you safe. And if someone grabs for your purse, by all means let go. Do you have copies of your passport and such, that you keep separate from the passport itself? Better to lose it than to be hurt. I'm glad to hear Ian didn't lose any belongings. That luggage distraction technique is interesting.

People sure can be tricky.

Meanwhile, back at the ranch, we have been enormously busy here, with so much going on. Where to begin!

I'll start with Laurel. Millie told me she wrote you about her. We have the final DNA test results: Not related. What a relief! Not because Ed and Michael are so greedy that they can't part with any of their fortune, but because it could have led to years, probably, of legal battles, wasted money and wasted time.

After finding this out, Ed stayed on a day in town and spent some time talking with Laurel. That's one of the things I love so much about him—he's compassionate, willing to look past people's masks to see the good underneath. He said she's actually a very nice woman. She's a bush pilot, just like her mom Rita was. When Rita had Laurel, Rita stopped flying just long enough to recuperate for a few weeks, and then started taking Laurel up in the plane with her. She couldn't afford a babysitter and had no choice, so Laurel was strapped in next to supplies and mail and customers, practically grew up in the air. "I learned to fly almost before I learned to walk," she told Ed. It's in her blood. On Rita's days off, the two would pack up a picnic, hop in the plane, and fly until they found a site that looked promising. They'd land, eat, explore, talk about life. Sometimes they'd camp out overnight, huddling in their sleeping bags while gazing in awe as the Northern Lights danced their eerie green dance in the night sky.

Laurel lived with Rita her whole life. She was just on the verge of moving out when they found out Rita had lung cancer and not long to live, so Laurel stayed and cared for her mom until the end. Rita didn't have very good health insurance—she was perfectly healthy before the diagnosis, exercised every day, never smoked, ate healthfully, never expected that she'd have reason to need great insurance at this time in her life—so the bills grew like mountains. The doctors told Rita about a new treatment that might help, but which wasn't covered by insurance. Cost of over a hundred fifty thousand, minimum. But when weighed against a life, what's a hundred fifty thousand? In their desperation and optimism, thinking Rita would live and regain strength and be able to help pay off the bills, they opted for the treatment. It may have given Rita a small amount of extra time but in the end, all it did was add to their already insurmountable debt. Laurel has sold off everything she and her mother owned, and now with still well more than a hundred thousand dollars owing, the only thing left to sell is her plane, which was her mother's plane. "I even tried entering the contest to guess when the Tanana River would break up," she told Ed; it's a contest in Alaska which any Alaskan can enter for a couple bucks, with a prize payout of nearly three hundred thousand dollars. "I was off by five hours." She didn't win.

And so it was desperation, not greed, that led Laurel here. But she's not related, and I don't know what she'll do any more than she does. Certainly selling the plane would bring in some money, but it would also take away her livelihood. What then? For Laurel, selling the plane would be like selling a part of her self. Is that really the best answer? But what else can she do? It's sad, Gran, it's sad. Money can't buy happiness but it certainly can help keep one from a certain range of despair, stress, and anxiety. I wish there were an easy answer for her.

And the opposite of despair brings us to my next topic: Laughter. We all could use some laughter—more laughter—on a daily basis, I think. Alexandra, wise woman that she is, recognizes this. She has begun our "out of the Box" experiments, and this first one involved all of Wishing Rock. She reserved a Commons room for this past Saturday and we were all told that if we liked laughing we should be there. Whether for curiosity of boredom or love of laughter, I'd say almost half the town showed up. And what did she have for us, you ask? Alexandra brought in a guest, a man who hosts a "Laughter Club" back on the mainland! Laughter Club? Yes, Laughter Club! Where the sole purpose is simply to laugh, nothing more, nothing less, to laugh for no reason other than the joy of laughter. He told us a bit of the history of Laughter Clubs and health benefits of laughter; I had no idea but there are thousands of such clubs (often, as with our session, associated with yoga) around the world!

I admit, the idea sounded a bit silly to me and probably more than a few others when we first heard it. The man told us we'd start off just by faking laughter while doing the laughter/yoga exercises, until we started to laugh for real, and then we'd just keep laughing. I, being quite hip, didn't want to look like an idiot and felt a bit foolish at first, doing the strange stretches and movements. But he had his methods and his props, and it didn't take us long to go from the forced hahas to the true guffaws. He had us going for almost an hour, all told, with a few welcome breaks now and again to catch our collective breath, and at the end my sides were literally sore. I haven't laughed that hard for that long in quite a while, and it was spectacular.

And what do you know, I was surprised to see Laurel there. I thought she'd have gone home, but apparently she's staying on a couple more days. She said being away from home makes her feel a little less frightened by all the angst that's hanging in the air at her home; has given her a brief respite-by-distance from the sadness, the memories. She told me Ed paid for her stay at the B&B in Moon Bay. He hadn't told me that. Anyway, I watched her a bit and while at first her laughter had a sort of restrained quality to it, by the end she was laughing as hard as anyone. I'm guessing she needed that. The best medicine.

I don't know if Alexandra is going to bring the Laughing Club man back, but I hope so. I don't know if anyone in Wishing Rock would want to take on the role of leading that sort of thing, but I think we all enjoyed it and would welcome an encore. It feels a bit strange: What did you do this afternoon? I laughed. Oh, you went to a funny movie? No, I just laughed, while doing yoga. It feels almost … I don't know, decadent? Superfluous? Wanton? Lavish? But I think it had tremendous value for our souls. Good call, Alexandra! She has such good ideas.

Or rather, she usually does. I think next week we're supposed to go try archery or some such thing. Alexandra says it's supposed to help us with focus since we all have so much going on in our lives, our attention spread so widely, but I have this image in my head of Claire accidentally shooting someone in the foot. The more I think about it, the more I worry it'll be a self-fulfilling prophesy. The more I try not to think about it, the more I think about it. Let's just get it over with! And who knows what comes next after archery. I live in fear.

As for Alexandra herself, she's doing okay, I think. Erin said she and Alexandra had a pretty in-depth conversation the other night, but aside from saying that Alexandra has decided to "live out loud" (Erin's words), she didn't say too much else about their talk. As for Erin, I can see that she's thinking a lot, and while sometimes that kind of over-thinking can be troubling, in her case it seems to be more like problem-solving; she's mulling over everything that's going on in her head and is going to come to a new understanding of herself and her life. She's pretty quiet about it, but you can tell there's activity in her noggin. A few days ago she went off to Seattle for the day, and came back with some new clothes—completely different from what she normally wears. A neckline more plunging, the colors more bold. Maybe she's trying on new selves to see what feels right.

Wait, is this midlife crisis? She's too young for that—I'm too young for that, we're too young for that! That can't be it. Must just be a phase. And not the midlife crisis kind of phase.

AND! Okay, the moment you've been waiting for: The Treasure!!!

Soooo, the treasure. This would, of course, be the treasure that Meriwether mentioned in a letter he wrote to Maddie some thirty-five years ago, a letter that Ben recently found down in the storage area. Extensive search parties have been going out to caves all over the north and east sides of the island for weeks, but no one ever found anything. I really think Ed and Michael were going to call it all off, but our Ben is a persistent young fellow. He went off alone one day and finally found it. He says it was hardly "buried" treasure but rather more "hidden behind and slightly underneath a rock" treasure. He was pretty sure it was Meriwether's toolbox because old Meriwether had a habit of engraving his driver's license on his belongings so they'd be returned if found, and the lid of this toolbox was engraved with numbers and letters starting with BROOKMB. Almost certainly Meriwether. Ben took us back to the cave and it's no wonder no one found it before, as a bush has grown up in front of it, blocking most of the mouth. I could imagine walking right past it without even seeing it. "I almost did," said Ben, "but a squirrel coming out of the cave caught my eye." Thank you, squirrel!

What is inside the box, what is inside, what is inside? Shall I tell you now? Or shall I make you wait? Oh all right, I'll tell you. Coins! Oodles of coins. Exactly what two small boys would have perceived as the greatest treasure ever. There are two mint sets from 1975 (the year Meriwether hid the treasure), one for each of his grandsons, and then a seemingly random assortment of other old coins, half dollars, silver dollars, all sorts of pennies and nickels and dimes. And, in a little sandwich bag, two of the tiniest little gold nuggets you ever saw. (Not that I've seen a lot of gold nuggets.) Ed speculates that Meriwether had them leftover from his years in Alaska, but I suppose we'll never know for sure. By face value, all added up the coins aren't worth much, but Ed is going back to Seattle tomorrow to look over Meriwether's will again and finish up some other business, and while he's there he's arranged to have the coins appraised. Maybe they'll find a real gem!

So that, Gran, is the latest goings on. That laughter club has got me thinking a lot. I think of myself as a rather happy person but I don't actually laugh every day as much as I think I'd like to. Being with Ed has certainly upped the amount I laugh; he just has a way with words, and the looks on his face, that put me into stitches. Still, I think maybe I want to be more conscious about laughing. That thing they say, that just smiling can improve your mood even if you're faking the smile … I think there's some merit to that. Something to think about, at any rate.

Keep us updated on your whereabouts! I think Ed has an inkling that he may want to visit his mother in Iceland sometime but I have no idea when. Having taken two trips this year I think I'll have to live vicariously through you for a while. Travel large!

All my love,
Ruby

Text from Alexandra to Ed
Sent: October 19, 2010

Ed, sweetheart, Ruby tells me you're in Seattle again; when are you back home? I need to talk. I've a bit of a conundrum. A dilemma. I need your thoughts and insights. Best shared over a cocktail in the privacy of my home. Let me know.

Text from Ed to Alexandra
Sent: October 19, 2010

A text? A text from Lex?!? Hold on while I check to see if monkeys have flown out my lower half. Lex, texting! And why do I feel like I'm in a rhyming children's book? I'm here today, gone tomorrow. Back in town tomorrow night. I can talk, though, want me to call?

Text from Alexandra to Ed
Sent: October 19, 2010

Ha ha, smart-monkey-ass. No, no need to call. Come by when you're home. Tomorrow night if you can, maybe? Or Thursday if tomorrow doesn't work. Friday may be too late. Or perhaps fate will work in its mysterious ways regardless.

Text from Ed to Alexandra
Sent: October 19, 2010

What's going on? You have me intrigued! Tell tell tell!

Text from Alexandra to Ed
Sent: October 19, 2010

Patience, my love, it's a virtue. I'll tell you soon enough. Any news on the coin front?

Text from Ed to Alexandra
Sent: October 19, 2010

Heading to the dealer in an hour after I leave the lawyer. Speaking of which, gotta go. Call if you need me!

Text from Alexandra to Ed
Sent: October 19, 2010

I'll talk to you soon.

From: Ed
To: Ruby
Sent: October 20, 2010
Subject: coinage

Hey babe,

Sorry I didn't call earlier; I found out a distributor was in town so I met up with him and we ended up out for drinks. Just got back to the hotel now. I'm assuming you're asleep, your dark eyelashes fluttering on your pretty cheeks, that little puff of breath, your frighteningly cold feet. Oh to have your cold feet next to me right now! Next to me, that is, mind you. Not on my legs, and certainly not above the calf. Damn, girl, your feet can get cold.

What's up with Alexandra, by the way? Do you know? She actually texted me earlier. Never got a text from that woman in my life, I don't think. Or only a few times at most. She isn't what one would call "concise" enough for texting in general. Likes her words, that woman. The brevity of texting isn't really her thing! Everyone is changing—Erin showing off her cleavage, Lex texting; what's next? Michael bleaching his hair? Too much change for this old man. Too much!

At any rate. The coin dealer. Are you ready for this? The 1975 proof sets are worth a ton! The dealer almost couldn't believe his eyes.

"Do you know what these are?" said he.

"Um, old coins?" said I. You can't get these things past me, Ruby! I was quite sure I was correct.

The dealer, however, was not impressed by my humor. In fact, he completely ignored my wit. "1975 proof sets with no-S dimes," said he.

"No-what whats?" said I. Pretending to be ignorant, to see if the man knew his business.

"No-S dimes. These are legendary. I've never seen them. Heard of them but thought they were urban myths. 1975 no-S dimes!" He shook his head. He went on to explain that all modern proof coins are minted in San Francisco, but the dies all come from Philadelphia. Philly sends the dies to Denver and San Francisco, which then punch in the "S" for San Francisco or "D" for Denver before striking the coins. However, in some rare cases, such as a very few 1975 dimes, someone forgets to punch the "S" or "D" or "P" (for Philadelphia) onto the die first, and a few coins get out without the designator. Thus a "no-S" dime.

The guy was clearly coveting my dimes, fidgeting a bit. Had I looked closely, I suspect I might have seen a bead of sweat forming on his brow. Obviously the same person who appraises them can't actually buy them—conflict of interest. I could see the struggle in him. But when I asked how much they were worth, he said he couldn't even begin to guess. As he'd said, prior to seeing these he hadn't even fully believed the 1975 no-S dimes existed. They're that rare. Someone will want them, he said; the trick is that you have to have two people who both want them equally badly, and are willing and able to bid each other up to get them.

He gave me the number of an auction house that deals with coins and offered the suggestion that to ensure rarity (and therefore increase bidding) we consider only putting one up for sale, if we're going to sell. Not a bad idea. I'll have to consult with Michael and the auction house and see what they think.

There were a few other rare coins among grandpa's treasure, as well. All told, not including the 1975 proof sets, he estimated the value of the other coins to be around $20,000. Not bad at all! Leave it to old Meriwether to purchase some mythical legendary coins, and hide them away for decades. Michael and I may have to give a dime or two (but perhaps not a no-S dime) to Ben for his time and effort.

I'm going to talk with Michael about maybe giving half the toolbox earnings, dimes included, whatever they may be worth, to Laurel. She could use a boost.

So, quick trip to the auctioneer tomorrow morning, then I'll be on the next ferry. See you tomorrow night (or rather tonight; it's late). Want me to make you something nice for dinner? Buy the ingredients and I'll cook it up for you!

Love,
Ed xxxxxx

From: Ruby
To: Carolyn
Sent: October 20, 2010
Subject: chili recipe?

Hey Carolyn!

Could you send me your chili recipe? The one you made the other week, the slow cooker one.

Thanks!!

R.

From: Carolyn
To: Ruby
Sent: October 20, 2010
Subject: RE: chili recipe?

Hi Ruby!

No problem. I love this recipe because I can dump it all into the slow cooker and forget about it. It's pretty straightforward but let me know if you have questions.

Slow Cooker Chili

Ingredients
- 1 lb lean ground beef
- 1 lb ground turkey
- 1/2 onion, chopped
- 1/2 tsp ground black pepper
- 1/2 tsp garlic salt
- 2 1/2 cups tomato sauce
- 8 oz medium or hot salsa
- 2 Tbsp chili powder
- 2 Tbsp chili seasoning mix
- 1 can cannellini beans, rinsed and drained
- 1 can kidney beans, rinsed and drained
- 1 can pinto beans, rinsed and drained
- Toppings: chopped avocado, sour cream, shredded cheese, corn chips, etc.

Directions
(You can use a different combination of chili powder and chili seasoning if you like; for example, all chili powder or all chili seasoning or somewhere in between. This is my preference and yields a rather spicy chili.) In a large sauté pan over medium heat, sauté the onions for a minute or two then add the ground meat. Sauté for about ten minutes, until the meat is browned and onion is tender. Drain the grease. Combine all ingredients in a 6-quart slow cooker and stir. Cook on low

for six to eight hours. Serve in bowls; top with avocado, sour cream, cheese, corn chips, or your favorite toppings. Also good served with a hearty bread.

From: Ruby
To: Ed
Sent: October 20, 2010
Subject: RE: coinage

Hey bubba,

Give Laurel half?! That's potentially a lot, isn't it? Do you have any idea what the dimes (or one dime) might auction for? Maybe you should wait and find out? Have you gone in yet?

Are you on your way back? Yes, dinner with just the two of us would be beautiful but you've had a long few days. I'll put chili fixings into the slow cooker—just got Carolyn's recipe from her—and it'll be ready when you get home. We'll have lots of leftovers to freeze, too! You can make me dinner some other time. I won't forget.

Game night? Scrabble? You know you want it.

xxx

From: Ed
To: Ruby
Sent: October 20, 2010
Subject: RE: RE: coinage

Game night! It's on, girl! Winner (me) gets a backrub. Qat, qintar, qadi, jaconet, jagua, jati, jiao. I'm on the ferry home now and I'm studying. I don't know what the words mean but I can spell them.

Watch out! I am taking Scrabble up a notch tonight, babe. I'm notching it. Watch. Out.

Saw the auctioneer. She has no idea how much the dime(s) would go for; they're so rare she had no frame of reference. She said easily five and maybe even six figures. She's going to try to get one into an auction that starts tomorrow, ends next week, online, modern coins only.

And yes, I'm sure it's the right thing to do, giving half to Laurel. Michael and I talked about it and we're in agreement. To maintain the value of the dime we put up for auction he and I will hang onto one dime for now, and give half the earnings from all the other coins and the other dime to Laurel. Michael and I each have more money than we'll ever need. And with the distillery and my investments, unless I spend like a moron I'll always have more money than I will ever need. The world doesn't need any more insanely rich people. The world needs more people living lives of passion, doing what makes them come alive. The world needs more happy people, not more millionaires. Flying is Laurel's passion and it's not right that she'd have to give up her plane if I can change that. Laurel didn't come into her debt by being careless with her spending; she came into it trying to save her mother. Her mother who, I might add, had a significant impact on Dad's life. I trust Laurel to be responsible with the money, and to pay it forward in whatever way she can, when she is finally able. People are inherently good, Ruby, but hard times can make them scared, and being scared can put people in survival mode, and being in survival mode can make people do things they might not otherwise do. But she's inherently good. I know good things will come of this. I can feel it.

From: Ruby
To: Ed
Sent: October 20, 2010
Subject: RE: RE: RE: coinage

"Notching it"? New phrase there, Mr. Jargon?

Okay, but what about all the other people in Wishing Rock who could use the money? Is it fair to give money to this woman you've just met?

❖

From: Ed
To: Ruby
Sent: October 20, 2010
Subject: RE: RE: RE: RE: coinage

Notching it. I'm coining (no coin pun intended) a new phrase. You just watch, soon all the kids will be saying it.

As to the money. First, it's our money and we can do what we want with it. Second, I've set up the grants; I'm going to be giving money to Wishing Rock people, too. Third, do you really think there's anyone in Wishing Rock I wouldn't help if they had insurmountable medical bills?

❖

From: Ruby
To: Ed
Sent: October 20, 2010
Subject: RE: RE: RE: RE: RE: coinage

Okay, fine, you made your point. As to your earlier question about Alexandra, no idea what's up. She came by the distillery looking for you and I told her you were out. She didn't say what she wanted. You have to tell me when you find out! I'm all curious now.

From: Ed
To: Ruby
Sent: October 20, 2010
Subject: RE: RE: RE: RE: RE: RE: coinage

You could ask her yourself, you know.
Ferry's about to dock; see you in a few! xx

October 22, 2010
Wishing Rock News
Millie Adler, editor
Another Guest Editorial from Ed Brooks

Hello people of Wishing Rock! I'm butting in on Millie's territory again to tell you that I've selected the first recipient of the ED grants! The fact that there was only one application is no commentary on the merit of the project. However, it does make me wonder, where are your dreams, people? Come on, let's make it happen! Don't be afraid to dream and dream big. This is your chance! Anyhow, with no further ado, the winner is: Walter Neumann!

Walter, one of Wishing Rock's newest residents, dreams of bringing culture to Wishing Rock. Good luck, there, Walt! I know these people. You have your work cut out for you!

There are two components to Walter's plan. I shall make a numbered list to illustrate this.

1. Community Band: Walter, once a music teacher, longs for a return to the podium. You, my people, are his guinea pigs in this

venture. Walter wants to create a community band, talent not required. Come as you are and he will mold you to his vision. You don't even need to have an instrument. Funds to purchase instruments are part of the grant. Walter will soon send out information about "auditions," though in his plan there's a place for everyone. Just a matter of figuring out what that place is. Tell him what you'd like to play and he'll make it happen. The community band will evolve with the help of its members. Stay tuned.

2. Wishing Rock Talks. You may have seen those videos online, people spreading great ideas in up to twenty minute chunks. Walter wants to host a similar weekend event here at Wishing Rock. Residents with something to say are encouraged to start thinking immediately and watch for Walter's calls for speech ideas. Walter will craft the perfect weekend with both local speakers and, if he can make it happen, some inspirational, interesting lecturers that he might ship in from out of town. His hope is to make this happen soon. I think Walter is going to be a busy man.

And, there you have it, the first ED grant. Walter will keep you informed hereinafter henceforth. We will have culture! Next they're going to make me use silverware. Where will this end?

Congratulations, Walter! And again, everyone else, get your applications in! I know you have a spark of a dream in your heart. Let it out. Next applications are due December 15. Don't make me come after you to get them.

Ed

From: Ruby
To: Pip
Sent: October 24, 2010
Subject: Checking in

Hey Pipster,

Just checking in, how are you? Almost through with the third month, right? Feeling okay? Will you guys find out if it's a boy or girl? Whether I'm going to be an aunt or an uncle? Hahaha.

So the annual Wishing Rock Cider Press Party was yesterday. We had good enough weather; a bit overcast but no rain, and this time of year that's all we ask.

And Jake was here.

How is it that I've moved on—I know I have, I absolutely love Ed, and I'm the one who broke it off with Jake—I've moved on but yet there were those butterflies, still? That little flutter in my heart on seeing him. Excitement? Fear? Nerves? Nausea?

And he brought a new girlfriend with him.

I know it's not fair to say he shouldn't date anyone else, especially since I broke up with him, but really, must he? It stung a bit. She was like a third of my age. Okay, not really. About his age. Whatever. I know, I know, I know it's not supposed to bother me. It's not my right, as the dumper, to care. But I do, somehow, I do care.

I've imagined what I'd do if I saw him with a new girlfriend. In my mind, the first time I saw Jake with another woman would go like this:

Me: "Well hello, Jake! So great to see you! You're looking good." (But in reality he would look sad, haggard, resigned.)

Jake: "Ruby!" (His eyes lighting up with hope and desire on seeing me. Poor guy.) "Great to see you! I swear, you look younger every time." (And he would be right.)

Me: "Oh Jake! Haha! You flatter me. Who's this lovely young

lady?" (She would not actually be all that lovely.)

Jake: (Remembering that there was someone else with him.) "Oh! This is Bunny!"

Bunny: (Chews gum.)

Jake: "She's a little shy."

Bunny: (Blank stare.)

And so on. I never could decide if it would be better for her to be smart (showing good taste on his part, retroactively complimentary to me) or an idiot (showing that he gave up on ever finding someone as brilliant as I am).

The reality of the conversation was that it was awkwardballs. It went thusly:

Me: "Oh! Jake! Hi!" I saw the woman by his side, her arm woven around his waist. Instantly I felt the flush of blood creeping up my neck and face. It was so quaint, wasn't it, when Princess Diana blushed? Not so with me. Makes people stare at me. Is there something wrong with that woman? She is red as a beet. Should we get help? Mortifying.

Jake: (Reaching out to hug me, so awkward, he caught me off guard and I somehow flung my hand into his nose.) "Ow! Hey, Ruby! Good to see you!" (Rubbing his nose.) "This is Ashley."

Ashley is young and confident and beautiful, looked charming as a peach, if peaches were known to be charming.

Jake: "Ashley's a first year medical student. Plans to go into pediatric." Squeezed his new squeeze to his side, kissed her hair. Beamed. He looked better than ever.

Wait: pediatric? As in kids? Which he hates? Does she know he hates kids?

Me: (Blank stare. Gauging the temperature of the heat which was radiating off my skin. Egg cooking? No. Wax melting? Maybe.)

Thank goodness Ed came over and saved the day. Gave Jake a hearty handshake and back-slapping man hug, and they had a moment of unspoken acknowledgement, forgiveness, reconciliation. They stood and chatted and Ashley laughed at the right times in her golden dulcet tones and I felt like I'd aged a hundred years.

Why, Pip, why? I'm so happy with Ed. I know I didn't make a mistake. I know I didn't. So why do these emotions swirl up like that? What causes that? And it's totally not fair to Ed. I couldn't do better than Ed. Am I just greedy?

Love, unfathomable. It should be so simple, but it's just not. I blame hormones. Probably perimenopause.

Oh, the party was fine, apple bobbing, cider pressing, potlucking, all the usual. I brought pumpkin bread, always well received.

In other news, Alexandra had a long chat with Ed the other night but neither of them will tell me what about. Hopefully I can get someone to spill the beans next week when I have Ed and Alexandra over for dinner for Alexandra's birthday. Just the three of us. Mark my words: I will get them to tell me, yes oh yes I will.

Let me know what's up with you! Miss you bunches. Hugs to all, big hugs.

xxx Rubister

❖

From: Pip
To: Ruby
Sent: October 25, 2010
Subject: RE: Checking in

Hey Ruby,

I thought we were past this anxiety? What happened? Could be hormones. Believe me, I know hormones.

These fears that you'll never have enough or never be enough—you have to let them go. Ed loves you—when you guys were over here, I could just see it in him, the way he looks at you, the way his body language is always sort of turned toward wherever you are, attuned to you, he's just aware of you keenly at all times. He's smitten and adores you and loves you unconditionally. But you have to trust that, and trust him, or you'll drive him away. You have to suck it up and just decide to let him love you, decide to let yourself love him, decide that you're going to trust it, and trust that if it doesn't work out, you are strong enough to get through the pain. You are. Don't let your fear sabotage a relationship with the greatest guy you've known. Lately I've been wondering if people sometimes cling to a feeling of anxiety simply because they're afraid that if they acknowledge any happiness they feel, that acknowledgement will cause the happiness to slip away. Embrace the happiness now, while you have it. What you focus on increases, right? Focus on the happiness, not the fears.

All's good here. I'm getting to know the neighbors more, which is good. Word is spreading that I'm a baker and I'm starting to get more jobs, but there's also a bit of territorialism and loyalty for another baker on the island who's a native on this Isle of Mull. It may take a bit longer before I'm accepted. I'm trying to find a way to tailor my offerings so I'm not so much competition, but rather complementary to what the other baker offers. There's plenty of room for growth in my business, but Gavin makes a good income and we'll be fine for now.

I'm still getting used to not having the stores and supplies I want easily on hand at a moment's notice. There are shops on Mull, of course, mostly over at Tobermory, but everything is so much more expensive. I've met a number of people who take empty suitcases on the ferry over to Oban, do their shopping there, load up the suitcases at the grocery store, and come back. It's cumbersome and it makes me really glad that Gavin has a boat and we're at least slightly more mobile. Still, he has a job to do and can't run back to the mainland every time I need sugar, so I'm having to learn to plan a little more. It's a bit of a learning curve, and one that might go more smoothly if I weren't so hormonal.

As for that, I've been feeling a bit frumpy and bloated. I'm not showing yet but my body definitely feels different. I still feel sick a lot, tired a lot, lightheaded sometimes, and cranky a lot too (Gavin will confirm), but I also feel calm and happy a lot. Like there was a spectrum of light that I viewed the world through before, and now that spectrum has shifted or something. I can't really explain it. Did I tell you my due date yet? Middle of April—right about tax day. Something good to look forward to instead of taxes. We haven't decided yet whether we want to know the gender. I do; Gavin doesn't. The question is whether we'll just go ahead and have the doctor tell me but not tell Gavin, or if we'll both be in it together, whether we know or not. It would be hard to know and not somehow slip and say "he" or "she." And if I knew, I wouldn't want to go on calling the baby an "it." Another compromise. I had no idea how many compromises there would be to making a marriage work! That's why they call it "making it work," I guess, rather than "making it easy."

Anyway, this is what I want you to do. First, this is something Gavin does when he's feeling stressed that he's taught me, and it's wonderful. When you wake up in the morning and are lying in bed, before you start fretting and worrying (and I know you do), start telling yourself, "Something fabulous is going to happen today. Something amazing. Today is going to be a spectacular day." Just say it to yourself over and over until you believe it. And then throughout the day you have to keep your eyes open for that something amazing, because invariably something amazing happens almost every day, if you're paying enough attention to the little things. Starting the day with that feeling of joyful anticipation, and then going through the day with your attention wide open like that, maybe I sound new-agey and Alexandra-esque (no offense to Alexandra) but I swear to you it makes for a good day.

And second, I want you to get a bunch of small pieces of paper, and on each of them I want you to write out one of your fears or insecurities. Then, take yourself out to that beach bonfire and burn them all. And take Erin with you and have her do the same. Maybe there's something in the air. These are challenging times, uncertain times, and I feel like people around the world are a little on edge. Breathe deep and believe in yourself. Love Ed, love yourself, love life, and life and Ed and yourself will love you back.

Wish you were here. The world is too big sometimes.

Love you,

Pip.

From: Millie
To: Erin, Alexandra, Ruby, Carolyn, Claire
Sent: October 27, 2010
Subject: Archery

Good morning, ladies! I'm just checking to make sure everyone survived our archery lesson last night. I'm almost shocked that aside from the huge bruise I have on the inside of my left arm, from where the bowstring attacked me, I feel fine. (Now I know to make sure that arm band doesn't slip!) I thought I'd have some sore muscles but I don't. I may try that again sometime! Maybe I'll take Walter along; I think he'd enjoy it.

What are we doing next, Alexandra, our fearless leader? First the laughing club (let's do that again!) then archery, and now …?

Don't forget you're all coming to my house on Saturday for Alexandra's birthday brunch. I'm making everything with a little help from Walter so don't bring a thing. Cinnamon rolls and fresh squeezed orange juice and champagne and scrambled eggs with some cheese and chives, some fruit and maybe some bacon, that should do it. If anyone has any special requests let me know now so I can be sure to have it on hand.

I forgot to ask last night, do any of you play instruments? Claire, you said you play flute, right? Walter is afraid no one will want to join his band. I told him that's silly. Even if only three people show up he can still do something small. It's a start. Any of you play, may I hereby encourage you to please "audition." I promise you'll be accepted. I don't think he'll be turning anyone away. He wants to get together a concert for Christmas so he needs to start ASAP. Anyone who wants to participate in the lecture series thing he's putting together, tell him even sooner. He wants to do that the weekend before Thanksgiving, which leaves him very little time! I doubt he'll have time to bring in outside speakers this time, but maybe for the second annual talks he can. If you have a topic you might like to speak on for ten or fifteen minutes, let him know. Public speaking, that's outside our comfort zones, right, Alexandra?

That's all!

M.

❖

From: Claire
To: Millie, Erin, Alexandra, Ruby, Carolyn
Sent: October 27, 2010
Subject: RE: Archery

Good morning, everyone! Before I forget, Alexandra, I've made Birthday Granola for you. Don't let me forget to give it to you. Carolyn, I owe you some for your birthday last month, too. Who else have I forgotten? It's been a hectic year. If you didn't get granola on your birthday, let me know. I made a big batch yesterday.

Ruby, I don't think I have your birthday on my calendar. When is your birthday?

Millie, yes, I do play flute and will certainly audition. I can't wait to play again!

I am pleased to report that I feel great this morning to, not a sore muscle in sight. Woke up and walked out on the roof and found myself pulling an imaginary bow. I'll be honest, I didn't really think I'd much care for the sport, but I really felt a rush of pride when I got those three arrows in a row right in the bullseye! If only I'd ever been able to repeat it. If anyone goes back to the range to do it again, let me know; I'd love to come along. Ben wants to go sometime, too. Great idea, Alexandra! Tell us, what is next? What great fun this is, trying all these new things. I am feeling invigorated and all my boys are jealous of our fun.

From: Alexandra
To: Claire, Millie, Erin, Ruby, Carolyn
Sent: October 27, 2010
Subject: RE: RE: Archery

Claire, I will admit I was very much hoping you'd make the Birthday Granola! I love that stuff. In fact, would you be willing to share the recipe? It's divine. It will be perfect with the Greek yogurt I've been hooked on lately. Rest assured I'll be by soon to pick it up.

Millie: Public speaking definitely counts as stepping outside your comfort zone. I could do a talk on intuition. I'll find Walter later and discuss it with him.

I'm delighted you all enjoyed the archery so much. Personally I felt something akin to relief, channeling all my focus into a singular point. I've felt so scattered lately. Archery was indeed a great choice, if I do say so myself.

I'm hoping you'll all be just as agreeable about what's next. The Moon Bay athletic center has a special on a four-week session of their "boot camp jump start." You know, those classes that are all the rage, where they kick your ass into shape and you come out looking like a million dollars. I'm sure it's that easy, right? This class has a martial arts focus, with kickboxing and the like, which I thought would be a nice twist. One hour a week, four weeks. Are you all in? Class starts next Monday. I called today to see if they still have room and they do, or if all six of us are up for it we could even have our own private group class.

What say you, warriors?

From: Erin
To: Alexandra, Claire, Millie, Ruby, Carolyn
Sent: October 27, 2010
Subject: RE: RE: RE: Archery

Boot camp? Oh good lord. All right, fine, I'm in.

From: Ruby
To: Erin, Alexandra, Claire, Millie, Carolyn
Sent: October 27, 2010
Subject: RE: RE: RE: RE: Archery

That sounds great! I've always wanted to do something like that. It would be fantastic if we could have our own private class. I don't mind looking like a fool in front of you all. If we're hiring out the instructor just for us, could we have him/her come teach at the gym downstairs rather than our all going to Moon Bay?

From: Millie
To: Ruby, Erin, Alexandra, Claire, Carolyn
Sent: October 27, 2010
Subject: RE: RE: RE: RE: RE: Archery

Do they have medics on site? I am not sure my old heart is quite
ready for boot camp, nor do I think I really need such a thing. I'm
a bit too old for something so trendy and strenuous! Would the
instructor hurt me if I took a slower pace?

From: Claire
To: Millie, Ruby, Erin, Alexandra, Carolyn
Sent: October 27, 2010
Subject: RE: RE: RE: RE: RE: RE: Archery

Alexandra: Birthday Granola recipe below.

All: I am in for the private class, but someone has to promise
to revive me if I faint! What the heck, Alexandra hasn't led us
astray … yet.

Birthday Granola

Ingredients
    4 cups regular rolled oats
    1/2 cup raw almonds, chopped
    1/2 cup raw pecans, chopped
    1/2 cup dried coconut
    1/4 tsp nutmeg
    1 tsp cinnamon
    1/4 tsp sea salt
    scant 1/2 cup maple syrup
    scant 1/4 cup oil
    1 tsp vanilla
    1/2 cup raisins or currants, optional

Directions

*   Preheat oven to 350 degrees. In a large bowl, combine oats, flax seeds, almonds, pecans and coconut. Mix together nutmeg, cinnamon, salt, maple syrup, oil and vanilla in a small bowl and pour over oat mixture. Mix ingredients thoroughly.
*   Thinly spread the mixture on two baking sheets covered with parchment paper. Bake for 10 minutes, stir well and return to oven for another 7 to 8 minutes until granola is lightly toasted. If using raisins, add them after the mixture is cooled. Store in a sealed jar.
*   Makes 7 cups.

Note: I rotate the baking sheets (move the one on the top rack to the bottom rack and vice versa) after the first 10 minutes. It prevents the top batch from getting too toasted.

From: Alexandra
To: Claire, Millie, Ruby, Erin, Carolyn
Sent: October 27, 2010
Subject: RE: RE: RE: RE: RE: RE: RE: Archery

Claire: Thank you for the recipe! I am going to make a batch very soon.

Millie: I'm sure no one will hurt you if you go a little more slowly. I'll double check with the instructor but I'm sure they'd be willing to work with each of us and our individual needs, especially if we're in our own private class.

Ruby: I'll find out if the instructor can come to us. It may be a matter of equipment. I believe giant kickboxing towers are involved.

I think that's almost unanimous. Carolyn, what about you? Are you in?

From: Carolyn
To: Alexandra, Claire, Millie, Ruby, Erin
Sent: October 27, 2010
Subject: RE: RE: RE: RE: RE: RE: RE: RE: Archery

Sorry, just in from a hike with Michael. Yes, sure, I'll give the boot camp a try! I'll tell you, Claire I know what you mean about your boys being envious of us; I think Michael is starting to get jealous of our outings as well. After I told him about our experience last night, he wanted to try the archery, too. He and I are going to go do it again sometime. I'll let you all know in case anyone else wants to come along. Claire, let Ben know that we'll be going soon and we'll be in touch if he's interested.

Millie, I might be able to speak on something at Walter's lecture series. I'll give him a call or stop by later and run the idea by him. I'll be interested to see what sorts of things people come up with! What a great idea!

From: Alexandra
To: Claire, Millie, Ruby, Erin, Carolyn
Sent: October 27, 2010
Subject: RE: RE: RE: RE: RE: RE: RE: RE: RE: Archery

That's everyone then! I'll schedule private classes. Since we're making our own group we may be able to set our own schedule on it. Send me the days of the week that will be best for you all and I'll get it set up. Look out boot camp, here we come!

Text from Ruby to Erin
Sent: October 28, 2010

Hey, have you seen Alexandra? I stopped by to say hi and can't find her.

❖

Text from Erin to Ruby
Sent: October 28, 2010

Haven't seen her. Have you asked Ed?

❖

Text from Ruby to Erin
Sent: October 28, 2010

Ed doesn't know. Something is up with Alexandra. He knows what but isn't saying. I'm going to figure it out!

❖

Text from Erin to Ruby
Sent: October 28, 2010

I am sure you will!

❖

Text from Ruby to Erin
Scnt: October 28, 2010

Want to join us? The dime auction ends at eight; we're going to await the final bids at Ed's with cocktails and hors d'oeuvres starting at about seven. Come by! The bids are getting really high! I can't even believe it!

Text from Erin to Ruby
Sent: October 28, 2010

Thanks, I was just sitting here thinking of going for a walk or down to the beach. Maybe I'll come by after, about 7:30. See you in a bit. x

From: Ruby
To: Pip
Sent: October 29, 2010
Subject: RE: RE: Checking in

Holy moly, Pip! I told you about the dime, right? Last night the auction ended. I still can't believe it. You won't believe it. I'm not even kidding you. One 1975 "no-S" proof dime. (They auctioned the whole proof set, actually, but it's only the dime that's worth anything.) Should be worth ten cents. People who collect coins are crazy. Do you have any idea how much it went for? Are you sitting down?

Three hundred seventy-five thousand dollars. Yes, you read that right. $375,000. Are you kidding me? Are you kidding me! Who in their right mind would pay $375,000 for a tiny piece of metal? And yet someone did. And Ed and Michael are going to give half of that plus half the value of the rest of the coins, to Laurel. Ed hasn't told her yet. She is going to freak out. That's insanity. Ed and Michael still have another dime just like it left.

Well, that will help Laurel's situation a great deal. She was going to have to sell her plane, her livelihood. It's more than her livelihood, really; it's the Cessna her mom used from the time Laurel was a little girl; it's filled with sentimental value, too, memories of her mother. I'm glad she'll be able to keep it.

I went out at lunch today and burned up all those bits of paper like you told me to. You're right about all that whatnot. And you're right about waking up and telling myself something fabulous was going to happen today. It started the day quite nicely. I started to believe something fabulous actually was going to happen! And who knows, it may still.

Alexandra's coming over in an hour for dinner, as is Ed. It's her birthday tomorrow so I wanted to have her for dinner. Tomorrow the poker gals are all doing brunch. It's an Alexandrafest.

Wednesday she has us all starting in on a boot camp class. If I'm still alive after the first session I'll tell you how it went.

Thanks again for your wise thoughts and your love. When did you get so mature? Maybe you're ready to be a mom after all.

Love you,
Ruby

❖

From: Millie
To: Adele
Sent: October 30, 2010
Subject: Hello, friend!

Long time no chat! I hear you might be heading back to bonnie Scotland soon. What is the news there?

I've just turned the dishwasher on, put the tablecloth in the wash, and vacuumed up after those messy ladies were here for Alexandra's birthday brunch, so I thought I'd take a minute to say hello and tell you the latest.

First, of course you'll have heard the big news about Ed and Michael's dime, worth more than a third of a million dollars! Meriwether, could you not have willed that dime to me? Haha! What a find! I think they've promised Ben, who found the treasure, a pretty penny or two. Were it not for him they'd have given up looking for it. Just amazing, literally one of the last possible places on the island. I suppose things are always in the last place you look; only a fool would keep looking. Still, it really was about in the last place they could have looked!

It's interesting to me to see that Ed and Michael are so keen to give all the coins away. Not simply because of the money, but rather because if it were me, I'd keep them for sentimental value. I like history, I like old pictures, I like being able to re-read letters from thirty years ago and I expect thirty years from now I'll enjoy it even more. I keep things. You never know when you'll want to relive those memories.

We talked about that this morning, actually. I'm a collector. Claire is a collector. When you visit you must look at her tea pot collection. Tom put up high shelves all around the top of the walls in the public areas at the Inn and in their kitchen, and her dozens of colorful, decorative tea pots and tea sets line the rooms. Absolutely adorable. She also collects vintage cooking tools, such as old egg beaters and potato mashers and rolling pins and cookie cutters and things that I don't even know what they do. She has those displayed on the walls of the Inn dining room as well, just a lovely collection that makes the room feel warm and cozy. Not disorganized or messy in any way but homey, nice.

Not all the girls think that way, though. Alexandra is something of a purger, but I wonder if that's in part because the memorabilia bring painful memories of the tragic death of her family, the loss of her dreams. Living in the past could be devastating to her, so I do understand her reasoning.

Carolyn is a purger, too. "If I don't need it, I don't want to store it," she said. "That's what the store is for. That's why it's called a store. They'll store it for you." Her storage area in our basement is probably the tidiest of all. "I don't understand the desire to keep all that old stuff," she said about letters and photos and the rich paraphernalia of a life well lived. I suggested that as she gets older she might change her mind. "I have the memories. I'd rather keep them." But what about when her memory goes? "Well, then I won't remember anyway, will I?" I don't understand that way of thinking. It seems that our history and ancestors are such an important part of who we are. I can't imagine not wanting to hang on to that. But, for Carolyn "It's just stuff. Clutter. I don't want to live my life in the past, reliving the lives of people from a hundred years ago. If I spend all my time organizing the detritus of the past, I'm not living in the present. I very consciously choose to live in the now, in the moment. What's done is done and really doesn't matter except in how it's formed who I am—and that is something I carry with me, not something I put away in storage."

To each her own, I suppose, but I like my memories and won't be throwing away my old albums any time soon. In fact, I think I'll go look through them again now. They make me smile; is there a crime in that? Remembering all the people I've been lucky enough to know, reminiscing on how things used to be. I enjoy that. I really think she'll change her mind when she's my age, but time will tell.

What really bothers me, I suppose, is that Ed and Michael are also both purgers, which means these memorabilia of Meriwether are in danger. Ben still has all those old letters (he tells me he hasn't found anything else of exceptional note), and I hope he'll hang on to them because I worry Ed and Michael would toss them into the recycling. That would be such a shame. My memories of Meriwether are among my favorites and I would hate to lose tangible reminders of the man. I once heard of someone who had kept journals from the age of twelve, and rather than risk someone coming along and reading them after she died, she went and shredded every one of them. A shame. Who could do such a thing? A crying shame.

On another note, tomorrow is Halloween! Time for the old Wishing Rock trick-or-treating fun. Each floor is assigned a "home" half hour where the people on that floor stay and answer their doors while all the other people from all the other floors come to them. That way everyone gets to trick-or-treat, but there are also people at home to hand out the treats. You will likely not be surprised to learn that we start early, about six in the evening, and at the end of it all we have a potluck. Speaking of which, I have to decide what to cook. I also must finish getting my costume ready tonight. I'm going as a palm tree. I have warm places on my mind!

Alexandra has decided we all need to go to an exercise "boot camp" in our efforts to support Erin (and Alexandra) through their tough times, so we will do that later this week; I think I heard it's on Wednesday but I'm not sure. I can imagine you know my reaction to this. But, I will support them if it kills me! Hopefully it will not literally kill me. Wish me luck. If you don't hear from me again it was nice getting to know you.

On that note, I'm off to slip into the past with my old letters and photos. Safe travels back to Scotland when you go. I asked Walter if he wanted me to tell you hello on his behalf. He said "I don't know her and she doesn't know me, but all right, if it would make you happy, tell her I said hello." I guess he has a point. At any rate, Walter says hello. And even though I don't know Liam, please pass on my love.

All my best,
Millie

From: Adele
To: Millie
Sent: October 31, 2010
Subject: RE: Hello, friend!

Hello, Millie,

Wonderful as always to hear from you. Yes, we've decided to head back to Scotland, probably next week. We're not done with Switzerland yet but both Liam and I feel we need a little time with family right now. I want to be with Pip through at least part of her pregnancy, and in talking with her she's been sounding a little homesick as well. Granny can help with that! Liam misses his family too, his kids and grandkids. The time is right to head back for a bit, and while we're there we can start planning the next journey.

Interesting discussion you all had. I can see both sides of the collector/purger debate. One thing with which I'm sure you'll agree, Millie, is that you and I came from more frugal generations. We didn't get rid of things like people do today. We had so little to start with that we learned very early not to waste. My father, for example, had an incredible knack for repurposing the scraps of life. We couldn't afford the extravagant collections people have today, and we never had so much that we found ourselves taking loads of items to charity or the dump. We had what we needed, and barely more. I think it turned some of us into collectors—people who felt they never had enough—and some of us into purgers—those of us who felt we always had plenty, and no need to collect more now.

I do keep some things, certainly. Letters from my husband are amongst my most cherished possessions, and I still have every one. I also will never give up the few letters my parents ever wrote me; even if I never look at them I like to know they're still around.

However, when it came time to consolidate my belongings for storage before I headed to Scotland earlier this year, I got rid of about ninety percent of the old photos I'd collected over the years. I kept some, but realized there were many that were simply taking up space. I was never much of a collector either. Some people say they find dusting meditative but it's always been nothing more than a bother to me, and knick knacks always need dusting. Still, over eighty years a woman accumulates some items that are infused with memories and meaning. They may not look like a correlated set to anyone else, but to me they show the footprints of my life's journey. These few special things, hardly any of which have any actual value, are priceless to me. They'll be with me until I die.

And, do you know, it isn't the trinkets that matter so much as the stories anyway. Having someone to share the stories with and having someone to hear the stories from. I remember so well one day when I was in my late sixties, sitting around at a family dinner talking with my siblings, and the question came up of what our parents did with the two older children when the time came for me to be born, since my mother did not labor long with me; I came very quickly. Did Dad pack them up and take them to the hospital with him? Did he drop them off at our grandparents? No one knew the answer, and we all looked around at each other with the sudden realization: There was no one left to ask; no one still alive who would know the answer. It's our stories that matter more than our trinkets, and the day you realize you will learn no more of your past because there is no one left to tell it, that day is a sobering day. That day you are slapped in the face with the finitude of time.

I eagerly await reports of your "boot camp." I admire you all for your loyalty to each other. Not everyone has such good friends that they would collectively submit to such torture in an effort to cheer someone up. I hope Erin perks up soon. One thing you learn the older you get, life is cyclical. Ups and downs, swings of the pendulum, that's just the way it is. It's easier to get through the tough days when you've been there and back so many times. I might like to add more years to this wonderful life, but I'd tack them on the end, not the beginning. The only thing I don't like about getting old is getting closer to the end, and losing so many loved ones along the way. That, and not being able to get around like I used to—I might like to have my young knees and young skin and young muscles back. I certainly do my best, though. Use it or lose it. I'm using it as much as 1 can!

Happy Halloween to you, my friend! Liam says to tell you and Walter both hello.

Adele

NOVEMBER

November 1, 2010
Wishing Rock News
Millie Adler, editor
Letter from the Editor

Dear Rockers,

Hear ye, hear ye! A quick note to let you know, the gauntlet has been thrown down. In a recent conversation amongst Carolyn, Claire, Tom, and Michael, apparently Tom and Michael got their peacock feathers up and challenged each other to a duel. A duel of baking. That's right, Tom and Michael, each convinced that he somehow through osmosis from years of watching his wife bake has himself become an expert baker, are having a bake-off.

The showdown will take place, wooden spoons will be wielded, flour will fly, on Saturday, fourth floor Commons, high noon. The challenge is threefold: best traditional cookie, best cake, best brownie/bar cookie. A prize has been decided upon: In addition to great prestige and bragging rights, the winner will be awarded a Golden Apron. Loser has to sew and present the Golden Apron.

Spectators are invited to bring potluck items to share whilst witnessing the wreckage. Don't bring dessert. There will be plenty! Hopefully some of it may even be edible! We'll see you there!

From: Ruby
To: Pip
Sent: November 2, 2010
Subject: The scoop

Okay, you're sworn to secrecy. Not that this is anything really secret but I don't want Erin to hear anything before the parties involved are ready to tell.

Alexandra still doesn't have her psychic powers back but that girl still has some good intuition. Last Friday I had her (and Ed) over for dinner for her birthday (which was Saturday), thinking "I'll get to the bottom of whatever is going on!" but apparently I was more transparent than I thought. She came in the front door with a look on her face that clearly said, "Honey, you do not have me fooled, and you're lucky I put up with you."

We mixed up cocktails and sat down in the living room for appetizers. (Ed made bacon-wrapped asparagus—surprisingly tasty! Recipe below. And you can justify it because: vegetables!) As soon as we were settled, Alexandra started right in: "Okay, what exactly is it that you want to know?"

"What do you mean?" I said, so coy I am!

Alexandra shook her head, smiling that soft amused smile of hers that I love.

"Well fine, then," I said. "What's going on with you? What's the big secret?" I mean, she seemed open to talking about it, so why not just jump in?

Ed held up his hands in a motion of deflection. "I didn't say a thing." This is true. He didn't say a thing. What kind of boyfriend doesn't tell me everything?

"I know you didn't, Ed." She wiped her fingers on a napkin, then smoothed out the fabric of her skirt on her lap. "It's nothing scandalous. I just found myself in a situation that I wasn't sure how to handle and I asked Ed for his thoughts."

Not scandalous? Surely that meant it was scandalous! My lady, you doth protest too much.

I raised my eyebrows and tilted my head toward her, ready to listen. "Tell me," I indicated with a nod of my chin and a wiggle of my brows.

Whereas she seemed so eager to talk at first, now she took her time. Scratched her nose. Pouted her lower lip for a moment, heaved a sigh.

"It's not easy, re-entering male-female relationships after avoiding them for so long," she said. "For one thing, it's unfamiliar. For another thing, the self-protection instinct is strong, so I'm finding it hard to accurately read signals. What might be signals, I assume are not. What might not be, I wonder if they might be. It's confusing. And there are other difficulties."

She stopped and looked at Ed.

"Difficulties?" I asked. That sounded undoubtedly scandalous.

"Mmhmm. Well, Wishing Rock isn't exactly the biggest pond when one is looking for fish," she said.

My mind whirred. Indeed, Wishing Rock is not the biggest pond. I could think of only a few eligible and available bachelors, and only one that might cause her consternation ....

"David!" I said, half question, half exclamation.

She nodded.

"David!" I repeated. "Are you dating David?"

"I'm not dating David," she said. "Not yet anyway. He heard about all our 'comfort zone' experiments, though, and how you all nixed the idea of dance lessons. He called and told me he had been thinking of taking some dance lessons. If I wanted to go, he'd go with me."

"David," I said, contemplating the ramifications. Then, "Erin." Sure, Erin dumped him, but dumping someone doesn't mean you're ready for them to move on. (Case in point: Jake.) We like to think a person can't survive without us, I think. We like to believe we were the one thing that kept them breathing. Not that we're so instantly replaceable. And while she dumped him, I'm not so sure she was actually over him herself.

"Erin. That's what I sought out Ed's opinion on. Certainly a person is allowed to take a class with another person without it meaning anything, right? Ed and I are a man and woman who are good friends, nothing more. I can go somewhere with Ed and no one raises an eyebrow, but that's because people know us and have grown used to our friendship. Why is it that in general if a woman goes out with a man that people assume it's a date? Can't it just be two people getting to know each other as human beings? Can't it just be two people who are curious to find out more about other people, and go do something fun together?"

The age-old question of whether men and woman can be just friends. Anyone witnessing Ed and Alexandra long enough would have to admit it's possible, but I know first-hand that it can take a bit for their significant others to really understand that it truly is platonic. I'll admit it, more than once I've been jealous of Alexandra, of her connection with Ed, of how close they are and how well they know each other. Sure, I want a guy who is loyal and knows how to keep a secret, and granted he and I have only been dating a few months, but I'll tell you, Pip, I couldn't help but be a little piqued when he wouldn't tell me Alexandra's "secret." I respect that he didn't betray her confidence, but there's this part of me that felt peeved and put off. Like he was picking her over me. He wasn't, I know. I absolutely want a partner who is respectful of other people's requests and privacy. But it did sting a bit.

"Is that all it was?" I asked. "Just a platonic night out? Was it platonic from his perspective too, or do you think he wanted more? Is that where you were last week, the night the auction bidding ended?"

"That's where I was the night the auction bidding ended," she confirmed. "We went to a dance class over at Moon Bay. "Ballroom dancing, some fox trot, some waltz, some rumba, just some basics. But we had a great time. I went in with the idea that it was nothing more than a chance to dance, have fun, and also get to know David. I don't know what his intentions were. I can't read minds." Anymore.

"So it was just two people out having purely platonic fun? That's the idea you went in with, but how did you feel coming out?" I asked.

To be honest, I don't think I've really seen Alexandra squirm before. She fidgeted and adjusted the hem of her shirt and played with the corner of her napkin. The answer was evident.

"It started out that way. That's all it is still. For now. But …."

Aha! Busted. "But you want more?"

"But I want to have the option of more. I don't know what I want yet. I don't want to hurt Erin but I also can't truncate my own life for someone else. Very few people in relationships aren't already someone else's ex. I wanted to get Ed's opinion on the topic because of his perspective on what happened with Jake and you, and him."

"Yeah, that wasn't ideal. Erin is in Jake's position on that one, except that she dumped David whereas I …. Well, 'dumped' is such a harsh word. I'm the one that called off the relationship with Jake." I still regret that my relationship with Ed almost ripped apart his friendship with Jake. It has healed some with time, but it's not the same as it once was. I suppose, though, that all friendships go through changes, ebbs and flows, no matter what. It's the nature of life. There are no guarantees that Jake and Ed would have been best friends forever if I hadn't come along. Something else could have happened. It seems that sometimes you have to trust that if a relationship is meant to be, then it will weather the storms. If it wasn't meant to be, then if one thing doesn't break it apart something else will. And true friendships can withstand some time apart, too, some time in which each person grows separately before they come back together and enrich the friendship with what they've learned about themselves in the meantime. I was thinking about that the other day, actually, an analogy of my heart as a giant parking lot. Some people come, park in my heart, and stay a while. Some people drive right through, decide the lot doesn't look right to them, and leave without ever stopping. Others bring their cars in once, park, and leave shortly thereafter. And then there are those reserved spots, for people who may not even show up all that often, but whenever they do, there's a place for them.

"I thought about talking with Jake to get his thoughts, but decided not to rub salt in old wounds," Alexandra continued. "Besides which, he might still be bitter enough that his opinion would be influenced by the residual pain. I knew Ed wouldn't judge me if I took a path different from however he might advise."

"Are you going to tell Erin?" I asked, imagining the conversation. On the one hand, Erin might not be so pleased. On the other hand, what could she say?

"Yes, but I'm not quite sure how. It's still too early between David and me; we're not dating or anything. But I don't want her to hear it through the rumor mill and wonder why I didn't tell her myself. People start jumping to conclusions before there are conclusions to be jumped to. Even if we're not 'dating,' people will make assumptions, and she'll get wind of it. It's awkward."

I had to agree. What would be the point of saying "I'm going to go have dinner with your ex-boyfriend, but I have no idea if it means anything to either of us?" It would just create more questions that Alexandra wouldn't be able to answer. Still, Erin is one of Alexandra's best friends.

"I think you should tell her," I said. "I know it's early and things still might not happen, but I think you should tell her."

And so, that was Alexandra's big mystery. She is going to tell Erin; I'm not sure how or when, or even how Erin will take it. I never got the feeling that Erin thought she would go back to David; the break-up had a much stronger feeling of conclusion. Erin needed to work on herself a bit, apart from David or anyone, and she's a smart woman. Even if she wasn't fully over him when she broke up with him, she had to know that David might well not be around still when she was ready again. That's the chance we take, when we let something go; it might not come back.

As for Alexandra and David, it's a pairing I never envisioned, and yet I think it has potential. They're both kind souls, gentle people, people who are more quiet about their passions. Maybe that's just the right combination for each of them. And it would be so great to see Alexandra in a relationship, since I know that's what she wants. She is kick-ass strong on her own, but her heart is telling her the time is right to find someone to share her life with, so I hope she finds it.

Time will tell. And then I'll tell you. Don't tell Erin yet, until you know she knows.

Let's see, other than that, Ed is on his way up to Alaska tomorrow to talk with Laurel, tell her about the dime auction, and hand over a check for half the earnings from the toolbox. I can't wait to hear her reaction. I can't even imagine. Changing the course of her life. Tomorrow night the poker gals are going to a boot camp workout. Keep me in your thoughts. I hope we survive.

Hello to my niece/nephew and to Gavin! I love you all.
Ruby

Bacon-wrapped Asparagus

Ingredients
Bacon
Asparagus
Dijon mustard for dipping

Directions
Preheat oven to 400 degrees. Snap woody ends off the asparagus spears. Wrap a slice of bacon tightly around a spear of asparagus. Place on parchment-covered baking sheet. Repeat with as much asparagus as you want to make. Bake for 25 minutes or until bacon is cooked. Serve with dijon mustard.
Ed's note: Asparagus is optional.

From: Pip
To: Ruby
Sent: November 3, 2010
Subject: RE: The scoop

Thanks for the bacon asparagus recipe. Gavin wants to try it immediately, taking heed of Ed's note. Brilliant man, my Gavin!

You said: "Apparently I was more transparent than I thought." I hate to tell you, Ruby: You're always more transparent than you think. Your face is an open book. You think with your face. No one is every really unsure where they stand with you.

So, Alexandra and David! Now I'm intrigued about this silent spelunking Casanova you have in your midst, wooing all the ladies before they know they've been wooed. He swoops in, takes hearts. Makes me think about something a friend of mine once said, long ago in high school, on looking at all the toothpaste options in the store. "We have too many options. I wish we lived in Russia." Sometimes, it seems, when your choices are limited it's easier to love what's in front of you.

Not to say that David is like bad toothpaste. I'm just saying you guys seem to cycle through the available bachelors. I suppose the more I get to know the people of Mull, the more I might find that to be true here as well. But maybe you all should branch out? Aren't there two other towns on that island? Moon Bay and that other one at the top, the small one ... Balky Point, is that it? You never know. Maybe someone's prince charming is up at Balky Point.

Alexandra's right. David could be perfect for her and if she holds back due to his having dated Erin, she'd never find that out. We're not fifteen anymore. Erin's an adult and if she doesn't like Alexandra dating David then she needs to look inside herself and ask why she would deprive someone else of happiness just so she can wallow in her own choices. That said, no one has said anything to Erin yet, so we shouldn't assume how she'll react.

I'm excited Gran is coming home. "Home," I suppose. Where does she officially live now, anyway? I'm glad she's coming back to Oban. I miss that lady. The whole family is excited to see both Liam and her. Plans are underway for a welcome home ceilidh. It's going to be a good time.

Keep me updated on the scandal! Love to all.

Pip

From: Ruby
To: Ed
Sent: November 4, 2010
Subject: Laurel?

Hey babe,

I'm at work. (Don't tell my boss I'm writing you from work). Do you know what I think would be a great improvement to my office space? (This part you can tell my boss.) Either a heated massage chair or a work station that somehow lets me work from a hot tub. Anything to help with this pain! Oh my gosh, Ed, I am in such intense pain. Did I actually agree to this?

Last night was our first boot camp class. I've figured out the instructor's primary goal: work us so hard that we become physically incapable of moving fast enough to murder him. I realize the term "boot camp" should have been a clue, but I thought it would be cute and fun, somehow. I don't know why. By the end of an exercise in which the instructor basically had me doing pushups while moving with my arms around the whole perimeter of the room, my vocabulary was reduced to five words: "are you effing kidding me?" (I may have used a substitute for "effing.") "Kick higher," he said while I was attacking the padded kicking tower with all the strength I could muster. "I'll show you a high kick," I think, "Just come a little closer."

His name is T.J. I think he goes by his initials so we can't track him down.

Immediately after the class I was actually mighty impressed with myself. From five minutes into the class until the moment we started to cool down, I alternately thought I was going to either throw up or die. Once it was over I was tired but thought, sure! Look at me! I can do this! I thought, I'm a little sore but nothing I can't handle. I'll take some ibuprofen when I get home and all will be well.

Oh, so naive.

This morning while washing my hair, I thought "why does my head have to be so far away from my arms?" And do you know my theory on why men might like working out more than women? Because men pee standing up. If, after an evening of boot camp torture on your thighs, you had to squat every time you had to pee, you might think twice about it too. I'd just barely started to sit when I found myself wondering if I might just hold it, after all.

Pain. Every cell is in pain. No, wait, I just did a mental full body scan. My eyelids are fine.

And we get to do it again on Friday! Wednesday and Friday this week, Monday/Wednesday/Friday the next three weeks. I seriously hope I don't die.

Before the beginning of the class Millie straight up told T.J. she was going to take it at her own pace, and if he didn't like it he could lump it. I'm wondering if I can convince T.J. when I see him on Friday that I'm actually thirty years older than I'd originally said, and I need to take the slow train too. Erin and Carolyn bopped through the class with hardly a care (it seemed). Alexandra and Claire were about at my pace. Erin isn't in yet and I haven't seen anyone else. I wonder how the others are faring.

In an interesting choice of timing, Alexandra asked Erin to come up to her room to talk after class. I hope that went well.

How did it go with Laurel?

xx

Ruby

From: Ed
To: Ruby
Sent: November 4, 2010
Subject: RE: Laurel?

Hey babette,

Your wish is my command. I've just been on the phone with the contractor, and the construction workers will be over to get right on that massage chair/whirlpool tub for your office space. Nothing is too expensive or impractical for the woman I love! They should be there in ten minutes. Promise! They're also bringing you a baby koala and a trampoline. Thought I'd throw in a few extras just for kicks.

Sorry to hear you're so sore. You can do it, though! I believe in you! What's four weeks? It'll fly by. Hang in there!

Yup, I went out to Laurel's house this morning. I called her up and she said to come on over. I don't know what she was expecting but it wasn't a check for two hundred thousand dollars.

First she was speechless, then she started crying silently. I went to the kitchen and got her a glass of water (why do people get water for crying people? Something to do? Trying to replace the water loss?), and by the time I was back she'd calmed herself down a bit. She asked me over and over if I was sure, if I wanted to be repaid, if I was sure. Yes, no, yes. It's yours.

"I've had to be courageous, put on a brave face, for so long," she said. "First through Mom's sickness and death, then through trying to figure out how to save myself from ending up on the street. Through it all I had no time or place to relax. Never a moment that a part of me wasn't worried sick. And now ... are you for real? Is this a dream?" She laughed. "I wish we were related, not because I want your money but because ..." She stopped, looked at the check. I noticed in that moment how quiet it was.

I've missed that quiet. Wishing Rock is quiet but in an island way; you can always hear the waves, the gulls, there's always something. Alaska is quiet in the way that only a vast, sparse, isolated land can be. I heard myself think; I could almost hear Laurel think. "Because you're someone I'd like to be related to," she finished.

She still lives in the cottage she lived in with her mother. It's a small but cozy log cabin. Laurel said it was built by a neighbor in the eighties, a retired man, a bachelor, halfway between a smitten suitor and a father figure to Rita, who said he was "bored" and took it on himself to create a beautiful space for them. A great room, kitchen, dining room, master suite downstairs. Upstairs a bedroom, bathroom, and a loft open to below. The kitchen table, a rough and rustic crosscut slab of a giant tree. Chairs made from beautifully carved tree stumps. Well-worn leather chairs in the great room, a rocking chair with a crocheted blanket draped over the back, a black iron wood stove in the center of the house, its pipe rising clear up to and out the top of the second floor. No stereotypical bearskin rug nor deer heads on the walls, but still, this is an Alaska home. I realize I'm in Alaska so I may sound crazy when I say her house took me back to Alaska, but it did; it took me back to my childhood, to growing up spending time in homes like this. Our own homes growing up were a bit different at times, but I knew so many people with homes exactly like this. I guess I do miss Alaska a bit. Moving to Wishing Rock was the right thing to do, but maybe, some day …. Maybe some day you should come up here with me on vacation. You should see this place (by which I mean Alaska, not Laurel's home). It's breathtaking.

While we were sitting at the kitchen table talking, suddenly I caught sight of a willow ptarmigan outside flying right into the snow bank, and then another right behind it. I pointed it out to Laurel. She smiled widely. "That's Mom," she said. I gave her a look. "Yes, it's a willow ptarmigan, but it's Mom, saying hello.

They do that, those ptarmigans—they fly into snow banks and burrow in. They don't walk up because if they did they'd leave tracks and their predators could find them. So they fly right into the snow. When I was little and first saw a bird do that, I screamed. I thought it was hurting itself. Mom told me about their habit, and we spent the next half hour dive-bombing ourselves into the side of some giant snow drifts, trying to burrow in like the bird had. After that the willow ptarmigan, especially in its pure white winter plumage, was special to Mom and me. I know, it's the state bird, it's common as they come, but to us it brought memories. Then later when I learned to spell ptarmigan I was all the more smitten, such a crazy way to spell a word.

"Before Mom died, we'd see ptarmigan around often enough, here by the house or out there in the meadow. But three days after she died I was sitting right here at this table for hours, and I swear to you, all day long there were ptarmigans out there, near and far, a constant flurry of them. I knew it was Mom's way of letting me know she's still here. And the winter white ones that crash into the snow," she shook her head, "that's Mom for sure."

Now I want to decide on a sign, something that after I die, people will know for sure is a sign from me that I'm still here and I'm okay. Butterflies? Rainbows? Too ordinary. I'll have to think of something else.

Anyway, the check is in Laurel's hands now, and I hope it will help. I know money doesn't solve everything but I do think this will cover all the bills and let her get on with her own life without being tied to the past by debt. She's been through enough.

I'm grateful that I have the means to give away money, but I wish I could give her back her mother.

I'm going to take another day up here to wander around the old stomping grounds. I'll be back Saturday, I'm guessing. I'll probably miss the big bake-off. If I do, cheer Michael on for me.

See you soon,

Love you.

Ed

From: Alexandra

To: Ed

Sent: November 5, 2010

Subject: revelations

Darling Ed,

How has your old neck of the woods been treating you up there in the cold frozen tundra? Ruby mentioned that you've been a bit nostalgic. Do you ever think of moving back? Wishing Rock would miss you desperately. I would miss you even more. Selfishly, I am going to say you are not allowed to move anywhere. Selflessly, I will say that if Alaska should ever call to you loud enough that you heed the call, you simply must be sure to have a guest room with my name on it.

I could perhaps use that guest room right about now. I am not the most popular person in Wishing Rock these days, after subjecting the girls to this boot camp. But complain as they may, they all went back to the second class yesterday. I don't think it hurts that young T.J. isn't so bad to look at, and he knows just what to say to motivate each person to push on to her best. That's what we're paying him for, after all. Having him all to ourselves is such a treat, and I mean that in a purely instructional sense. I'm not entirely sure Claire needs quite as much help and guidance as she has been requesting from our Instructor Charming, but who am I to deny a friend a simple pleasure?

Wednesday after class, I took advantage of Erin's exhausted state and invited her up to my room to talk. I was hoping physical fatigue might lend itself to emotional candor. And also that if she were angry with me, she would be incapable of inflicting bodily harm. (I failed to consider that if she did try, I might be incapable of escaping. Lucky for all parties involved, the need to fight or flee never came up.)

Noting our post-boot camp aromas, we agreed to each shower before our chat. Once she was squeaky clean and refreshed, and I was as well, Erin came over, both of us in our flannel pajamas, our warm robes, our cozy slippers.

Not wanting to start right in about David, I began by asking how she has been as of late.

"I'm fine," she said, running her fingers through her short, dark hair, still slightly damp from the shower. "Actually, I'm embarrassed. I'm embarrassed to be the center of all this attention. I appreciate the thought and the kindness, of course, but I'm embarrassed to have everyone focused on me. I'm embarrassed to have shown such weakness. I'm embarrassed that people now know I'm not as together as I want everyone to believe. I'm embarrassed to have all my messy dichotomies exposed. I'm embarrassed that everyone now knows I don't have everything all figured out, as I should by this advanced age. As everyone else seems to have."

I had to laugh. "Erin, Erin, Erin! No one has it all figured out, believe me. Some people are better masters of disguise than others, but no one has it all figured out. At best, people learn not to worry so much, or they learn to cope better, or they learn what to ignore. But we all have our issues. We all have our messy dichotomies.

"The thing is," I continued, "each of us is too busy being the center of our own universe to really much notice whether anyone else has it all together. Furthermore, anyone's assessment of whether someone else has it all together has far more to do with that person than the person being judged. Bitter, angry people will always find fault. Kind, compassionate people will always give others the benefit of the doubt, or at least try to. Neither is a true expression of reality. It's all subjective and to that degree, it doesn't matter."

"But now everyone knows I'm a mess," she said. "No more pretending to be perfect, I guess."

Perfection, why does anyone strive for this, when it's a moving target anyway? Who defines it, who decides?

"I hate to tell you, my love, but no one thought you were perfect to start with. The only person whom any of us thinks is perfect is ourselves, and that's only when we are righteously comparing ourselves to someone who has gotten our proverbial goat."

We talked a bit more on the topic. I think she's generally okay, just going through one of the troughs of life. She did admit that however reluctant she may have been to go try archery, the laughter club, the boot camp, and so on, she does feel better when she gets out to try something new. I think that's the key, Ed. When times are tough the best thing we can do is attempt that which we are sure we cannot do, that which stretches and challenges us. I really believe it. There is strength and confidence in both attempt and accomplishment.

Finally we moved on to David.

"About David, then…." I said.

"Alexandra, don't start in on me about David. I know you all think I should have stayed with him but it just wasn't working for me. It wasn't the right time. I know he's a great guy, you all have told me that a million times, but he's not right for me, not now."

Hmm. I cleared my throat. "Well, that's not exactly what I was going to say." I explained how he'd invited me to the dance class, how we'd gone, how I'd had a great time, how I didn't know where it was going but I was hoping to find out.

She was clearly taken aback. "Are you asking me for my permission?" she said. "I don't know ... I don't know that I want to give it."

Reminding myself not to escalate the tension but rather to respond with as much love and understanding I could muster, I said, "I'm not asking. We're adults, we both know that. I wanted to give you the courtesy of being the one to tell you. As I said, I don't know where this will go. I don't know if we'll date. What is dating, anyway? Where does not dating end and dating begin? We enjoyed each other's company, and that's enough for now. David is an interesting man. Fascinating, really. Did you know he's one of the few people in the world ever to gain entrance to Lechuguilla Cave in Carlsbad Caverns, in New Mexico? He heard about its discovery when he was a young teenager, and instantly became determined to see it. That's how he got started in spelunking, actually. In his early twenties he started petitioning the powers that be to let him go in. It took him five years but he finally got approval. He's promised to show me the photos. From his descriptions, it sounds absolutely magical."

"I didn't know that," said Erin, her brow furrowing. I wondered what they had talked about all that time they were together, or if Erin had had her defenses up from the start. Everyone is fascinating, Ed, if you only get them on the right topic. Everyone has passion in them, whether or not they know it or believe it. You just have to be patient, listen, ask questions. Eventually you'll find it.

I went back to the point at hand. "This is difficult, for both of us," I said. "I don't want to hurt you, you know that. My intent in getting to know David better is not at all to hurt you."

"Couldn't you wait a while? I mean, just a few months, maybe?" she said.

I didn't answer, but let her chew on her thoughts for a while. I got up, made us both some cocoa with a nip of Irish cream for good measure, handed Erin's cup to her, and snuggled back into my couch.

Finally, she spoke. "Sometimes, it's hard knowing I have to be an adult about things. It would be so much easier to tell you you're simply not allowed to date him and if you do you're awful and horrible and the worst friend ever."

"I understand," I said. "And while I know that logically there's no reason for me not to spend time with David, I was concerned for your feelings. It's awkward."

"Wishing Rock sometimes seems really really small," she said.

"I think it's good for us," I said. "In bigger cities, if someone crosses you, you can just avoid them rather than deal with it. Here, we have to face each other, like it or not. If we can't learn to live with each other, we'd fall apart. I think small communities by necessity cultivate kindnesses. Or at least tolerance. And maybe more honesty. True feelings will come out sooner or later when there's nowhere to hide."

"Maybe I need a break from all this honesty," she said. "I could do with a little anonymity sometimes, a little more space between me and everyone's prying eyes."

We talked a bit more about that, about her thought of maybe living somewhere else for a few months. There's merit to the idea; we all need some space to think sometimes when our hearts are raw. She isn't making any decisions this year but come 2011 we may be sending her off for a bit. We will see.

And so, I survived the talk. Strange, isn't it, how telling people the truth can sometimes be so frightening? Our hearts. We don't give them enough credit. They are, after all, quite hearty, are they not? Isn't that where the word comes from? Our hearts can survive so much more than our fears are willing to throw at them. Or if we get precise about the seat of emotions—disregarding the continued debate on where that may actually be; for our purposes I shall declare our souls to be our emotions' home—if the soul is the seat of our emotions then we are paying even less due. For souls are, after all, eternal, and certainly they can weather a rejection or an angry friend now and again within a single lifetime.

In the same vein, perhaps we don't give friends enough credit sometimes either. I was worried about how Erin would react to my news about David, and not completely unjustifiably so, but it seems life will go on. As with you and Jake, time will heal. Time and love heal all wounds. The earth continues to turn, the sun continues to rise, we each continue to stumble our way through. I will tell you this, though: The solution to all of it, the fears, the worries, the anger, the madness, is love. Love and forgiveness, rinse and repeat as necessary, love, forgiveness, love.

I'm sorry you'll miss the bake-off. Wish you could be here; this will be fun. I do love our people. We have good people, Ed. Be safe on your journey home, and I'll see you soon.

My love,
Alexandra

From: Erin
To: David
Sent: November 6, 2010
Subject: Alexandra and other entanglements

Hi David,

You all are at the bake-off right now as I write this. Alexandra told me this week about you and her. Don't worry, she doesn't have you married off in her mind or anything; she just mentioned that you're spending time together and she wanted to be the one to tell me, regardless of what happens between you two. She didn't want me to hear through the Wishing Rock grapevine, and that grapevine is extremely short. If she wanted to tell me first, she had to tell me quickly. That's all. Anyway, I didn't think I was up to a public function where the two of you would be together just yet, so I hopped in my car and found myself up at the lighthouse at Balky Point. This island isn't conducive to long drives, is it? The lighthouse, though, that's symbolic enough. Maybe it'll help guide me through the fog. No, there's no wifi up here, of course. I'm typing this up on my laptop and will send it when I get home. As you may have discovered by now, the door's always unlocked at the lighthouse, so I've climbed up to the top. It feels good to be up high. Somehow it feels like it gives me clarity. False confidence, probably, haha.

So, birthday buddy. You know, no matter what happens in life, wherever our paths take us, when I think of you I'll always smile to think that we're birthday buddies. I remember the day I found out … I thought it was fate's hand sending me an indisputable sign, that you were the one for me for now and for all time. Look no further, Erin, you have found your true love.

But life's not a fairy tale. If it was a sign, maybe I read it wrong.

I'm not sure where to start or even what I want to say. I guess … I guess I want to apologize. I know I didn't give you a fair chance, and I know I hurt you when I broke up with you, and I'm sorry.

I like to believe that I'm strong, that I can conquer anything. When I run each morning, sometimes I get such a high that I feel invincible. As it turns out, though, I am no match for timing. You are a wonderful man and I was so lucky to spend those months with you. The timing was wrong, though. That sounds so lame, has always sounded lame when I've heard other people say it. Doesn't love conquer all? Apparently not. You found me just before this time I'm in now, whatever this time may be, but in this time I think I need to be by myself. Or maybe I don't. Maybe that's a cop-out, an excuse. Maybe what I need is to be with someone and to learn to let people love me. I'm sure at some point you've heard those dating rules I made—that I'd never start dating someone between Labor Day and my birthday, because it's just too awkward to start

dating someone December 10, or February 1, and then have to figure out what sort of Christmas or Valentine's Day present is right
for someone with whom one is in an intimate relationships, but for
such a short time; what gift appropriately defines the status and
strength of the relationship. I still believe I'm right; it absolutely is
awkward to figure those gifts out. But the more I look at it the more
I realize those are the rules of a person who is putting boundaries
on her heart, boundaries on love. The more I look at my past relationships, the more I see that this bears out. I made barriers, not
bridges, because I was afraid of letting people in. Is anyone not
afraid of that? I'd think we're all afraid. Some people are just better
at pushing through the fear. Some people are better at believing it
is worth getting to the other side. That's where I want to be so I
need to do some self-exploration, I think, silly as it sounds to write
that. I need to figure out what I want, and convince myself that I'm
stronger than I think I am.

I know you don't need my blessing to date anyone, including
Alexandra, but you have it anyway. She's a wonderful woman and
she's just come through her own barriers to realize she wants more
from life too. Where she goes with those discoveries, I hope to
follow. In the meantime, you are lucky to spend time with her,
and she with you, and I wish you both all the best.

Erin

From: Millie
To: Adele
Sent: November 6, 2010
Subject: RE: RE: Hello, friend!

Hello, Adele!
I'm just in from the Challenge du Jour—Michael and Tom

facing each other in a bake-off. People had a grand time, so much so that I think we need to make this an annual event and get more men involved. It was half cooking show, half comedy hour!

It all began when Michael and Carolyn had Tom and Claire over for dinner one night. Michael and Tom were praising their wives' baking prowess when somehow the topic twisted and each of the men started claiming their own such skills match—nay, surpass!—the ladies'. Thus the gauntlet was thrown down, and the challenge was on.

The rules were basic Wishing Rock rules—meaning, mostly, there were very few rules. The men had to do the baking them-selves and in the fourth floor Commons kitchen area, and supply their own ingredients, but other than that anything went. Noting that skill on one recipe does not a baker make, the men agreed to a three-pronged match, with each baking a cake, a cookie, and a bar cookie/brownie. Judges would be the peanut gallery of what-ever potluckers showed up.

Come noon today, the fourth floor Commons was packed. It is raining today, no surprise, and what else is there to do here on a rainy day? The men had a captive audience, and a hungry one. Not hungry in the spiritual, existential sense. Just hungry. Lunchtime.

In case you are curious, the men made the following:

Cake:

Michael—pumpkin spice Bundt cake

Tom—flourless chocolate torte

Cookies:

Michael—Carolyn's molasses cookies (the one she won't ever give out the recipe to)

Tom—chocolate chip cinnamon chip oatmeal

Bar cookies/brownies:

Michael—chocolate caramel brownies

Tom—magic seven layer bars

Tom had Ben distract Michael while Tom hid Michael's flour. Michael caught Tom just as Tom was pouring Michael's sugar into a container so as to switch it out with salt. Michael engineered audience involvement by getting them to unwrap all the caramels for his chocolate caramel brownies, and ran around hugging every person in the room, sitting in laps or giving floury neckrubs to gain favor. Eventually through the afternoon of chaos the goodies were baked, the potluck was eaten while the baked goods cooled, and then judging commenced. In the end, Tom's cake won out over Michael's, but Michael's cookies and brownies won, so Michael was declared the winner. And we still can't get that molasses cookie recipe out of Carolyn!

Never a dull moment here, we're now gearing up for Walter's Wishing Rock lecture series. I've seen the ideas people are putting forth for their talks and I have to say, I think we're in for a good weekend! That will be the weekend before Thanksgiving. Walter is trying to come up with a witty acronym for it. Wishing Rock Ideas and Theories, perhaps? Thus WRIT? Though that would be better for a writing series, but we don't always do things the way we're supposed to here on Dogwinkle. Ben says he'll video record the talks and put them all up on the Internet, so I'll send you the links when he does.

Meanwhile, stay tuned for possible breaking news on Alexandra and David. They're not being secretive about a blossoming friendship, but nor are they advertising it much. I do know that Alexandra had a chat with Erin about it, but other than that I don't think either has said much to anyone. The walls have eyes, ears, and mouths around here, though, so I'd say anyone who is paying attention (which is just about everyone) has noticed a special spark between the duo. So far I believe they've gone out dancing once, and have shared a dinner once at a restaurant downstairs and once at David's home (but who's counting?). I've also seen them off on a walk or two together, and I've heard rumors that they went out driving together. Do you suppose they were necking in the back seat? Haha! Well, I hope so. I'm delighted for Alexandra that she's found someone to give her a little attention after all this time, a little spark, and while I don't think Erin is too excited about it, I also don't think she's going to put up a fuss. I will keep you informed of any developments.

Thank goodness your email follows you around. I can't keep track of where you are these days. Let me know when you're back home. Walter and I just may visit sometime yet.

All the best,
Millie

Text from Erin to Ed
Sent: November 7, 2010

Hey, doesn't your mom live in Iceland? Does she happen to have a guest room for one of your ex-girlfriends?

Text from Ed to Erin
Sent: November 7, 2010

She does live in Iceland, and she does have a guest room. Which ex-girlfriend? You? What's up?

Text from Erin to Ed
Sent: November 7, 2010

I have a sudden urge to move to Iceland for a few months. Or rather, I have a sudden urge to get away, and Iceland sounds good.

Text from Ed to Erin
Sent: November 7, 2010

It's pretty dark there right now, you know. Almost all day dark, for a while yet. Maybe summer would be a better time to go?

Text from Erin to Ed
Sent: November 7, 2010

I'll think about it. But do you think your mom would be up for a guest?

Text from Ed to Erin
Sent: November 7, 2010

I don't know. I'll get in touch with her and see what she says. You doing okay there?

Text from Erin to Ed
Sent: November 7, 2010

I'm good. I also might enjoy getting somewhere where everyone isn't asking me ten times a day if I'm okay.

Text from Ed to Erin
Sent: November 7, 2010

That won't work, you know. No matter where you go we'll still care about you and worry about you, like it or not. We have ways of asking you ten times a day whether you're okay, even if you're not just down the hall. I'll ask ma and let you know.

Text from Erin to Ed
Sent: November 7, 2010

Thanks, Ed. You're all right.

Text from Ed to Erin
Sent: November 7, 2010

This is true. So are you. Take care of yourself, Erin.

From: Ruby
To: Erin
Sent: November 8, 2010
Subject: ICELAND?

You're moving to Iceland??
    Where are you? Aren't you supposed to be at work by now? Did I forget a distributor run?

From: Erin
To: Ruby
Sent: November 8, 2010
Subject: RE: ICELAND?

Ha, that news actually moved more slowly than I expected.

Yes, I'm on the ferry, distributor run. Back this afternoon.

No, I'm not for sure moving to Iceland. I was thinking it might be good to get away from things for a while. I don't really want to watch David woo Alexandra. Just some time away would be nice. Maybe Iceland. Maybe Croatia. Maybe Greece. Maybe Italy. Who knows.

From: Ruby
To: Erin
Sent: November 8, 2010
Subject: RE: RE: ICELAND?

I was going to say you can't run from your problems, but I suppose if the problem is having to watch your ex woo your friend, then maybe you can. We don't know that David is going to woo Alexandra. Maybe they won't date after all. When would you leave? What would you do in Iceland/Croatia/Greece/Italy/other? Maybe you could just move to Seattle for a while. Pull a reverse Ruby. How long will you be away?

Actually, if you're bound and determined to go somewhere, you could always go to Scotland and stay with Gran or Pip, I'm sure. It'd be cheaper, and they'd love to see you. Or even Gavin's sister in Ireland, Pip says they're nice. I'm trying to think who else I know abroad. Too bad Gran's out of Switzerland, that would be gorgeous!

From: Erin
To: Ruby
Sent: November 8, 2010
Subject: RE: RE: RE: ICELAND?

I haven't decided anything yet (thus Iceland/Croatia/Greece/Italy/other). It's just a thought.

I saw David and Alexandra together in the hall. Body language. It doesn't lie so much. They may not be dating yet but I think they're heading in that direction. Has this been going on longer than the last few weeks? When did she start spending time with him? For all I know they've been having secret lunches for a year. Doesn't it seem quick? Why did she have to pick him? Why do I have to be mature about it? And, frankly, unless some new men move to the island, I'm going to have to go to Iceland/Croatia/Greece/Italy/other to find someone, because there aren't a lot of single men here.

To answer your questions:

I don't know when I would leave, but probably not until after the new year.

I don't know what I would do there. Visit the tourist spots. Do what the locals do. Meet people. Write bad tragic poetry. Throw bread crusts at ducks. Drink wine. Take pictures of sunsets. Buy bright scarves and woolen sweaters. What does a person do anywhere?

I don't know how long I'd be away.

I appreciate the Pip/Gran idea. I'll think about it. Much as I like traveling solo it's nice to have someone familiar to come home to, even away from home.

Don't jump the gun. I'm just thinking. I'm not trying to run away from my problems, you know. We all need space sometimes. Wishing Rock was that space for you, and it worked out okay,

right? Maybe I'll find my Ed in Iceland/Croatia/Greece/Italy/
other. Mostly I just need to think. You know how when you were
young and people were trying to teach you confidence, and anytime someone would hurt you people would say things like "It's
not you, it's them," or "They're the ones with the problems"? Well,
I think that part of maturing is realizing that sometimes, it is you.
If the same thing happens over and over, maybe it's you. With all
these relationships I've had ending the way they have, maybe it's
me. I want to go somewhere, away from everything, and think
about what I want out of life, and what I'm doing to get in my
own way, and how to stop that. So I'm thinking that should take
an hour or two. Haha.

From: Ruby
To: Erin
Sent: November 8, 2010
Subject: RE: RE: RE: RE: ICELAND?

You're right. At some point we have to acknowledge that if something isn't right in our lives, it's up to us to fix it. No one else can.
I hope you do find your Ed, and yourself, and whatever else you're
looking for. I would really miss you but I understand. If you go,
you have to promise you'll come back.

From: Erin
To: Ruby
Sent: November 8, 2010
Subject: RE: RE: RE: RE: RE: ICELAND?

Don't worry. I'll at least visit.

Ferry's docking; talk to you later. Don't forget, boot camp tonight! No escape!

November 9, 2010
Wishing Rock News
Millie Adler, editor
Letter from the Editor

Dear Rockers,

Have we all recovered from the bake-off festivities of the weekend? I think I had a sugar hangover for a bit there. And it's not even December yet! Congratulations, Michael. Well done, you've proven your prowess. Now, of course, we will expect you to take over all baking duties from here on forward!

For the musicians amongst us, and the would-be musicians, Walter's community band is taking shape. If you haven't spoken to him about it and are interested in participating, get in touch with him. Practices will take place Tuesday nights in our auditorium, with extra practices as needed leading up to the first concert, late in December. If you want to be in the band but have no experience whatsoever, don't let that stop you! This band is about the joy of playing, of participating in a group effort, of having fun for the sake of having fun. There are always tambourines to be tamboured, or maybe you could play the spoons or washboard. If you want to have fun and make music, don't delay.

Other exciting news! Our council met yesterday and decided it's time for a Wishing Rock Open House. This is not to say that you all aren't lovely people, but our Box is only a bit more than half full, and a few more characters might liven the place up. The plan is to try for an Open House when Wishing Rock is in its full holiday glory, sometime in December. The council wants to try something new, and stage a condo or two with furniture and decor to help people see the rooms in a warm and welcoming light. If you'd like to help with the Open House Committee please contact the council immediately.

Millie

❖

From: Adele
To: Millie
Sent: November 11, 2010
Subject: Back home

Hello, my Millie!

We are home. I've officially moved in with Liam. Last we were here, I was always at his home anyway. This is much nicer, having my things with me rather than having to go back for a forgotten pair of socks or extra reading glasses or whatever I might have left behind. His house is plenty big enough for the both of us so we have room to get away from one another if need be.

I will say this: it is so much easier to travel around Europe from within Europe. I do love my dear Washington state, but flight times from there to here are unbearable. From within Europe it's all just a hop, skip, and a jump. If I were back home, I might only get to see my great grandbaby once or twice a year if I were lucky. Living here, I'll be able to pop over at a moment's notice. I can't tell you how glad I am to be able to be with Pip right now, especially since the rest of her family is so far away. But then, I do miss all the family back home. I'll surely come to visit home and Wishing Rock sometime, and I can't wait to meet you when I do. Oh and yes, absolutely, you and Walter would be welcomed here with open arms! Has Walter traveled much? We would love to show him around. Scotland is quite accessible by car, and of course

Gavin has the boat to take us to all the islands whenever he has the time. Come visit! You will love it here.

What is the news on Alexandra? I heard whisperings of a new Romeo in her life? Also, has she regained her psychic abilities yet? She must feel naked. Or that feeling when someone has been at your side, and they leave, and suddenly where their body had been touching you feels very very cold. She is a strong woman, though. I am sure she will find her way.

Off we go to a dinner party at the neighbor's. We've quite a busy schedule, dinners all week to welcome us back. If I get to bed before midnight once this week I'll consider myself lucky.

All the best to you and tell your Walter I said hello.

Love

Adele

❖

From: Millie
To: Adele
Sent: November 12, 2010
Subject: RE: Back home

Adele,

So good to hear from you, and glad to know you are safe at home again. There really is no place like home, wherever home may be.

Alexandra! Adele, I tell you, I did not see this one coming. It's the quiet ones you need to worry about! I didn't know David had it in him. Do you know, he's such a solid, logical type that it surprises me somewhat that he'd be interested in a psychic. On the other hand, he didn't start dating her until she lost the gift. And on the third hand, Alexandra is a woman worthy of anyone's love. I'll tell you, I don't know why those voices all went away; I am not privy to the ways of the beyond. That said, frankly, I'm glad they did. I had no clue

Alexandra was in a shell until she started to come out of it. That woman is more alive than ever, glowing, and it's a joy to behold. I know she was scared when her life changed so dramatically, but it seems she made the choice to grab life by the horns and take it on, risk it all, jump in with both feet, and so on and so on, all the appropriate metaphors. She is a woman on fire, dynamic, and leading the way for the rest of us. This theory that happiness comes from taking risks, I am on board with it. I was settled into my comfortable life but with Alexandra we've all been out trying new things, and I've never had so much fun. The joy comes not from the achievement but from the efforts, and the efforts with friends. Boot camp alone would be insufferable, but sharing and laughing about boot camp afterward with other casualties bonds us together. Alexandra's new life has brought new life to us all, and I'm grateful. Very likely that liveliness could be what caught our David's eye. And so now we help Erin find her own peace, and we move ever onward.

Perhaps Walter and I will start planning our dream trip to Scotland. Do you plan to be there a while, then? We couldn't make it out before spring, and I don't imagine the weather there is at its best until then (or later) anyway. Half the fun is in the planning, though. A visit, I shall plan!

My best to you and Liam,
Millie

❖

From: Ruby
To: Pip
Sent: November 13, 2010
Subject: Changes

Hey Pip,

Everything falls apart. That's how it seems sometimes, everything is going along great and then suddenly everything falls apart. But then, maybe it's a matter of perspective, of where you're standing. The moment when at the time everything seemed to be falling apart, in hindsight might actually be just the moment when everything started to fall together.

Here I finally feel my life is just right, Ed is … what's the word even. Ed is amazing. I'm in a community I couldn't love more, I have friends who mean the world to me, I'm starting to feel settled, starting to trust and feel safe, starting to believe in my own happiness. And what happens? Tension between Alexandra and Erin since Alexandra is dating David. (They haven't admitted it yet, but if they aren't they will be soon.) Erin is determined to move away for a bit after the new year to sort through her heart and her priorities and what she wants from life. I guess I can't blame her. I did the same thing, after all. Wouldn't it be nice, though, if the people around us could all live their lives in accordance with our own needs and wishes? I want Erin here with me, but it's not about what I want (though I can't see any reason why it shouldn't be). Makes me think of the cave times, back when people traveled by foot and finding a new home wasn't as easy as searching online. I'll bet people really thought twice about moving away back then, breaking the hearts of the people who loved them. Sure, the whole saber-toothed tiger thing might have made things a little more exciting in those days, but the people, they stayed together. None of this crazy moving five thousand miles away.

I miss you.

That said, now that I'm feeling more settled here I'm starting to think about what more I might want out of life. I was talking with Carolyn about Ed's ED grants the other day, as I have no idea what my dream is.

"Do you know what you would do with a grant?" I asked her.

"Obviously it wouldn't be right for me to get a grant," she said.

"We have more than enough ourselves. I'm not applying."

"No, I know. I'm not either, even though Ed's money isn't mine. It would look weird. But I don't even know what my dream is. How do people figure that out? Do I have to go to Iceland too?"

"You don't have to go to Iceland. You also don't have to have a dream. Some people need dreams and goals, something to strive for; others are perfectly happy letting each day unfold as it may. Who's to say that either way is right? Maybe the first set reach their dreams, but the latter set might be more open to something spontaneous. You don't have to have a dream to be worthy. There's no 'right' way to live."

"But do you know what you'd do if you had the money?"

Of course, she does have the money. "It's more a matter of time and motivation, I guess. It would be fun to create my own line of preserves, food products, things that walk the line between food and gift. Gourmet isn't the word I'm thinking of. Homemade, unique, flavorful twists, things with heart. Packaged with attention to beauty. Products that recognize and honor the fact that nourishment, food, is a gift from the earth. Carolyn's Creations or something. That's what I'd do."

But me, and Erin too, we haven't a clue. Maybe it's okay to go through life day to day without a real goal or dream, but it does sometimes seem like society says otherwise. What if setting goals is just a way of setting people up for failure, so they'll feel inadequate, so they'll go out and buy something, spend lots of money, to make them feel acceptable again? What if goals are just a conspiracy to make people unhappy? And we're all buying into it?

You have a dream, I know you do. A bakery. Right? What happens when you get to your goals and dreams? Do you have to make a new goal, have a new dream, to be happy? Do we always have to be striving? Is it never okay to sit and be content with what we have?

Ruby

From: Pip
To: Ruby
Sent: November 14, 2010
Subject: RE: Changes

Rubes,

Way to turn dreams into a conspiracy theory, there. You figured it out! You win the prize! Individual people's goals are just Corporate America's way to make more money for themselves. Rebel against The Man! Do nothing! Don't dream! Don't let them win!

You are being silly. You are right in one respect: It's not about the goals. What it's about, in my humble opinion, is fulfillment, finding your own personal meaning of life. If your happiness comes from not knowing what the day ahead holds, then so be it! Live life as an endless surprise. If Carolyn's happiness comes from making those gift food products, then she should do that, and part of doing that successfully means having a plan that defines how she's going to get there. That's where the goals come in. Measured steps leading to the dream. If you don't know what your dream is, I don't think you have to force it. The question is, do you know what makes you happy, what fulfills you, and are you spending your time on that? In the end, I suppose that's more important than having a grand dream or vision. Spending each day doing things you love, with the goal being spending as much of the day as you can doing things you love. Maybe these things will culminate in one grand end result and maybe they won't but it's the individual moments that make up life. And if knowing what you want is the egg, dreams are the chicken. The egg comes first. You don't have a dream and then decide what you want in the world. You figure out what you want, and then figure out how shape that into a dream.

Yes, a bakery is my goal. Not so much because I want the bakery but because it's a means to what I want: being able to spend my time baking, and being in charge of my own destiny. I'm not good at having a boss. Remember those office jobs I had? Every time someone asked me to make a copy I'd think, "For serious, you can't make a copy yourself? What are you, an idiot?" Not the best attitude for office success. So for me, baking all day and being my own boss means having a bakery. A few years from now, my dream might change. Like you said, everything changes. Things fall apart so new things can fall together. Circle of life.

You think too much and you fight the flow too much. Let life happen, Ruby. Trust that it will all be okay. Trust yourself.

Look at me giving advice. I'm going to be such a great mom. I hope. I hope I don't scar this child for life somehow. I hope this child is resilient enough to recover from all the mistakes I'll make. Resilience. Resilience is key. If you have resilience, you can survive anything.

I miss you too.

Pip

❖

From: Ed
To: Alexandra
Sent: November 15, 2010
Subject: David

Well, well, my mysterious Miss Alexandra! Do you know what time it is? 3 a.m.! Something woke me up so I was out of bed when I heard the stairwell door close in the hall. I looked out the peephole of my front door, and saw you heading down the hall. Verrrrrry interesting, young lady. Coming up from David's room at this hour are you? Question one: What were you doing there so late? Question two: Why didn't you stay? Question three: Are you ever going to tell me your first name, Miranda? Abigail? Florence?

Hope you were having a good time down there, girl! Fill me in!

Oh, I almost forgot. You never told me the results of your career guidance searches. Any leads? Have you found a new career?

From: Alexandra
To: Ed
Sent: November 16, 2010
Subject: RE: David

My, my, the walls have eyes and ears even in the dark wee hours, do they! Were you spying on me? Had you actually gone to bed or were you up late waiting for me to pass by? Silly Ed.

Yes, I was down at David's place. He made me dinner, a lovely chicken cordon bleu affair with a rich and caramely crème brûlée for dessert (David is a master with the kitchen torch). Then we played cribbage for a while (he's quite good but I still won), and chatted, and talked about the past and the future and the present. We may have kissed. Ha, Ed, I'm a schoolgirl. I haven't kissed anyone in a very long time. Lucky for us both I remembered how to do it. And then we chatted some more and then I said I felt it was a bit early in the relationship for me to be there so late, so I headed home. I had a lovely, lovely evening. I'd forgotten this feeling. Giddy. I have not been giddy for years. It makes a person want to draw smiley faces all over everything. Giddy, giddy, giddy. Not in love, not that far yet. Just happy to be living, and happy to be doing so with David nearby. He's a quiet one. It takes a while to get to know him. But I am glad to be taking that time. Being with him feels right.

And yes, I am glad you asked about the career. I had meant to tell you I think I've found a post-psychic path that is right up my alley: Something to do with the study of the brain. It's all part and parcel, really, with what I was doing before. The brain is a fascinating organ, and in my past work I've had the blessing of having a less-than-common glimpse into some of its rarer workings. More specifically, I might aim for work that gives me the opportunity to study intuition. A person doesn't have to be psychic to have excellent intuition. Where does it come from? I've been reading up on it. It works for us even while we're sleeping, did you know? And our whole bodies are involved in intuition, if we're paying attention (or even if we aren't). Studies prove that we can sense things even before our logical, conscious brain knows it. How does that happen? I'm not sure exactly what course I'll take in my study of intuition, but I do think that is the right path for me. I just have a feeling.

Don't worry, my darling, I'll tell you my full birth-given name one of these days. It's just a bit more fun making you work for it.

xx Alexandra .... if that is my real name.

From: Alexandra
To: Claire, Millie, Carolyn, Erin, Ruby
Sent: November 17, 2010
Subject: Next adventure

Ladies, as our boot camp ends next week on the day after Thanksgiving (so timely!), I've been dreaming up our next adventure. What do you all think of curling? Not the hair, the ice sport. There's a curling club in Seattle that has regular open houses. We could go make a weekend of it. Interested?

From: Claire
To: Alexandra, Millie, Carolyn, Erin, Ruby
Sent: November 17, 2010
Subject: RE: Next adventure

One time a woman from a Canadian curling team stayed at the Inn. She told me that the first time she tried curling, she nearly pulled a groin muscle. Apparently she loved the sport enough to go back, though, because if I remember right she had won some championships!

From: Ruby
To: Claire, Alexandra, Millie, Carolyn, Erin
Sent: November 17, 2010
Subject: RE: RE: Next adventure

From boot camp to groin pulls? Maybe we could do something this time that doesn't involve maiming ourselves? Poetry reading or knitting or cake decorating? Fingerprint art?

From: Erin
To: Ruby, Claire, Alexandra, Millie, Carolyn
Sent: November 17, 2010
Subject: RE: RE: RE: Next adventure

Curling sounds great. I wonder if people curl in Iceland. You would think, right?

From: Claire
To: Erin, Ruby, Alexandra, Millie, Carolyn
Sent: November 17, 2010
Subject: RE: RE: RE: RE: Next adventure

Oh, Erin, are you really going to move to Iceland? Can't you find inner peace here? Maybe there's a place up at Balky Point where you can get just far enough away, but we can all still be together on poker nights?

From: Erin
To: Claire, Ruby, Alexandra, Millie, Carolyn
Sent: November 17, 2010
Subject: RE: RE: RE: RE: RE: Next adventure

I don't think Balky Point will quite do this time. I may be going to Iceland, or maybe Greece, Croatia, Italy, Australia, New Zealand …. Just somewhere.

From: Ruby
To: Erin, Claire, Alexandra, Millie, Carolyn
Sent: November 17, 2010
Subject: RE: RE: RE: RE: RE: RE: Next adventure

You've added Australia and New Zealand to the list now? So really you just want to be anywhere but here?

From: Erin
To: Ruby, Claire, Alexandra, Millie, Carolyn
Sent: November 17, 2010
Subject: RE: RE: RE: RE: RE: RE: RE: Next adventure

A literal journey to accompany the impending journey of self discovery. Maybe one helps the other along, like a prompt: Oh yes,
my feet are actually moving, so I should be moving on the inside
as well.

Ruby, are you still in touch with Dan? Wasn't he Australian?

From: Ruby
To: Erin, Claire, Alexandra, Millie, Carolyn
Sent: November 17, 2010
Subject: RE: RE: RE: RE: RE: RE: RE: RE: Next adventure

Dan was a Kiwi. New Zealander. No, I'm not still in touch with
him, but if you want me to contact him I will. I'm sure he must
still know people back home, maybe someone you could stay
with. It is summer there right now, after all. Maybe I will come
with you. It's getting cold here!

From: Millie
To: Ruby, Erin, Claire, Alexandra, Carolyn
Sent: November 17, 2010
Subject: RE: RE: RE: RE: RE: RE: RE: RE: RE: Next adventure

I'm late to the party, but I'm here! Erin, go where your heart takes
you. Live now rather than regret it later. Follow your intuition.
Right, Alexandra? We will be here (unless we follow along to New

Zealand! That sounds wonderful!). Walter was showing me that online video chat thing. We can keep up with you that way. We will miss you but we will always be your family!

As for curling, I would love to. I was an ice skater in my youth, you know! Got a third place ribbon once when I was eight! I love the ice!

From: Erin
To: Millie, Ruby, Claire, Alexandra, Carolyn
Sent: November 17, 2010
Subject: RE: RE: RE: RE: RE: RE: RE: RE: RE: RE: Next adventure

I'm not gone yet! Give me time! I have to work it all out first.

You were an award-winning ice skater, Millie? I had no idea! How is it that we've been together all these years and I didn't know?

From: Alexandra
To: Erin, Millie, Ruby, Claire, Carolyn
Sent: November 17, 2010
Subject: RE: RE: RE: RE: RE: RE: RE: RE: RE: RE: RE: Next adventure

We all contain multitudes. It has taken our lifetimes for each of us to become who we are; there will always be mysteries in each of us, whether intentional or not.

From: Claire
To: Alexandra, Erin, Millie, Ruby, Carolyn
Sent: November 17, 2010
Subject: RE: RE: RE: RE: RE: RE: RE: RE: RE: RE: RE: RE:
Next adventure

So says the woman who refuses to tell us her name! If this is going
to become a philosophical discussion, I'm afraid I have to go. Full
house tonight, I've got to get the Inn ready! I'm in for curling, just
let me know when. Have a good evening, all!

From: Alexandra
To: Claire, Erin, Millie, Ruby, Carolyn
Sent: November 17, 2010
Subject: RE: RE: RE: RE: RE: RE: RE: RE: RE: RE: RE: RE:
Next adventure

I will research the December and January open house dates and let
you all know, and we can plan from there. Will be in touch soon.

November 19, 2010
Wishing Rock News
Millie Adler, editor
Letter from the Editor

Dear Rockers,

   The weekend you all have been waiting for is here! It's time for
our Wishing Rock Ideas and Thoughts Lecture Series! I myself am
absolutely excited. Who knew Wishing Rock had so many experts
on so many fantastic topics. Every one sounds so interesting.

Lectures will all take place Saturday in the auditorium. The line-up is impressive for a first year, I think! Schedule is as follows:

10:00 a.m. Life on Other Planets / Tom

10:30 a.m. Laughter as a Path to Happiness / Michelle

11:00 a.m. Break

11:15 a.m. Alaska from Above, a photoessay / Laurel Payne

11:45 a.m. A New Approach to Education: A Student's Perspective / Ben

12:15 p.m. Potluck lunch

1:15 p.m.   Geocaching as Metaphor for Self Discovery / Nathan

1:45 p.m.   The Myth of Perfection / Carolyn

2:15 p.m.   Break

2:30 p.m.   The Lechuguilla Caves, a photoessay / David

3:00 p.m.   Expressing the Inexpressible through Music and the Importance of the Arts / Walter

3:30 p.m.   Intuition / Alexandra

Talks will be up to twenty minutes each with a short time for Q&A after each. I am looking forward to seeing you all there!

Millie

From: Adele
To: Millie
Sent: November 20, 2010
Subject: Hello

Millie,

How wonderful about Alexandra and David. I get bits and pieces of news about her from various sources and it does sound like she's found some peace again. I'm so glad for her. She's a lovely young woman.

Your lecture series sounds delightful. Wish I could be there but I'll be eagerly awaiting the videos. Sometimes I think about how far the world has come so fast and it's amazing to me. We didn't have phones at my house when I was a girl, and now I can watch a video of someone on the other side of the world, online or on my phone even if I could figure that out. What will come next? Will all our brains be connected with microchips? That may be a little more than I need. A little mystery and a little slowness are good things.

I didn't recognize a couple names on the lecture list. Naturally I don't know everyone there, having never even visited, but it threw me off! Who are these people? I'd like to hear about them.

The guest room is waiting for you and Walter? Or do you need two rooms? We can arrange whatever you need. Come on over!

Adele

From: Millie
To: Adele
Sent: November 20, 2010
Subject: RE: Hello

Hello, Miss Adele!

I say good evening, you say good morning. I think its not quite dawn there as I write this. Good morning to you!

We had a wonderful time at the lecture series. Everyone was just brilliant. I admire people who are willing to get up and speak to a roomful of people, even if it's a friendly room full of people they know. That might make it harder rather than easier, actually.

You probably were referring to Michelle and Nathan as the people whose names you didn't recognize? Were there others? Yes, even in a town with just a hundred people or so, we all know each other of course but there are people we are closer to and people we don't know as well. The lecture series today was an opportunity to hear the thoughts of some people I haven't spent much time with, and that was a bonus I hadn't expected. Overall I would call the day a success, and I must give great credit to Walter for making it happen and bringing all these people and ideas together.

You will have noticed, of course, that Laurel Payne was on the lecture list as well. Of course you recognize her name; she's the woman who came to Wishing Rock claiming to be a half-sister to Ed and Michael, and left not a relative but a friend. As a "thank you" to Ed and Michael, she put together the most spectacular slide show of pictures she has taken over Alaska from her bush plane. Truly stunning. I think we all left her talk wanting to fly up there with her. Sometimes the beauty of this Earth of ours is absolutely incredible in the true sense of the word—unbelievable. Breathtaking, magnificent, awe-inspiring, beyond description. Beautiful. The way Laurel put the show together, and the few words she added, such poetry. It was a lovely tribute. I think I may have seen the start of a tear in Ed's eye. Hopefully Alaska won't call him home like Iceland (or Greece, or Italy, or …) has called Erin away. I like to have my family around me.

Will you be celebrating Thanksgiving over there? I know it's not a Scottish tradition, but it's such a nice tradition, aside from the eating so much you can't move, that I think it's worth exporting it (or importing it, since you are there). There's never a bad time to be grateful.

I hope you're settling back in well there. Have a wonderful week, Thanksgiving or no!

Love,

Millie

Text from Alexandra to Ed
Sent: November 21, 2010

Where are you?

❖

Text Ed to Alexandra
Sent: November 21, 2010

I'm over at Michael's. What's up? When you text, it worries me.

❖

Text from Alexandra to Ed
Sent: November 21, 2010

Come over. The voices are back. Ed, they're back. Everyone's back.
My husband, my children, all the voices, all the everything. It's
back. David's out spelunking, I can't reach him. Come over.

❖

From: Ruby
To: Pip
Sent: November 22, 2010
Subject: Alexandra

Pip!
    How are you? I'm awake a bit late today, we're all a bit tired
from celebrations last night: Alexandra's psychic abilities have returned! Just like that, they came back! Claire had an impromptu
dinner party to celebrate (no one staying at the Inn last night) and
we were up until two in the morning. (She served us the most
delicious stuffed acorn squash; recipe follows.)

"I was taking a bubble bath, of all things," said Alexandra, "meditating on the peacefulness, sinking into it. To be honest, that sort of silence is something I hadn't had for twenty years. Spirits, I love them, but they'd often pick times like that to make themselves heard. When they all left and I was devastated and lost, I consciously chose to focus on what I did have rather than what I didn't have. Peace and quiet, that was one of the blessings. It scared me at times, but if I could relax into it, when I could relax into it, it made me feel … infinite, somehow. As if the voices were like clouds in the night sky, and without them I could see forever.

"Anyway, I was in the bathtub feeling infinite when I heard something. I sat up and looked at the door, thinking maybe David had come home early from his day out in the caves and let himself in."

I glanced over at Erin at this point, who of course was there, and saw her draw in a slow breath, close her eyes. If the air around a person can close off somehow, the air around her did. She suddenly seemed inaccessible. I know she doesn't begrudge Alexandra her happiness, but I also know she feels hurt not to have that sort of happiness for herself.

"It wasn't David," continued Alexandra. "I knew it wasn't even as I looked to see if it was. It was Jimmy." Jimmy, her husband, who had died all those years ago.

"He started talking to me. 'Did you miss us?' he asked, his energy playful. In that moment I realized the aching loneliness of a reunion where there is no one to hug, no one to make physical contact with. It was like a reunion in my brain. I felt awkward, actually," she laughed, "How quickly we adapt."

"Conversations with people on the other side aren't exactly word by word, sentence by sentence," she explained. "But the gist of the conversation was that they left for my own good. They— Jimmy and my children Charlie and Chloë—thought I wasn't living my life, but rather was clinging to them and their memory. They were right, of course. I suppose I knew it in a way, too, but it's hard to let go. At first it was impossible, and then I just grew used to it.

"When who you think you are is stripped away completely, you find out who you really are," she said. "I thought I was living large in the world. I mean, I was traveling, I had great friends," (we all nodded and mumbled our agreement), "I had a fulfilling career. But the fact of it was, much as I loved traveling, I was usually alone. It sounds exotic and adventurous, exploring the world solo, but every time I'd see a grand sunset in a new landscape, or look out over a city from atop the tallest building in town, or go to dinner, all of this alone, I'd just feel like something was missing. I would talk to Jimmy and the kids a lot at those times. And they knew I was using them as an excuse to keep from taking the risk of being alive in the real world with real people who might reject me. They knew. And they decided to take drastic measures to push me out of their world and back into my own.

"The laughter club and the boot camp and all those things, Jimmy told me, were a start, an indication to them that I was taking the leap, but it wasn't until they saw that I'd taken a chance on risking my heart again that they decided it was okay to come back home." She blushed a little. In an act of intimacy that surprised me from him, David, who was sitting next to her on Claire's couch, reached out and took Alexandra's hand. "That human connection. That's what we're here for. That's what I'm here for, anyway. My happiness comes from connecting with other people. I'd convinced myself that I had everything I needed, but I knew I wanted more, or different.

"I don't want in any way to imply that a person has to have a significant other to be happy. You have to be able to be happy in who you are and in your solitude, as well. Another person can't make you happy; you have to do that yourself. But being happy with someone, that was something I wanted, and now, it's something that I have."

She looked at Ed. "The reason I changed my name was because the names we gave my children, Charlie and Chloë, were patterned after my own name. Hearing my name became an impossibly painful reminder that they weren't here, physically, on this Earth anymore, so I started going by my middle name. I just became Alexandra. But," she said, "I was born Charlotte Alexandra Day, became Charlotte Alexandra Day Sparks when I married Jimmy. My name is Charlotte."

And so Alexandra, as we'll still call her, is back to her old self, but renewed and made better, reborn. Pip, I think things could get pretty serious between her and David. I know, it's still early days, but you know how I like to read faces. Their faces just go together. They are a good match.

As for me, work and then a nap, and then an evening in cuddling with Ed and letting him pamper me in ways I've yet to determine. Just over a week to my birthday; I've been giving him good hints for a while now about the many ways he can make me happy. I think he's catching on.

I was thinking about what you said about goals and dreams. You're right. (Yes, I admit it!) It's about doing what you can to find that joy. I thought about the times that I'm happiest, and for me it's those times like last night, times spent with people I love, talking and laughing and sharing. To me, the meaning of life is to be found in sharing it with other people. My dream isn't a bakery, or a food products business, or to spend my time on a bush plane in Alaska. My dream is to spend as much time as I can with interesting, funny, thoughtful, compassionate people, and my goal now is to figure out what I need to do to make that happen. Who knew, I do have a dream! I guess dreams come in all shapes and sizes too.

Go over and give Gran a hug for me, and tell Gavin and Liam hello too. You can give them hugs for me if you like. Love to you all,

Ruby

Claire's Stuffed Acorn Squash

Ingredients

1/2 cup dry wild rice mixture or brown rice mixture
1 1/2 cups Cheddar cheese, shredded
4 acorn squash
2 Tbsp butter
1 large apple (about 1 cup) diced
2 large onions (about 2 1/2 cups) diced
1 Tbsp sage
2 Tbsp lemon juice
1 cup dried cranberries
1 cup pecans and walnuts, chopped
1 lb cooked sausage (optional)

Directions

Note: Quantities of filling ingredients can be adapted to personal taste.

1. Cut the squash in half and clean out seeds. Oil baking sheet and bake, cut side down, until tender. Scoop out some of the pulp to make room for the stuffing. Save the cooked pulp to put back into stuffing mixture.
2. Cook rice according to directions. Add cheese to warm rice and mix well. Set aside.
3. Melt butter. Add apples and onions and sauté until tender. (Add sausage, if using.) Add sage and sauté 2 more minutes. Add rice, squash, lemon juice and mix well. Add cranberries (reserve a few for garnish) and nuts and continue mixing. Fill squash shells and bake (filled side up) for about 25 minutes. Sprinkle with a few cranberries.

From: Ed
To: Alexandra
Sent: November 23, 2010
Subject: The return of self

Lex,

Wow, now that I know your name, what will I do with my spare time? Mystery revealed. Quite a story, Lex. I get it now, why you decided to go by your middle name. It's funny, we think we know people but there's so much more even to the people we know and love the most.

There's something I want to say. I couldn't figure out how to say it other night, or even what it is that I wanted to say, so I've been working on it, trying to get it just right.

I well remember when you moved here. Of course I thought you were an amazing woman, and I was right. But you resisted all my charms and we settled into this friendship. Clearly that's as it was meant to be. We think we know what we want but in the end we really do get what we need. Even being as close to you as I was, though, I was somehow blind to the fact that you weren't living a full life, that you weren't as happy as I would want you to be and thought you were. If it had been me, you would have (as you on more than one occasion have) taken me aside and challenged me to dig deep to figure out what was blocking me from my potential. But I, being a knucklehead, never even thought there might be reason to challenge you, and I guess I want to say I'm sorry. I let you down.

That said, I'm truly happy that you are so happy now. Because, Charlotte Alexandra Day Sparks, your being happy is important to me. Even I could see it at dinner at Claire's: David adores you and you adore him. Those fates of yours, they did some good work this time. It's enough to make a manly man get all sensitive and say: Life, it really is pretty good.

Love you,

Ed

❖

From: Alexandra
To: Ed
Sent: November 24, 2010
Subject: RE: The return of self

Ed,

I know this wasn't your intended effect, but your letter made me laugh. Ed, Ed, Ed! My burly manly brusque rough Ed! Where have you gone, and who is this über-sensitive Ed you've replaced him with?

You have no cause to feel bad. I myself didn't realize something was amiss; how could you have known? And what's more, the older I get the more I believe that we all have to learn our own lessons anyway. Good advice is a lovely thing but we don't learn from advice; we learn from falling down and scraping up our knees and bloodying our noses and not wanting to get back up but getting up anyway, and learning that being knocked down isn't what defines us; it's the getting back up that counts. You could have come to me and said all the right things and given the best guidance and I still would have taken my own path. Yes, as brilliant as you are, I might have followed my own mind. It's the way we humans are. Each of us thinks we are smarter than the rest, and thus we are destined to make our own mistakes no matter how many warning signs others may place in front of us or how many helpful hands are held out. Each of us has our own tightrope to walk, our own ship to sail, our own cliffs to jump off of. My choices and path are my own. You need feel no guilt.

And yes, there's more to everyone than what we see on the surface, or even what we see of our dearest friends. That's why we have to be kind to everyone. You may not know everyone's battles but every one of us has scars. Every one. If, as I believe, happiness lies in connection with other people, then by corollary, loneliness comes from isolation. We can isolate ourselves even in the midst of a crowd, by putting up barriers. Finding fault in everyone we encounter is a way of trying to protect ourselves from getting close to people. Everyone has a story. Everyone struggles, everyone wants to be loved. Our instinct when other people start to reject us is to reject them back, isn't that natural? Better though to forgive and embrace them in a cloak of compassion. We don't have to take every lost soul into our own circle of companionship—it's simply impractical to try to fully engage with everyone we meet, and misguided to think that if we are kind enough to everyone our personalities will be compatible—but we do, I believe, have a responsibility to mentally wrap everyone in kindness. We all struggle. We are all simply doing the best we know how.

I am so glad to have my "psychic powers," as you call them, back, but I could not be more grateful for their having gone away, for a while anyway. I might never have found myself if they hadn't. When I first lost those voices, Ed, I panicked. I tried to hide it, but inside I felt terror. I'd had those guides for so long, I was frightened that I wouldn't be able to navigate the world on my own. For a while, it was a self-fulfilling prophesy. That panic kept me from being able to feel or trust my natural human intuition, the intuition that every one of us has, psychic or not. As I started to accept that maybe this would be my life now, I started to realize that I do still have that intuition. It was my trust in that intuition that led me to David, to trust that he has a role in my life, for a good long time, I hope. Ironically, all those psychic powers I had were blocking me from clearly seeing my own life. Blocking me from realizing I wanted more. I suppose because I knew that "more" comes with a price. Asking for more means risking not getting it, being disappointed.

We want life to be "up" all the time and we are scared when we're down. Life isn't a straight line. If we're challenging ourselves, if we're growing, then we're going to be uncomfortable sometimes. If we're risking our hearts, we'll be hurt. If we love, we will on occasion be rejected. If we try, we will sometimes fail. If we bring friends into our lives, we have to be prepared to occasionally forgive. None of us is perfect. Our best intentions may hurt other people and our most well thought out plans may lead to our own misery. I made the mistake of thinking a busy life was a fulfilled life, but I was completely neglecting the most basic of my own needs: to love and be loved by someone special. I am not saying everyone needs that—some people need space, as Erin needs space right now—but I know I want that companionship. A ship to sail along with me, committed to be there through the rough waters and smooth.

And I need good friends, too, friends like you, to sail along with me. Losing my voices made me realize all the more how insanely lucky I am, how grateful I am, for people like you and all the other incredible people in my life. It would be remiss of me not to tell you. Words cannot describe, Ed, how much you mean to me. Thank you for your friendship. I love you.

A.

From: Ruby
To: Gran
Sent: November 25, 2010
Subject: Giving

Gran,

Today I woke up, turned on my phone, and found I'd received two texts left earlier in the morning.

From Claire: "Your sense of humor."

From Alexandra: "Your dedication to continuing to learn and grow."

I was puzzled, but figured I'd ask them about it later.

Opened my door to go over to Ed's for a light Thanksgiving brunch before the big Thanksgiving shebang this afternoon, and found he'd taped a dozen notes to the outside of my door:

"Your smile."

"Your laugh."

"Your backrubs."

"Your creative mind."

"Your courage."

I asked Ed about it and learned about the most fabulous of Wishing Rock traditions I've yet discovered. Every Thanksgiving, all day long, the people of Wishing Rock send each other notes, leave voice mails, send texts, whatever way they can think of to communicate, declaring the many ways they're thankful about each other. Claire makes pancakes for her family and pipes words made of blueberry sauce on them. Carolyn makes personalized pumpkin spice fortune cookies for her family and friends. Michael carves short sentiments into driftwood and leaves them at select people's doors. The post office is closed today, but late Wednesday night each year, Millie slips small notes into everyone's mail boxes. No one is left out of the day. There are enough residents committed to the tradition that even the few people who don't choose to participate find notes of gratitude on their doors or voice mails or phones. And it's also an unspoken agreement that nobody tells the people who have moved in since last Thanksgiving that this all is going to happen, so we newcomers are blessed with that added element of surprise and joy.

Downstairs in the lobby, a couple days ago I noticed someone had put up a giant sheet of paper, blank, but no one would tell me what it was for. Today when I passed by it I saw that someone had written in bold blue letters at the top: "I AM THANKFUL FOR…." And people had begun to fill the page, writing in ink of all colors: "My family." "My health." "My mother surviving her cancer." "My new bathroom." "Carolyn's cooking." "Wishing Rock potlucks." "Mysteries." "Buried treasure." "Books." "Ed's various attempts at making new liqueurs." "Cupcake pops." "Beach bonfires." "Down-filled slippers." "Pillows." "Hot tea." "Croquet." "Discovering new caves." "Bats." "Bees and fresh honey." "Gardens." "Hoedowns." "Life."

I felt surrounded by, embraced by, engulfed by, gratitude. All these messages of gratitude, all these people taking the time to tell each other what they mean to each other, what things in the world make them stop and feel wonder, what small joys they deeply appreciate.

I remembered earlier this year, when Pete wanted to get back together with me, and he talked about telling people you love them while there's still time. The challenge in that, though, is that sometimes it seems there's no "right time" to take a conversation into that serious place where you can express those deep thoughts. It can feel a little creepy to tell people you don't know well that you nonetheless appreciate their place in your life, their work, their way of being. What I appreciate so much about this tradition is that it made all that completely acceptable. It's the perfect opening to let someone know what you're thinking. It's lunchtime now and I've found myself with misty eyes of joy almost all day. All this love and kindness. It's almost more than I can bear.

The other day I was out on the beach, thinking, beachcombing, looking again for wishing rocks to add to my collection. A man came along, a stranger. Probably someone waiting for the ferry. He saw that I was looking for something, and said, "Any good jewels here?"

I paused. I realized I wasn't sure what he meant by "jewels." He could mean sea glass. He could mean nice rocks. He could mean actual jewels, rings that slipped off the fingers of poor hapless souls and such. He could mean wishing rocks.

I said, "I think so. To me there are."

He smiled, nodded, and walked on.

As I continued looking for rocks, I thought of a few additions to my Wishing Rock Theory of Life:

1. Different people are looking for different things. Sometimes the way to find exactly what you're looking for is to change or expand what you're looking for. You don't always know what you want until you find it. I started out collecting wishing rocks, but I had to start another collection too of other beautiful items I've found, rocks with wonderful patterns of spots or colors, sea glass aged to that gentle glow you can only get from the ocean, all sorts of wonderful objects. Focus is good but if you get too focused, you might miss out on something amazing.

2. To get what you want, you can't just sit on the sidelines. Wishing rocks, and life and dreams, are not Mohammed's mountain. They will not come to you if you don't go to them. Knowing what you want is one thing, but you have to do the work, you have to go out and make your dreams and wishes come true, make your life what you want it to be.

3. Just as no two people are exactly alike, no two rocks are exactly alike. Their beauty is in their variations. Some are more obviously gorgeous than others, but each one has something

in it to admire, if you look carefully enough. Even if you never know it, every rock has a story, where it came from, what forces shaped it, how it got here, where it's going next.

4. Because the rocks are more vibrant when they're wet, I often go rock hunting right at the edge of the water. With every wave, some rocks are swept in and some are taken away. Just like in life, people come and go. You have to appreciate the ones that are there, when they are there, because they could be gone in an instant.

I'm thinking today about where I was just one year ago. Pete had just dumped me. I felt broken and wasn't sure I'd ever be right again. And yet today, I feel overdosed on blessings, overwhelmed with satisfaction. I'm so blessed, Gran.

Do you know what it is? Of course you know, you've lived long enough to know this. It's perseverance. One foot in front of the other, day after day after day. When the road is long you just keep walking. The only difference between a person who finishes a marathon and one who doesn't is that the person who finishes never quits. If you just keep going, keep on keeping on through the hard times, you get through it. One foot after the other. We get through.

So, Gran: Your sassiness. Your smile. Your heart. Your indomitable spirit that has us all on our toes trying to keep up with you. Your kindness. Your compassion. Your ability to listen to me endlessly through all my dramas and insecurities and fears. Your love of adventure. Your willingness to try new things. The way you don't judge. They way you laugh. The way you love. I am thankful for all these, and so much more.

Come visit us soon! Happy Thanksgiving.

All my love and so much gratitude,

Ruby

More by Pam Stucky

FICTION

Mystery

Death at Glacier Lake

The Megan Montaigne Mysteries
Final Chapter
A Conventional Murder
The Caramel Crow
Sent to Death

The Wendy Grace Mysteries
X Marks the Murder

Middle Grade / Young Adult Sci-fi Adventure

The Balky Point Adventures
The Universes Inside the Lighthouse
The Secret of the Dark Galaxy Stone
The Planet of the Memory Thieves
The Perils of the Infinite Task

Adult Contemporary

The Wishing Rock Series
Letters from Wishing Rock
The Wishing Rock Theory of Life
The Tides of Wishing Rock

From the Wishing Rock Kitchens: Recipes from the Series

NONFICTION

Travelogues

**The Pam on the Map Series
(wit and wanderlust)**
Pam on the Map: Iceland
Pam on the Map: Seattle Day Trips

FOR MORE INFORMATION
pamstucky.com

Thank you for reading

www.ingramcontent.com/pod-product-compliance
Lightning Source LLC
Chambersburg PA
CBHW052024240626
47153CB00006B/1947